D1250116

Superstoe

Also by William Borden

PLAYS

Don't Dance Me Outside

Turtle Island Blues

Meet Again

When the Meadowlark Sings

Sakakawea

The Consolation of Philosophy

Makin' It

*The Only Woman Awake Is the Woman
Who Has Heard the Flute*

Loon Dance

Tap Dancing across the Universe

The Last Prostitute

POETRY

Slow Step and Dance

Superstoe

A NOVEL BY

William Borden

Orloff Press
BERKELEY, CALIFORNIA

Copyright © 1967, 1968, 1996 by William Borden.
First published by Victor Gollancz, London,
and Harper & Row, New York.
This edition published in the United States by Orloff Press.

Orloff Press
P.O. Box 8536
Berkeley, CA 94707-8536

United States Constitution, First Amendment:
Congress shall make no law respecting an establishment of religion, or prohibiting the free exercise thereof; or abridging the freedom of speech, or of the press; or the right of the people peaceably to assemble, and to petition the Government for a redress of grievances.

Printed on acid-free, recycled paper
Manufactured in the United States of America

Book design by Zipporah Collins

Publisher's Cataloging-in-Publication Data
Borden, William, 1938–
  Superstoe / William Borden
    p. cm.
  ISBN 0-9642949-5-8
  1. Political satire, American—Fiction.   2. United States—Politics and government—Fiction.   3. Universities and colleges—United States—Faculty—Fiction.   I. Title.
  PZ4.B7297 Su4   1996
  814.54—dc20   95-70750

5 4 3 2 1

for
Nancy

Contents

At last I came to the conclusion
that all existing states
are badly governed
and the condition of their laws
practically incurable,
without some miraculous remedy
and the assistance of fortune;
and I was forced to say,
in praise of true philosophy,
that from her height alone
was it possible to discern
what the nature of justice is,
either in the state or in the individual,
and that the ills of the human race
would never end until
either those who are sincerely
and truly lovers of wisdom
come into political power,
or the rulers of our cities,
by the grace of God,
learn true philosophy.

PLATO,
Epistle VII

PART ONE

The Idea

1   It was Superstoe's idea to take over the government and reform society.

The idea came on a Saturday morning, at one of the Friday evening dialectics.

Superstoe, Adams, and Furth met every Friday evening. They had begun meeting long before, when they were teaching at the university in Great Spoons, North Dakota.

But when the new president came to the university, Benjamin Franklin Adams, who taught philosophy, quit. He moved to Crossbar, North Dakota. To pass the time he taught himself Russian, Polish, and Hebrew. He was sixty-one years of age.

A year later Paxton S. Superstoe was fired.

Lazarus Furth quit.

They moved to Crossbar and began teaching in the high school.

Paxton S. Superstoe was short, portly, and bald. His eyes, which were blue, were a boy's eyes set candidly in a middle-aged face. They were wide, wondering, certain, and innocent;

they laughed, but one wondered what they laughed at. His nose was unobtrusive, his teeth were sound, and his lips mischievous. He had a semicircle of clipped, gray hair around his head, like a tonsure; he had short, nervous fingers; and he walked with a peculiar, quick, flat-footed gait.

Furth said Superstoe looked like an aging, unimportant cherub. Adams said he was an angel who had fallen for the hell of it and was on his way to a new solar system for the fun of it and was neither damned nor holy because he thought the two were the same.

He had translated the Linear A, the Phaistos disc, and five Easter Island tablets, and had written a monograph explaining his Unified Field Theory of Linguistic Evolution; all had been rejected by the publishers. At Crossbar High School he taught English (all four levels), Latin, Spanish, and mythology.

Lazarus Furth had a B.S. from MIT and a Ph.D. from Caltech. He taught algebra, geometry (plane and solid), trigonometry, physics, chemistry, and biology. He had offered to teach geology, astronomy, and ecology as well, but the school board had rejected the proposal.

Furth had a lean and hungry look. He stood five eleven in his brown uppers, his mouth was wide, his cheekbones were high, his nose was hawklike. He moved with the ease and relaxation of a camel. (When he was twenty-one he began studying ballet. After two months he was locked out of the studio and his money was refunded.) His black hair was crew cut twice a year, and it grew straight up. He had never owned a comb.

His brown eyes, behind thick, rimless glasses, wore a puzzled look. He took for granted the stupidity of most human beings and the illogicality of causality, but, on the other hand, he would at times look suddenly at a tree, or a cloud, or Superstoe, or a paper clip, with incredulity. Adams called him an Epicurean ascetic. Superstoe said he was a giant standing on the shoulders of pygmies. Furth merely retorted, "All philosophy is a footnote to Heraclitus."

When they first came to Crossbar, they held their dialectics at the Saddle Up Bar and Grill, above which Furth had a room containing a bed, a table, a chair, a hot plate, and three thousand books, abstracts, and journals. But after one meeting they moved the dialectics to Adams's house, where they could talk all night.

Benjamin Franklin Adams lived in a gray, unpainted farmhouse eight miles southwest of Crossbar. His living room was lined with bookshelves. But, with the exception of one corner of one shelf, the shelves were bare.

Twelve volumes stood in that corner. Two were the *Dialogues of Plato*, in Greek. The other ten volumes were hand-bound in black leather; their contents were in longhand, in brown ink, in Adams's elegant, eighteenth-century script. The ten volumes were entitled

T	J	R	T	T	L	H	L	P	I
R	U	E	A	H	I	I	O	L	N
U	S	A	L	I	S	S	V	A	Q
T	T	D	K	N	T	T	E	N	U
H	I	I	I	K	E	O		S	I
	C	N	N	I	N	R			R
	E	G	G	N	I	Y			I
				G	N				E
					G				S

The thickest volume was TALKING; it was 198 pages. The thinnest was LOVE; it was two pages.

Adams was six and a half feet high, broad-shouldered, solid, and quick-tempered. He had a mean handlebar mustache. It, like his full head of hair, was white. His smile was grim. No one had ever seen him laugh. He loved to hunt and he hated to fish. Superstoe said he was a Moses who refused to remove his shoes. Furth said he was an Agamemnon without a Trojan War.

After a few months the dialectics moved to Superstoe's house. It was there he conceived his idea.

Superstoe lived in another abandoned farmhouse, two miles north of Adams's. Superstoe's house was crammed with books. The largest room, which Superstoe, with a bottle of Haig and Haig, had christened the Dialectic Room, contained the most important books—the complete Loeb Classical Library, scholarly texts in Greek, Latin, and a dozen other languages, dictionaries, and volumes in philology, philosophy, history, economics, law, and literature.

On Friday evenings either Superstoe or Furth prepared the dinner. They would eat at the long oak table in the center of the Dialectic Room, and then Superstoe and Furth would clear the table and return with pewter cups and three bottles of John Jameson.

Adams would light a cigar and flip the match into the red chamber pot at his elbow. Superstoe had painted the chamber pot; he had painted the outhouse the same color.

Once Adams's cigar was lit, Superstoe would clang his cup against the chamber pot, as if calling them to prayer.

The chamber pot fascinated Superstoe. As they talked, and thought, late into the night and the following morning (often the dialectics lasted until Sunday noon), he stared at it, his eyes unfocused. One night, while Adams was outside relieving himself, Superstoe climbed onto the table and urinated into the pot.

When Adams returned, Superstoe was seated.

Adams tossed his cigar butt into the pot—which, it was understood, was to be used exclusively as an ashtray. The cigar butt splashed.

Curiously Adams peered into the pot. He sniffed. He looked at Superstoe. Superstoe smiled and blinked questioningly. Adams filled Superstoe's cup from the pot and handed the cup to Superstoe. Superstoe ran out the door. Adams followed. Superstoe fled to the outhouse and bolted the door.

Adams, his breath frosting in the autumn chill, contemplated the fire-engine-red house. Then he backed his car against the door, set the brake, and returned to the house. He and Furth continued to talk until breakfast, after which Adams returned to his home on foot.

Sometimes Jason Johanneson came to the dialectics. He was Adams's cousin. He owned Adams's house, and Superstoe's house, and the land between and beyond them, as far as he could see. The land was so flat that to see a three-foot hill would be more surprising than to see a herd of mastodon grazing in the wheat.

Johanneson was nearly as tall as Adams and almost as bald as Superstoe. His only schooling was four years in a country schoolhouse, but between the ages of fourteen and nineteen he read the *Encyclopaedia Britannica* and *Webster's Unabridged Dictionary*. Now he read the *Congressional Record* and collected and studied maps. He was at the dialectic when Superstoe conceived his idea.

After Adams had lit his cigar, and after Superstoe had clanged his pewter cup against the tin chamber pot, Furth would swirl his whiskey until drops fell to the floor and would pray: "All hail, majestic rulers of the universe and guardians of the mysterious deep."

"*Pax vobiscum,*" Superstoe would reply.

And then they would drink, and begin the dialectic.

2   They talked of piety, truth, justice, happiness; the world, the universe; energy, matter, and soul; the good, the beautiful, the sublime; the ethical implications of Markov processes; the relation between quasars and deoxyribonucleic acid, between anti-matter and evolution.

But they also talked of America, of government, of human nature, and of the future. It was at one of these dialectics that Superstoe's idea was born.

It was the hour preceding dawn. They had agreed the world was in a hopeless condition. Furth had just urged Adams to publish his ten volumes, and then he had very slowly lowered his eyelids, sighed, and slid onto the floor. He usually urged Adams to publish his ten volumes just before he passed out. His head thumped against the table leg.

"Alas," said Adams, drinking.

Superstoe plopped a pudgy finger in a puddle of spilled whiskey. "Publish?" he asked softly.

Adams looked meanly into his cup.

"No," Superstoe went on. "They've learned to castrate anything honest. They've learned to disarm dangerous books."

Silently Adams nodded agreement.

"A few reviews, a little publicity," Superstoe continued, "that's all it takes. They don't kill their Socrateses any more, they applaud them."

"Those were the good days," Adams sighed. He pulled at the tips of his handlebar mustache.

"Oh, yes, they're clever," Superstoe said. He withdrew his finger from the puddle and sucked it. "If Socrates were alive today—if you were to publish your manuscripts—"

"Now, now."

"They'd need no hemlock."

"No."

"They'd interview you on three television networks ..."

"They'd give me a weekly show in prime time."

"They'd paint your portrait and slap it on the covers of three or four magazines I refuse to name ..."

"Don't name them, please."

"You'd make the *New York Times Magazine* ..."

"Lord, yes."

"They'd pay you lots of money . . ."

"God forbid."

"And they'd say you were the greatest thing to hit town for centuries. And you wouldn't accomplish a thing. They wouldn't change."

"How often must I tell you?"

"I know, Ben, I know. Human nature never changes. But it does surge and ebb."

"Granted."

Furth began to snore. Johanneson twiddled his thumbs and stared at Furth's head, which had rolled against his shoe. Adams and Superstoe stared dejectedly at the John Jameson label.

Superstoe raised his head. He squinted out the window, as if trying to fathom something in the dimness of the approaching dawn. He looked out the window for some moments, and then he began to speak.

"Ben, if we could get control, we could use their perversity. We could make this into the proper kind of world. All we need do is get control."

"That's ever the dilemma," Adams said.

Superstoe sat up straight. His voice rose in volume. Still watching the gray images through the window, he said, "If we established a firm control, disguised as benevolency to placate the masses . . ."

"That wouldn't be difficult."

"If the world were in our hands, the whole world . . ."

"You and Mahalia Jackson."

"We'd have to lay our plans carefully."

"Indeed."

Superstoe sprang to his feet and ran around the table. "We'll ride the tide of the times!" he cried. "Like a surfboard!"

He tripped over Furth's legs.

Adams raised his cup and toasted the two bodies. "For everything there is a season," he said in Hebrew.

Superstoe sat up. "We'll beat them to a lather and let them gallop to *our* goal!"

"Whip the surfboard to a lather," Adams observed to the bottle.

Superstoe scrambled to his feet. "We'll make our plans. We'll ..."

"Why don't you make breakfast?"

"Wake Lazarus! Here, Lazarus!" He tugged at the galluses of Furth's overalls. "Lazarus! Lazarus! We're going to take over the government!"

Furth smiled and rolled over. Superstoe emptied the bottle of whiskey over Furth's head. Then he dashed to the kitchen and began opening drawers.

Johanneson followed Superstoe into the kitchen and fried eggs, bacon, and potatoes. Superstoe, singing "I've got de whole world in mah hands," dropped bread into the toaster, started the coffee, and carried butter, jam, plates, and utensils to the table.

The aroma of the bacon roused Furth. When Johanneson brought the eggs, he had recovered his chair.

"You smell like a distillery," said Johanneson.

Furth inhaled. "It's a lovely smell," he said. He slid four eggs onto his plate.

Superstoe plopped into his chair.

Furth remarked, "Paxton looks as if he's had an orgasm."

"An idea," said Adams.

"It's the same thing," said Furth.

Superstoe waved his fork in the air. "We're going to take over the world!"

Furth chuckled and speared three slices of bacon.

"We are the greatest gathering of intellects in the world!"

"Of course," said Furth.

"Pass the toast," said Adams.

"We have spent years," Superstoe drove on, "talking. We have talked about virtue, we have talked about evil, we have talked about talk ..."

"Where's the coffee?" asked Adams.

"But we have yet to *do* anything!"

"Get the coffee," said Adams.

Superstoe stood on his chair. Thrusting his fork aloft like Liberty's torch, he proclaimed, *"We shall reform the world."*

3 Superstoe had his good days and his bad days at Crossbar High School. Mondays and Tuesdays, and sometimes Wednesdays, were his bad days. It was as if the shock of returning to the classroom after a weekend of dialectic were too great. Thursdays and Fridays were his good days.

He abhorred human contact on his bad days. He sped, eyes on the ground, from class to office, and locked the office door. When the bell rang again, he waited until the noise died in the hall, and then he sped back to the classroom.

He dreaded speech on those days. He abandoned his lectures. He assigned themes or exercises to be done during the class, or he gave a test. Or he wrote questions on the board in his illegible scrawl, pointed to the question and then to a student, and waited for the answer. He had been known to wait forty-five minutes. If, finally, no answer came forth, and if the student was a girl, he scrawled her name on the board and after it drew an F. If it was a boy, he hit him on the side of the head with a textbook.

If, on the bad days, he happened to meet someone in the hall late in the afternoon after classes, he would duck into an empty classroom and hide there until the person had passed. He might pop into the rest room. For some time it was thought he suffered from chronic diarrhea.

But on his good days he became garrulous. He would corner a colleague who was on his way to class, or lunch, and explain once again the basis of his Unified Field Theory of Linguistic Evolution. Or, when he was working on his Survey of the Schools of Psychology, he would elucidate the theories of Binzwanger or Adler or Wertheimer.

In class he was equally loquacious. He beguiled the forty-five minutes by reciting Ovid in Latin to an English class or by reading Petronius in Latin to his Spanish class. Sometimes he sang songs and did a soft-shoe around, and occasionally on top of, the desk, using a pointer for a cane and the wastebasket for a hat.

One spring, when the gardener was cutting the grass beneath his classroom window and he couldn't be heard above the roar of the mower, he threw erasers, chalk, books, and finally a chair at the gardener. When that failed, he took his class outdoors and seated them on the grass, in the path of the mower. When the gardener descended from the mower to protest, Superstoe handed him the textbook, climbed onto the mower, and drove it through the rose bushes.

Only a handful of intimates knew anything of his past. Everyone knew he had a master's degree from Wisconsin, but everyone didn't know he had worked three years on a Ph.D. and then left when his adviser advised, "It's certainly an original idea, but I suggest you confine your dissertation to a more limited topic and compose it in a more conventional manner."

Most people thought he must be a determined bachelor, like Furth, but in fact he had married while a graduate student, become a father eight months after the wedding, and, after leaving graduate school, supported his mother-in-law for seven years, until she died.

His son died at eleven years of age. Two years later his wife was committed to an asylum. She never left it.

After teaching at the university for eight years he was promoted to assistant professor. He was never promoted again.

The year after Adams left the university, Superstoe gave the son of an influential state legislator an F in English. The boy was ineligible to play hockey. In March, when the rest of the faculty pulled green contracts from their mailboxes, he found his empty.

Furth charged into the president's office and threatened to resign if Superstoe's contract was not renewed.

"We'll be sorry to lose you, Furth," the president replied.

Fortunately the new high school in Crossbar had just been completed. They desperately needed teachers. Johanneson was then a member of the school board.

4 Furth and Adams were accustomed to Superstoe's schemes. His decision to take over the government surprised them no more than his drawing lewd pictures on the high-school blackboards one night.

Nevertheless, when Adams entered the Dialectic Room the following Friday, he stopped in surprise and cracked his head on the lintel.

Superstoe pushed him aside and darted into the room. "This," he announced, spreading his arms, "is our material. To plan taking over the world."

Piled neatly on the table were a dozen reams of paper—white, blue, pink, and yellow paper—dozens of spiral notebooks, pads of lined paper, pads of unlined paper (four sizes), pads of graph paper, a ruler, a protractor, a pair of compasses, ballpoint pens (red, blue, black, and green), and three dozen pencils sharpened so recently they could smell them.

Superstoe, wearing his gray sweatshirt, brown corduroy pants, and sandals (at school he wore a brown suit, a red plaid shirt, a green striped tie, blue socks, and green suede loafers), held one hand up, index finger extended. "Now," he began, as if commencing a lecture, "the first thing to remember is that we must be ruthless."

"But not cruel," Furth said, sliding into his chair.

"Of course not," Superstoe replied.

Adams strode to his chair. "Where the hell are my cigars?"

Superstoe pointed. The chamber pot sat on top of the box of cigars. On top of the chamber pot lay a loose-leaf notebook. Embossed on the notebook was a red cougar, and around the cougar was printed the legend GO CROSSBAR COUGARS.

"Paxton, why have you cluttered the table with this crap?" asked Adams.

"I told you. To draw up our plans for taking over the government and reforming society."

Adams sighed and lifted the notebook off the chamber pot. Inside the chamber pot he found a paperback copy of the *Vita Nuova*. "I thought," he said, "tonight we might begin by discussing the apparent need for comedy in human existence."

"No no no no no, we're discussing revolution!" Superstoe cried.

"You can't take over the government," Adams said, removing the pot and extracting a cigar from the box.

"Why not?"

"It's impossible."

Superstoe turned to Furth. "I cannot stress too much the importance of positive thinking."

"This isn't South America," Adams said. "You don't even have an army."

"We don't need an army. Once we take over, we'll have the U.S. Army. And the Marines."

"Revolution is unconstitutional," Adams said.

"Oh, we won't do anything unconstitutional."

Adams was ripping the seal from a bottle of Jameson.

"Every four years the President takes over the government," Superstoe explained.

"You're going to run for President?"

"I'm not that crazy." Superstoe balanced his cup on his head. "We could reform society by creating a crisis," he went on. "If the populace were shocked and frightened, they would put themselves into the hands of a strong leader."

"Who?" asked Adams.

"Me," replied Superstoe. "All we have to do is decide how to cause a crisis, and how to get control."

Adams filled his cup. "We might discuss Thucydides tonight," he said.

"Whom do we know in government?" Superstoe asked. "Have any of our students gone into government, Lazarus?"

Furth stared at him, shocked.

"Ben!" Superstoe cried. "We know Bryan Knutson! You know him very well, don't you? Senator Knutson."

"I know him."

"He was in the state legislature when you were revising the curriculum at the university. When did you see him last?"

"Last summer. He wanted me to come to Washington."

Superstoe gazed at Adams in ecstasy.

"Despite his obtuseness, Bryan occasionally recognizes genius. He wanted me to join his staff."

"Well, there we are!" cried Superstoe.

"Do you recall the story of the violation of the Hermae?" Adams began.

"We'll join Knutson's staff," Superstoe continued, "and elect him President. He'll appoint me Secretary of State.

Then we'll kill him, the Vice President, and Congress, and I'll succeed to the presidency. Or Ben—you're the oldest. It's your prerogative. We'll have him appoint *you* Secretary of State. Then we'll reorganize things, and we'll be the first council of philosopher-kings to rule in America. Or anywhere."

Adams swept a pile of notebooks off the table. "Will you stop this bullshitting, Paxton?"

"Benjamin, I am quite serious." Superstoe dipped his finger in Adams's whiskey and drew a wet circle on his head. "Now, once Ben is on Knutson's staff, how shall we create a crisis? How shall we get Knutson elected President?"

Furth looked up. "That's easy," he said.

"Good," said Superstoe. "How?"

"Germs."

"Fine. That's settled. Now what?"

"Germs?" asked Adams.

Furth replied, "I could wipe out this state, Minnesota, and South Dakota with the cultures I'd find in the university medical lab."

"Come now," said Adams.

"I could get anything I wanted from Ed Watt at the university. If he didn't have it, I could order it from the American Type Culture Collection in Washington."

"Order germs?" cried Superstoe. *"From the government?"*

Furth grinned. He scratched his head with the point of a pen. "We'd start epidemics," he said. "Give Knutson bits of information—let him think we were his private, super FBI. He'd make speeches, become famous, be nominated for the presidency. His party's out of office; it doesn't have a leader. The election's a year from this fall. That will give us time enough. There are a lot of things we could do. A lot of stories we could tell. Plots, intrigues ..." He smiled dreamily.

Disdainfully Adams flicked ash onto the Cougar notebook. "You can't go around killing people."

"We wouldn't have to kill people," Furth said. "We could cause crop failures, spread livestock epidemics. Very few people would die. If that's what you're concerned about."

"It doesn't concern me a great deal," Adams replied. "But I don't believe it's possible."

"It would be a home-brew germ warfare," Furth explained. "Knutson would say it was a foreign power; that would embarrass the administration. Or he'd say it was an internal plot, fomented by the President to cause a crisis to ensure his re-election." Furth jotted some symbols in the notebook. He chewed the tip of his pen. "We could start the plague," he mused, "as in Thucydides."

Adams drained his cup. "You're as crazy as Paxton," he said.

5   The people of Crossbar thought Furth was eccentric, too; but they didn't ridicule him, as they did Superstoe. His eccentricity was of a different sort.

Shortly after coming to Crossbar he began wearing bib overalls to school. That night the school board called an emergency meeting and summoned Furth.

"Did you hire me to teach or to be a fashion model?" he asked them, looping his thumbs through his galluses.

"We think it makes a better impression to dress more conventionally," said Tom Clark, the International Harvester dealer.

"Then hang a suit in front of the blackboard and let it teach Euclid."

Frank Sigulrud, who owned the Happy Corral Bar, across the street from the Saddle Up, and had made a fortune selling his land to the government for the Minuteman Missile complex, said, "I thought you were teaching math and science."

The next week a letter appeared in the Crossbar *Courier.* In it Furth asked why the school board was ashamed of the North Dakota farmer, since the farmer wore overalls. "What's good enough for the North Dakota farmer is good enough for the North Dakota teacher," the letter concluded.

His resultant popularity with the townspeople was brief, however. On Easter morning, while half the town was in the Lutheran church and the other half in the Methodist and Baptist churches, he led a black bull to the steps of the Lutheran church. He carried a hibachi he had borrowed from Superstoe.

He built a fire in the hibachi. Then, as the worshipers, accompanied by the joyous tolling of the bell, descended the steps, he slit the bull's throat, ripped open its abdomen, and placed the heart on the coals.

Teaching in the high school did not prevent his study of the latest mathematical and scientific developments.

He lectured and drew examples on the board by rote, at the same time reading books and journals in mathematics, physics, biochemistry, biophysics, microbiology, ecology, and several other fields. He might enter the classroom carrying not the algebra textbook but *Theoretical Petrology, Nuclear Pulse Spectrometry,* and *Lectures on Ergodic Theory.*

Sometimes as he lectured he invented, and tried to solve, insoluble problems. When it looked as if he might have a solution, he stopped the lecture in mid-sentence and jotted equations on the board. Once he worked on a problem through trigonometry and biology and on into the night. When one blackboard was filled, he moved to the next classroom.

The solution came at two in the morning, in the home economics classroom. He turned and resumed the lecture, wondering why the class had left and why it was dark outside.

Grading occupied little of his time. After the first day he knew if he had any student worth his attention. If he did, he gave the student extra work and carefully examined his proofs. The other papers he marked either C or F, without looking at them. He told Superstoe, "They'll forget it in a month. I'm not going to break my ass pouring water through a sieve."

While he was a student at Caltech he wrote a paper, under the pseudonym of Matthew Bumm, which refuted Goedel's Theorem. The paper was published in a respectable journal.

The effect in mathematical circles was one of horror and dismay.

But six months later peace was restored. Another paper, by a certain Fillmore Thumb, appeared and revealed the flaw in Matthew Bumm's logic.

6   The Monday morning following the dialectic in which Furth proposed the germ-warfare plan the principal of the high school phoned Adams. He asked, "Where are Furth and Superstoe?"

"How the hell should I know?"

"I thought you might know."

"No."

"They're not at school."

"I suspected."

"What?"

"Would you call me if they were?"

"Oh. Of course. Have you any idea …?"

"No."

"You don't think there's been an accident?"

"No."

"It's very mysterious, isn't it?"

"They're mysterious individuals."

"Yes, they are. I wonder if they'll arrive later."

"God knows."

"Yes, we must trust in the Lord. I suppose I'd better find substitutes. The trouble is, I don't have anyone ... Do you suppose you ...?"

"No."

"Do you think I should notify the police?"

"Nonsense."

"Well, thank you very much, Mr. Adams."

Curious rather than disturbed, Adams climbed into his car and drove to Superstoe's house. He expected to find them playing go or making up a scientific-linguistic crossword puzzle. They had done that another time. Once they had cut school and painted an abstract mural on the side of the barn, over the Harold's Club advertisement.

But Superstoe's red jeep was gone. The house was empty. A greasy skillet and two plates lay in the sink. Coffee grounds had been spilled on the floor.

More uneasy than curious, he drove to town. He found Furth's motorcycle in the service station next to the Saddle Up. He climbed the stairs to Furth's room and unlocked the door. It was empty. *Principles of Epidemiology* lay open on the unmade bed.

Friday afternoon Adams drove to Superstoe's. His uneasiness had passed. Now he was merely curious again, and confident. They had never missed a dialectic.

At dusk the jeep roared into the drive pulling a rented trailer.

Adams watched Furth tear into the kitchen and evacuate the refrigerator. When it was empty, he scrubbed it thoroughly.

Superstoe carried in boxes marked GLASS FRAGILE HANDLE WITH CARE THIS SIDE UP.

Furth brought in several small cartons and placed them in the refrigerator.

Superstoe eyed the cartons dubiously. "Are you sure it's safe?" he asked.

"Safe as fried chicken."

Adams examined one of the cartons. It contained a bottle. The bottle bore a label with a red border. ROCKY MOUNTAIN SPOTTED FEVER was printed on the label.

Johanneson arrived. "Have a nice trip?" he asked.

"Excellent," said Superstoe.

Furth reached into his pocket and dropped a quarter into Johanneson's hand. "Here's your change," he said.

Johanneson looked at the coin and then at Adams. "I gave them a thousand dollars and all I get back is a quarter," he said. He shook his head sadly.

"You what?" Adams turned to Furth. "What the hell have you been doing?"

"They said they were going to Washington," Johanneson said. "I thought you knew."

"We flew," trilled Superstoe, flapping his wings.

Furth studied the boxes Superstoe had carried in. "Now we need paint, cement, and lumber," he said. "You're good at those things, Ben."

"Just what do you have in mind?"

"I'm going to fix up the barn. Knock out the stalls, patch the cracks, maybe we should plaster the walls, lay a cement floor, have electricity run in, install light fixtures ..."

"And then?"

Furth scratched his head. "Then get to work," he muttered to himself.

Impatiently Adams tapped one of the boxes. "Could you be more explicit?"

"What?" asked Furth absently.

"What are you going to do in the barn?" Adams shouted.

"Make germs," said Furth. "And things. Make the barn into a lab. Haven't you been listening?"

7   Before the barn was completely renovated, the Crossbar *Courier* reported an outbreak of smallpox in Washington, D.C. The Public Health Service observed that many
persons neglected to acquire regular smallpox vaccinations.
They advised revaccination every three years.

It was Sunday morning. Superstoe read the newspaper as
he ate. "It says," he said, "a high-level military authority has
suggested the smallpox might be the work of enemy agents,
the beginning of a clandestine biological warfare offensive."

Furth heaved the griddle upward, twisted his wrist and
torso, extended one leg, lunged, and missed. He nearly
dropped the griddle in Adams's lap. "It's the wrong type of
griddle," he said.

"The government," Superstoe read, "denies the possibil-
ity."

- "It's like trying to solve a differential equation with high
school algebra. You must get another griddle."

"So you can start an epidemic," Adams said. "That doesn't
prove you can take over the government."

Furth observed the pancake oozing on the linoleum floor.
"Some sort of experiment was necessary," he said. He
poured more batter onto the griddle.

Reading, Superstoe stabbed with his fork.

Adams gave an incoherent cry.

Superstoe looked up. Adams's fork was poised over the
plate of bacon. His eyes were closed.

"Did I stab you, Ben?" asked Superstoe. Adams nodded
without opening his eyes. "Are you praying?"

Adams's eyes opened. "I am," he replied. "And you are
included in my prayers."

Furth stared at the circle of batter erupting on the griddle.
"The President's popularity increased two percent," he said.

"You see, Ben?" asked Superstoe.

Adams inspected the four points of blood on the back of his hand. "I see," he said.

"Now all you have to do is tell Bryan Knutson you'll join his staff."

"I have no desire to join Bryan Knutson's staff."

"Teamwork is the first requisite for success," said Superstoe.

"I have no intention of being Knutson's flunky."

"The Secretary of State has lots of fun," said Superstoe. "Parties, receptions, a nice office. I've read he has a private elevator. Is that true?"

"I wouldn't know."

Fascinated, Furth watched the circumference of the pancake blacken.

"Isn't that pancake done yet?" asked Adams.

"No," Furth replied. He watched the pancake smoke. He was thinking.

"It's smoking," Adams said.

"What?"

"The pancake!"

"I haven't flipped it yet. You know Fermat numbers are very interesting things."

Adams closed his eyes in despair.

"I'm worried about Ben," Superstoe said. "He's praying a lot."

"It's a bad sign," Furth agreed. "Approaching senility."

"I am the only sane being in this room!" Adams roared.

"That's what's wrong with you," said Superstoe.

Furth poked at the circle of charcoal on the griddle. "Do you really think we're crazy, Ben?" he asked.

"Of course we're crazy," said Superstoe. "That's why we don't watch television."

"The pancake seems to have burned," said Furth.

8   The laboratory was completed. The cement floor lay a bit unevenly, and they blew a fuse the first time they switched on the lights—bare bulbs suspended from the ceiling—but Furth pronounced it an admirable lab.

Furth carried the equipment into the lab. Then he looked around. "I seem to have forgotten to order tables," he said.

That night he and Superstoe drove Johanneson's largest truck to the state park twenty-two miles away.

They carried the picnic tables into the lab and Furth began to remove the benches.

"Now," said Superstoe, "all we need do is write to Knutson, and see that Ben joins his staff."

9   Ben Adams was born in North Dakota. His father grew sugar beets in the black soil along the Red River of the North.

Adams learned to read at the age of three. When he was ten, an older friend complained of all the books he had to read at the state university. "There must be five hundred books in that library," the boy said.

Every Saturday thereafter Adams hitchhiked or walked the fourteen miles to the university.

When his father died, his mother moved to Great Spoons. Every afternoon Adams walked straight from the high school to the university library, where he read until it closed.

One evening, as he sat at a reading table, a hand fell onto the page. Adams looked up. He recognized the professor of classics. "What are you doing with the Greek lexicon?" he asked.

"Learning Greek," the boy replied.

So the professor tutored him, without payment, first in Greek and then in Latin.

A year and a half later Adams entered the state university. The professor began to invite him to his house on Friday evenings; the philosophy professor, a history professor, and sometimes the French professor and a mathematics professor came. They talked, and they drank sherry or port.

When Adams graduated, they wanted him to go to Harvard graduate school.

But his mother had remarried. Her new husband had sold the farm, invested the money, and lost it. Thus after classes at Harvard Adams worked. He worked as a librarian, a bookstore attendant, a waiter, a carpenter's apprentice, a plumber's helper, a garbage collector; in the summers he dug ditches.

After two years and four months, telling neither Harvard nor his mother, he took a job as a stoker and sailed to Liverpool. He took two changes of clothes, a trunk full of books, and a briefcase full of manuscripts.

He spent six months in London, six months in Paris, two years in Leipzig; then a year in Paris, a year in Rome, two years in Amsterdam. He attended lectures, he talked in cafés, he lived in attics, he read books, and he worked—as a tutor, furniture mover, translator, ditch digger, dishwasher, plumber, butcher, gravedigger.

Then he traveled to Norway. He lived there two years, first working as a farmhand and later as a lumberjack. In the spring of his second year he began writing. He produced twelve volumes written in longhand in brown ink. He bound the volumes in black leather.

He decided he was ready to teach. He returned to America on an immigrant ship and began teaching philosophy at the City College of New York and, two nights a week, Norwegian at Columbia. He was thirty-seven years of age.

He met a woman teaching physics; she was thirty-eight. He married her and engendered two girls in two years. Four years later they moved to the University of Maryland, where he read a paper to the Baltimore Philosophers' Club.

A professor from Johns Hopkins, Samuel Podorinsky, heard him read it and suggested he expand the paper into a book. Adams was reluctant, but Podorinsky insisted. Adams began to write.

As he was typing the final draft, a book by a well-known scholar appeared which in effect duplicated Adams's book. Adams threw his manuscript in the garbage.

A little later he reread the twelve volumes he had composed in the Norwegian forests. He decided two of the volumes were superfluous. He threw them away.

One evening, as Adams was returning to his rented Baltimore house, he passed a boy sitting on the pavement holding a stub of chalk in his hand. A right triangle with squares projecting from the sides was drawn on the sidewalk. The sides of the triangle were labeled x, y, and z.

Adams took the chalk and began writing equations. The boy said, "I know that proof."

"What's the problem, then?"

"I'm looking for a new proof."

Adams raised his eyebrows. "Why?"

"I just am." The boy seemed surprised one should ask.

Adams handed him back the chalk. "How old are you?"

"Almost eleven."

"What's your name, boy?"

"Lazarus Furth."

Twelve years later, while Furth was at Caltech composing Matthew Bumm's attack on Goedel's Theorem, Adams was talking to Podorinsky in a Baltimore bar. It was three in the afternoon. Podorinsky had just returned from the American Philosophical Society convention in New York.

"Don't you have a class now?" asked Adams.

"Indeed I do," Podorinsky replied. "And my lecture is taped, and the tape recorder is sitting on the podium. My reader is taking attendance. You should have gone to the convention, Ben."

"Why?"

"I saw some fascinating burlesque shows. Interviewed the strippers. Fascinating convention. I was gathering material for a new book." Podorinsky wrote detective novels under a pseudonym.

"At one show—where was it?—the Heat Wave, I think— I saw Pillsbury, chairman of the department at North Dakota. Know him?"

"No."

"He's looking for someone to take his job. I told him about you. He said the job is yours if you're crazy enough to want to go back to North Dakota. He's moving to Arizona."

"I'll go."

At North Dakota the president of the university was impressed with Adams. He encouraged Adams to revise the philosophy curriculum.

Adams met Bryan Knutson, a state legislator.

Adams tried to hold Friday evening dialectics.

The faculty thought he meant Friday evening parties. Even after he kept the lights on, refused to play records, and locked the bedroom doors they thought he meant parties.

Then one night he deposited an economics professor and the wife of a graduate student on his lawn in three feet of snow. Returning to the house he discovered the motor running in a car. Inside the car he discovered an English professor and a dramatics instructor. He threw them in the snow, too.

Then no one came on Friday evenings—until one night, several weeks later.

Adams was grading papers on "The Allegory of the Cave as Applied to North Dakota." He heard a timid knock on the door, and in walked Paxton S. Superstoe.

Superstoe looked around, blinking. "Oh," he said, "I'm sorry."

"What about?"

"I was told you held dialectics Friday evenings."

"I do."

"It's over then?"

"It's just begun."

Superstoe removed the brown package from under his arm and exposed a bottle of John Jameson. "They drank at the Symposium," he said. "I thought ..."

"Of course."

"It's James Joyce's favorite."

"It's mine too."

"What are you discussing tonight?"

"What would you like?"

"The Good."

Gradually others came to the Friday-evening dialectics. Superstoe brought Ivan Borozov, the Russian instructor. Borozov had a bald head, flushed cheeks, and one eye. He drank a pint of vodka every morning with breakfast. He had escaped from Russia during the Second World War, killing, on the way, four Communists and two Nazis, and losing his left eye in a fight with a Frenchman in a café. He strangled the Frenchman. In Russia he had taught philology. In America he bought a glass eye and taught beginning Russian, intermediate Russian, and scientific Russian.

Then Ed Watt came. He was an M.D. who taught psychobiology at the university, conducted cancer research, and for ten years had been writing a book on Laurence Sterne. He was forty years old, smoked meerschaum pipes, and was wont to say, "I don't believe in God, but if he did exist, he'd be an M.D."

A year later Arthur Pall came, fresh from graduate school. Pall was a red-haired, good-looking, charming Machiavelli. He had a B.S. in chemistry and an M.A. in history. He had written his thesis on Renaissance murders and assassinations. His hobby was inventing poisons, for which he used Watt's lab. Once he destroyed a series of Watt's cancer cultures; he didn't tell Watt, and Watt thought he had discovered a cure for cancer.

Isen Timothy Zorr came. He was blond and blue-eyed and better looking than Pall and even more concupiscent. He looked younger than Pall, though they were both twenty-four when they came to the university. Zorr taught English, said he was writing a book on sexual imagery in Emily Dickinson's poetry, played the harpsichord, and tried to seduce the girls in his classes. He could argue with Adams, however, as keenly as Watt or Superstoe.

And of course Lazarus Furth came—"For some sensible conversation," as he told Adams.

"Why the hell come here?" Adams asked him. "You could get a job anywhere."

"Hell, Ben," Furth replied, "it's all a fucking game any how. If I work for industry, I'll have to kiss somebody's ass; if I go to Princeton, I'll have to specialize. Shit, I've got thirty specialties now."

At the time, none of them—Superstoe, Adams, Furth, Watt, Borozov, Pall, or Zorr—suspected they would one day rule.

With the encouragement of the president of the university, and—thanks to Knutson—money from the state legislature, Adams created a program for exceptional students. Special courses were initiated.

Furth lectured on "The Structure of Everything," and conducted "Seminar on Insoluble Problems." Adams taught a year's course on the first page of the *Euthyphro*. Superstoe conducted classes on "Evolution—Physical, Biological, and Linguistical" and "Psychology from Abrahms to Zweig."

Watt taught "Artistic Insanity," Pall taught "The Ethics of Violence," and Zorr supervised "Literary Classics": his students read pornography.

Adams, Furth, Watt, and Borozov led a colloquium on "Thinking."

Then after one year a new president came to the university. He terminated the program for exceptional students.

He told the legislature, "From now on this university will produce useful citizens. We're not going to waste our time and money turning out eggheads."

That same year Adams's older daughter, Sophia, joined the Roman church, left Reed College, and entered a convent.

Two months later, as if not to be outdone by her sister, his other daughter, Rachel, ran off with a Fuller Brush salesman. By the end of the year his wife had left for New York.

He asked Johanneson if he would hire him to help on the farm.

"No," Johanneson said, "but you come live in one of those empty houses and I'll pay your bills."

"No."

"Look at it this way," Johanneson said. "Every Jewish family is supposed to support a scholar. We're cousins. You're a scholar."

Adams agreed.

Adams's and Johanneson's grandmother had been named Sarah Goldstein.

10 Superstoe's letter to Knutson was mailed in May.

In June, with school dismissed for the summer, Furth spent his days in the lab. He nurtured his cultures, and he studied.

Every day more books arrived—volumes on bacteriology, immunology, epidemiology, hygiene, public health, infectious diseases, pathology, pharmacology, livestock diseases, crop diseases.

Meanwhile, as Furth made notes on rinderpest, Superstoe filled stacks of notebooks with writing. He sat at the table in the Dialectic Room. He wrote hurriedly, sometimes in blue ink, sometimes in black, often in red, occasionally in green. At times his thirty-nine-cent ballpoint halted, and he chewed the end of the pen or tapped it against his forehead as if hoping to flush an idea from its neurological burrow. He had composed a list of national and world problems by going through one Sunday's edition of the *New York Times*. He arranged the problems in alphabetical order, and then he proceeded to solve each problem in turn, jotting the solutions in the notebooks. He showed the notebooks to no one. As each was filled, he placed it under his bed.

Adams's life continued unchanged. He sometimes borrowed a few of Furth's books; he continued his study of the Arabic language; he argued with Furth about Ideas. (Adams maintained that Ideas could be considered to exist everywhere, as if they were an ether or a field analogous to an electromagnetic field. Furth argued that Ideas were coded in the deoxyribonucleic acid and that wrong ideas occurred through mutation.)

Adams seemed unconcerned with the plans. Perhaps he still thought they would come to nothing. Perhaps he was merely waiting. His thoughts—save for his intellectual thoughts—he never communicated.

Furth expressed concern at Adams's lack of interest. But Superstoe advised confidence. "When the time comes, Ben will act," he said.

Then on a hot July afternoon, as Adams and Furth strolled along the dirt road to Johanneson's house and Superstoe pedaled his bicycle in circles around them, Superstoe said, "Did I tell you, Ben? I wrote Knutson for you."

"The hell you did."

"Your signature is very easy to forge."

"Good God, Paxton."

"You have just received an answer from him. He wrote he'd be here sometime next week."

Adams gave the bicycle a shove and Superstoe skidded to the dirt. Furth leaped nimbly over the obstruction and they walked on.

Superstoe wrestled the bicycle off his bare chest. "You are not Samaritans!" he cried.

The pedestrians walked calmly on.

"Paxton!" Adams cried.

"Ever been goosed by a bike?" inquired Superstoe.

"I have been the butt of many jokes," Adams replied. Superstoe raced ahead.

"There are two kinds of people," Furth remarked.

"The Superstoes and the non-Superstoes," Adams said.

"There's only one Superstoe."

"Thank God."

"There are two kinds of people," Furth repeated. "The intelligent, individualistic, creative kind and the unthinking kind: the masses. Our aim is to create a society of the former and eliminate the latter. Heretofore every utopia has aimed at stifling intellect, creativity, and—" he paused, watching Superstoe, hands on head and feet on the handlebars, slide into the ditch—"eccentricity. They've been no different from existing societies."

They reached Johanneson's house. Superstoe opened the refrigerator and suggested a wienie roast.

"Beer?" asked Furth.

"Not much," replied Superstoe. "I'd estimate fifty cans." He threw three cans to Furth. Furth handed one to Adams. Superstoe handed Adams the opener.

"However," said Adams, "genius arises from the masses. If you wipe out the masses ..."

"Wipe?" asked Superstoe.

Adams took the towel and wiped the beer from his eyes. Superstoe grabbed the erupting can, but it slipped through his fingers. Adams began wiping his trousers.

"Nothing of the can," said Furth, his opener sinking into the can with a pop and a sigh.

"Kind," Superstoe corrected.

"We shall be," said Furth. "We simply won't let them have babies. They'll enjoy sex more that way."

Johanneson joined them, and they had their wienie roast, and they drank beer, and they contemplated. Evening settled down onto the lawn, where they sat in canvas chairs in the cool green air. A mourning dove cooed. Two meadow larks flitted over their heads, from east to west, and a rabbit hopped from behind the barn. The stillness and the coolness were soothing and idyllic.

"Are you aware of the Indo-European root 'dhlgh'?" Superstoe asked suddenly. No one answered.

"It meant to carry out one's responsibilities," he continued. "In German it became 'pflegen': to become accustomed to, to bestir oneself. The Germans grew used to responsibility, which is typical. But the English did something curious. In Old English 'pflegen' turned into 'plegan' or, as it is sometimes found, 'plegian,' which meant to play. Isn't that interesting?"

Adams dropped his cigar ashes into Superstoe's beer can.

"You see," Superstoe went on, addressing the rabbit, "the English, from which I am descended, turned 'work' into 'play.'" The rabbit hopped into the windbreak of trees. "It's the sign of a higher nature to turn work into play." He reached for his beer can. "I wonder if Bryan Knutson turns work into play."

11 Furth was in the barn-laboratory when he heard the car pull into the driveway, but he continued to peer into the microscope. It was four days later, and the temperature was 103. He was wearing only red-and-white-striped boxer shorts and sneakers.

Superstoe, wearing white bermudas, was lying on a towel on the grass. He heard the car, but he didn't look up. He assumed it was Adams.

A sonorous voice boomed, "Anybody home?"

Superstoe craned his neck and saw, shimmering in the heat waves, a Lincoln Continental. He clambered to his knees and found two trouser legs, neatly pressed, before his eyes. Erect, he saw a white shirt and a silk tie. A hand reached for his bare, sweaty stomach.

"Afternoon, friend. My name's Bryan Knutson."

Superstoe pulled a blue bandanna from the pocket of his bermudas and wiped the perspiration from his forehead and his palms. Knutson's hand slipped into a pocket for safety. He asked, "Where's Adams? Went by his place but ..."

Superstoe held up his right hand, palm outward. Having silenced him, Superstoe pulled Knutson's hand from its pocket and shook it firmly.

"Bryan Knutson," Superstoe enunciated. He held the hand in both of his. "Yes." He breathed. "Yes, I am Paxton S. Superstoe. I expected you." He relaxed his grip and the hand retreated to the pocket, to jingle coins.

"Adams told you ..."

"No."

"He wrote me and ..."

"Senator Knutson," Superstoe intoned, "Mr. President."

Knutson smiled deprecatingly.

"No," Superstoe resumed, again raising his hand. "Ben did not tell me. He did not have to. Come into the kitchen where it's cooler and have a beer."

"Well ..."

"I knew you were coming. Last night I had a dream. I don't have them often. I inherited the faculty from my mother. She experienced a premonitory dream before her death. And before my father's death. And before my brother was shot down in the war."

Superstoe had been an only child.

"Last night I dreamed you would come today. And that you would be elected President a year from this November. And other events as well. Remember, Lincoln dreamed of his assassination."

They entered the kitchen. Superstoe safely opened two cans. He handed one to Knutson and tapped his against it. "To the election," he said. He sat. Knutson sat.

"Now, Bryan, the first thing you must do is acquire competent advisers."

Knutson leaned back and opened his mouth, but Superstoe went on. "You must weed out the self-seekers and replace them with experts devoted to your election."

Again Knutson opened, then closed, his mouth. "We've watched you carefully, Bryan. You've proved your greatness. All that remains is to show it to the people. You mustn't hide your light under a basket. In ten years you, not George Washington, will be known as the father of his country. Now come with me."

Superstoe stopped him at the door. "You forgot your hat."

Knutson retrieved his hat and followed.

"This is Lazarus Furth. Lazarus, President Knutson."

Furth looked up wildly from his microscope, as if looking for the button that would make the laboratory disappear.

"Lazarus knows more about germs, chemicals, and nuclear energy than any man living. He has refused offers to work for industry; he has refused offers to work for the government; he has refused invitations from the Princeton Institute for Advanced Study. I doubt very much if he will even consent to join your staff. Now come this way."

Cooling his legs in the breeze from the Lincoln's air conditioner, Superstoe directed him to Johanneson's farm.

Adams, driving Johanneson's truck, turned into the drive before them. "We've been helping Jason," Superstoe explained. "Last week two of his hands put one another in the hospital in a fight over a girl. The third ran off with the girl."

They had volunteered to help Johanneson, even though neither Furth nor Superstoe had ever driven a tractor. Up and down the fields they went, forming the left half of a wedge. Johanneson was in the lead. Adams came behind him and to his left, then Furth, hunched nervously over the wheel, and then Superstoe, singing "Bringing in the Sheaves."

At dusk of the fourth day black clouds piled up in the east. They mowed all night, seeing by the headlights. But Superstoe's light burned out.

They found him that morning in the middle of a field of sunflowers.

"Hell, I don't want it."

"I thought you did," said Knutson.

"What made you think that?"

"Your letter ..."

"Oh that damn letter ... Why should I be your adviser? You wouldn't take my advice."

Knutson set his beer can on the table between them. They were sitting on Johanneson's porch, and they could hear Superstoe fussing in the kitchen. "I've always valued your advice, Ben," Knutson said.

"You'll be President soon. You'll have a staff of Rhodes scholars."

Knutson smiled. "Everybody thinks I'm going to run," he said, raising his beer can.

"I don't give a damn whether you run or not."

Knutson set the can back on the table. "I haven't decided ..."

"Shit, Bryan, you decided before you were twelve."

"We'll run some surveys first ..."

Adams crushed his empty can in one hand and threw it into the yard. "Do that."

Superstoe joined them, carrying a can in each hand and a third balanced atop the two. Under one arm was a newspaper. "There's a nice editorial welcoming you, Bryan," he said. Knutson smiled automatically. "Opposite the astrology chart." Knutson grabbed the paper.

12   On Labor Day Superstoe was in Washington with a key to Knutson's Senate office and a pass admitting him to the building.

The next day he flew back to North Dakota. He jogged down the flight of steps, hurried across the runway, entered the small terminal, tipped his hat to Adams, who was in the boarding line, and said, "Your office is first to the left. *Au revoir.*" He vanished out the opposite door.

Adams started after him, but the crowd pushed him forward and onto the runway.

Outside, Superstoe yelled: "Lazarus!"

"Evening, Paxton."

Superstoe jumped and looked behind him. "I thought perhaps you had left," he said.

"Had a Coke."

They walked to Adams's car. "Ben looked surprised," Superstoe remarked.

"I believe he thought you'd gone to Minot. You left a note to that effect."

"Oh, yes."

"Get the office cleaned up?"

"Oh, yes. You should see what I found in one desk!"

"What?"

"Dirty pictures."

"Just lying in the desk?"

"The drawer was locked. I'm afraid I ruined it."

"The picture?"

"The desk. I'll show you the pictures when we get home."

They reached the car. Equations, Superstoe observed, were drawn in the dust on the hood. "Did you solve it?" he asked. Furth shook his head.

13   "Ben, I can't have this sort of thing."

"What sort?"

"My office ransacked. My ..."

"I don't know a thing about it."

"You come in here and move out my three top aides ... desks broken into ..."

"I just got here, Bryan."

"Well, who the hell?"

"Have you seen this?"

"What is it?"

"Found it in my desk. A report on your aides."

Knutson opened the folder and began to read. "Jesus H. Christ," he whispered. "Is this true?"

"Hell, I don't even know the men's names."

"Who wrote this?"

"Is it signed?"

Knutson found the last page, read, and muttered, "Respectfully submitted"—and then cried, "How did he get this information?"

"He's indefatigable."

"My God, I'm glad I found this out now. This would have queered my chances ..."

"Don't thank me."

"It's hard to believe."

Adams shrugged.

"No, I mean it's hard to believe Superstoe could have gotten this information."

A green-eyed, red-haired youth, wearing a blue turtleneck, a tweed jacket with elbow patches, desert boots, and khaki pants, stepped into the office.

"Morning, Ben," he said simply. "Where's my office?"

"Arthur Pall," Adams said to Knutson.

Again the door opened and a straw-haired youth carrying two large suitcases stepped inside and cried, "Art, you son of a bitch!"

"Isen Timothy Zorr," Adams said.

"You sex maniac!" Pall shouted.

"Ben!" cried Zorr. "How are you? Hi, Senator Knutson!"

"Ben," asked Knutson, "what the hell is going on?"

"Staff moving in, Bryan," Adams replied.

Superstoe had found Arthur Pall at a teachers' college in southern Illinois. Pall hadn't replied to the cryptic letter. He replied to the cryptic telegram with "Whatever it is No." Finally Superstoe phoned him, explained the code in Latin, and sent a telegram in the code.

Pall called Superstoe, collect. He said, "You're nuts."

"Be in Washington two days after Labor Day."

"Why, it's impossible."

"Certainly, Arthur. Knutson's office is number 283."

"I'm happy here."

Superstoe laughed heartily.

"I'm an associate professor already," Pall said, "and I'm sleeping with the dean's wife, who's a little older but a nice piece."

"That's wonderful, Arthur. In ten years you'll be dean yourself, and ever after you'll preside at the annual summer picnic. Goodbye."

Pall left the Labor Day picnic at noon—left the dean's wife wading in the stream, fresh jelly in her rubber diaphragm—

drove home, packed a bag of clothes, and drove to the airport. The ticket agent told him all flights were filled.

"But my mother, dear mother, died suddenly," Pall explained.

The ticket agent nodded solemnly and then smiled and lifted the phone. "We'll take care of you," he said.

Pall still wore his shorts, tennis shoes, and sports shirt.

It took Superstoe several days to track Zorr. He had returned to graduate school at Berkeley, left after a semester to teach at a junior college in southern California, and after a semester there gone to Paris to write a novel.

A cablegram found him in care of the Paris office of the *New York Herald Tribune*. Another seller handed him the cablegram as he stood before a café on the Champs Elysées. He read it, handed his twenty papers to a woman walking past, collected the money cabled to the bank, and caught a plane.

14   Adams sent them the letter attesting his security clearance. Superstoe framed the letter and hung it in the Dialectic Room. Above the frame he hung a small American flag.

The Xerox duplicator arrived. Superstoe made copies of the classified papers sent by Adams, and Furth read them in the evenings.

During the day Furth labored in the laboratory. Now and then he drove Superstoe's jeep to the university to pick up more cultures from Watt.

They had resigned from Crossbar High School.

Superstoe was ecstatic over his retirement. The first few days he wandered about the house and lab inventing songs. He sang:

The man who taught Latin
Went out at night cattin',
And he met a virgin whore.

"Ho-ore," Furth chorused.
Superstoe sang:

She said are you ready
to go to the beddy
And try it one time more?

"Mo-ore," Furth chorused.

The man who taught Latin,
He said can you fatten
My tool just a little bit more?

"Mo-ore."

She said to her Teddy,
Oh my aren't you heady
To think I'd know such lore.

"Low-ore.

Said he to his kitten,
I am not kiddin',
Get down and lie on the floor.

"Flow-ore."

Oh my but I'm smitten,
Indeed I am bitten
To see you ...

"An electric blow-er."
"An electric blower?"
"We install it in the rear of a panel truck," Furth explained, "and blow germs or crop killers or whatever from it."
"Won't somebody notice?"

"We'll do it at night."

"Will that prevent detection?"

"I hope so."

"There's nothing more conspicuous than a blower," Superstoe said.

"This will be a secret blower."

"All right, then."

15 Superstoe was watching Furth and Johanneson tighten nuts and fit pipes. He had helped assemble the first truck, but Furth had asked him to desist when he discovered the fan had been installed backward.

"I always wanted to be a truck driver," Superstoe said. "But, I always found the food was worst where the truckers ate."

"The world is full of myths," Furth said.

Superstoe was sitting on one of the dozen metal drums that lined the wall of Johanneson's barn. The drums contained weed killer which would also destroy wheat, rye, and barley.

"Which truck am I going to drive?" asked Superstoe.

"I didn't plan on us driving them," Furth said.

"You've invented a robot to drive them?"

"Maybe Ed Watt can find us some men."

"Won't that be dangerous?"

"That's why I don't want to drive one. It'll be the most dangerous part of our plan."

16 Ed Watt entered Johanneson's barn one Saturday morning in November. Superstoe was at home reading Grotius.

" 'Lo, Doc," said Johanneson.

"Where's Lazarus?" asked Watt.

Johanneson tilted his head. Furth appeared from beneath the truck.

"I thought you were doing epidemiological research," Watt said, "not mechanical engineering." He inspected the truck.

Furth stood and wiped his hands on his overalls. "Didn't I tell you?" he asked.

"I brought a new virus," Watt said. "I thought you might be interested."

"I am."

Watt opened the rear door of the other truck. He walked along the row of drums, now piled two high. He climbed into the cab of the first truck and examined the tanks, pipes, and compressor. "You know what somebody could do with these?" he began.

"That's what we're gonna do," Furth said.

Unperturbed, Watt sat on a stool and packed his pipe. "Why?"

Furth took a fan belt down from a nail on the wall above Watt's head. "We thought we'd take over from the government," he said.

"I wondered why Ben went to Washington." Watt lit his pipe and puffed for half a minute. "Think it will work?"

Furth stretched the belt on a compressor. "Just have to find out."

"Hmm."

"Haven't anything better to do. Have you?"

Watt puffed for a few seconds. "I suppose not," he said. Furth disappeared beneath the truck. "But," he added, "I'm not eager to get caught."

"Neither am I." Furth's voice came from beneath the truck. Then his head appeared. "We'll need some help. Guys to drive these trucks. They ought to know chemistry and bacteriology." He slid out from under the truck and stood up. "Paxton thinks they ought to know Plato, too, but that's a lot of crap."

"How many?"

"We'll have three trucks. Two to a truck."

"I'll see what I can do."

Four weeks later Furth received a letter from Watt. It read:

Dear Lazarus,

David Silvers and Robert McAllen, grad. students in biochemistry. John Lee, ass't. prof. biochem. Fritz Wilson, grad. student in bacteriology.

I think one expert per truck will be enough. You have 1.33 for good measure. You also have Laurence Miller, math instructor, and Jack Smith, English instructor. They can learn whatever bacteriology they need to know quickly enough.

They've read Plato.

It will be less suspicious if they leave at the end of the semester. Can they stay out there with you? Maybe in Ben's house.

Ed

Furth replied:

Dear Ed,

Yes.

Can we trust them?

Laz

Watt answered:

Dear Lazarus,

I think so.

Ed

17   Superstoe sang at the top of his lungs: "God rest ye merry, gentlemen, let nothing you dismay, remember Christ our sayay-vure was born on Christmas day!" He thrust the plug into the socket and the tree, festooned with balls, icicles, strings of popcorn, and a dried Hawaiian lei, lit.

"*Semper fidelis,*" said Superstoe, congratulating the string of lights.

Furth dropped the armload of beribboned packages at the foot of the tree. A beard of cotton was taped to his cheeks. The red chamber pot, inverted, sat on his head.

Preceded by a blast of wind and snow, Adams entered the house.

"Welcome home!" cried Superstoe.

"How's Washington?" asked Furth.

"Drunk, when I left."

"I saw Lazarus's letter to Santa Claus," Superstoe said. "Do you know what he asked for?"

"A Guggenheim?"

"Botulin. Rickettsia. Viri. Fungi. Mosquitoes. Houseflies —*Musca domestica.*"

Solemnly Furth handed the packages around. For each of them a box containing vaccines and a hypodermic syringe from Watt.

For Adams, cigars from Johanneson, a microfilm camera from Furth, and an epic poem in iambic tetrameter from Superstoe.

For Furth, a sweater from Johanneson, the latest volume of bacteriological abstracts from Adams, and Sears, Roebuck long underwear from Superstoe. "For those cold days in the lab," he explained. On the seat DO NOT TREAD ON ME was stenciled beneath a coiled rattlesnake.

For Superstoe, a *Playboy* calendar from Johanneson, a top hat (for the inauguration) from Adams, and a gas mask from Furth.

Johanneson arrived and found a box of bills from Furth, a catalogue of citrus-fruit seedlings from Superstoe, and a Chinese atlas from Adams.

On the table in the Dialectic Room Superstoe arranged plates, utensils, and goblets. He wore Levis, sneakers, a gray sweatshirt bearing the face of Johann Sebastian Bach, and the top hat.

He returned to the kitchen and removed three bottles of Gewürztraminer from the refrigerator. "First course," he said. He removed a cottage-cheese carton. "Salad," he said. He reached again into the refrigerator.

"Good God no!" Furth cried from the stove.

Superstoe cracked his head on a tray of ice cubes.

"That's not cottage cheese! That's San Joaquin fever!"

"Does it go with white wine?"

"It goes with embalming fluid."

"We'll have it with the Pinot Noir." He replaced the carton and removed another. "Do you suppose this is cottage cheese?" he asked.

"Open it and see," said Furth.

Superstoe gazed at the carton. He placed it in Furth's hand. "You open it and see."

Setting the bottles before him and handing him a corkscrew, Superstoe asked, "What does the President eat for breakfast, Ben?"

Adams weighed the corkscrew in his palm. "Cheerios."

"Really?"

Adams reached for his cigar, which rested in a red, white, and blue aluminum ashtray announcing KNUTSON THE NATIVE SON.

"Does he drink orange juice?"

"Grapefruit."

"With sugar?"

"Artificial sweetener."

"Coffee?"

"Caffeine-free."

"Does he have stomach trouble?"

"Ulcers."

"I've never read that."

"Neither have I."

"Did he tell you he had ulcers?"

"He did."

"The President told you?"

"Hell no. Knutson."

"Well, what has the President told you?" Superstoe had sat down. His face was as serious as a boy's inquiring into the adult world.

"The President, Paxton, has told me nothing."

"He says nothing at breakfast?"

"What the hell's breakfast got to do with it?"

"I thought you breakfasted with the President, along with the other government leaders."

Superstoe disappeared into the kitchen. Furth, beard removed but chamber pot on head, emerged with hot hors d'oeuvres: shrimp and clam puffs.

Johanneson sprang to life, after tenderly placing his atlas beneath the tree.

"You made the Cheerios up then," said Superstoe.

Adams chewed and swallowed. "Not at all. Knutson appears congenitally incapable of keeping his mouth shut."

"Oh dear," said Superstoe.

"Why say that?" asked Furth. "How else do we get information?"

"Hot," breathed Superstoe.

Salad of orange and grapefruit sections and cottage cheese, garnished with pimentos and bathed in a French dressing created by Furth, followed. Only Superstoe failed to eat his.

At the next course he appropriated two servings of fillet of sole meunière.

Grandly Furth bore the roast goose from the oven. Humbly Adams carved it. Watching the juice ooze from the blade of the knife, Superstoe licked his lips.

Superstoe bore in mashed potatoes: a block of melting butter spread from the center of the mound.

Furth entered cautiously, watching with terror the brown steaming gravy lap at the sides of the bowl.

Again Superstoe entered. Gallantly he rested the bowl of sweet potatoes—islands of burnt ochre in a sea of sweet sauce—before Johanneson. Johanneson caressed the bowl.

Furth presented the peas: emerald spheres, exhaling steam, with mushrooms snuggling amidst them. He sat. Superstoe sat.

They ate.

When the goose had been eaten, Furth removed the carcass and brought in a turkey. Empty wine bottles filled the windowsill.

Furth stepped through the door bearing a blazing dish. He set it on the table and stepped back with satisfaction. Superstoe sang a chorus from Handel's *Messiah*.

The blaze died, leaving pockets of flame spurting from the rim of the dish. Furth divided the plum pudding into quarters, and Adams uncorked another bottle.

The table stood bare except for the four snifters, the bottle of cognac, and the chamber pot. Johanneson snored contentedly.

Adams examined the red tip of his cigar. "The time has come," he said, "to talk of many things."

"Of murder and disease."

"And secrets and intrigues," added Superstoe.

Adams described the progress in Washington: Knutson's dependence on Zorr as a speechwriter, Pall's accumulation of data on the private lives of government officials.

Furth enumerated his plans: deploying the trucks and their supplies throughout the country, sabotaging fertilizer and feed.

They agreed on signals and code words.

Finally Johanneson interrupted. "I was just thinking," he said. "What happens if we get caught?"

"Would they let us hold dialectics in Leavenworth?" asked Superstoe.

No one spoke.

"Well," said Superstoe, "nothing but dying is done without danger."

"Aren't you worried?" asked Johanneson, his brow furrowed.

"Why should I be?" Superstoe answered. "Here I am, wit, scholar, raconteur. I've led a life of ridicule. I've taught courses I could have taught before I was out of high school. I'm a linguistics specialist teaching ninth-grade grammar. A scholar of psychology who has been asked to teach health and safety. A man who writes Latin as gracefully as Cicero who has never been able to take a class beyond Caesar's *Bellum Gallicum.* I'm about to take over the world. Should I hesitate out of fear? I've lived twenty-five years of my life in North Dakota. Do you think prison frightens me?"

Furth filled the four snifters and they toasted Superstoe.

Then Superstoe's eyes lit up. "Let's go rape Miss Thippleson," he suggested.

Miss Thippleson was fifty-nine years old and taught history, home economics, and physical education at Crossbar High School.

"I would rather rape a rusty battleship," Furth replied.

"But think of the joy we'd bring to her life," said Superstoe. "Remember it's Christmas."

"I'd forgotten," said Furth. "We must make sacrifices so the sun will return and melt that goddamn snow."

"Then we'll sacrifice Miss Thippleson," said Superstoe.

Furth considered. "I don't think the sun would accept Miss Thippleson."

"She *must* be a virgin."

"I think she would drive the sun into another galaxy."

"What shall we do then?"

"That question," said Furth, "has been asked before. And the answer is, invite the sun to dinner. Kill a bull for him."

"Bob Foster has cows," said Superstoe.

"A cow will do," replied Furth.

Furth and Superstoe pulled on coats, hats, and galoshes. As Adams opened another bottle, they forged into the snow and climbed into Johanneson's pickup.

They sped down the snow-free roads—the roads were built higher than the fields so the winds would sweep the snow off. "We'll take the cow to Miss Thippleson's and sacrifice it there," Superstoe suggested.

"All right," said Furth.

"And then we'll rape the old bitch."

It was beginning to get light when they arrived at Bob Foster's. The dogs woke him. His head and his shotgun emerged from the door.

"Merry Christmas!" Superstoe cried.

The shotgun protruded farther.

"We just want one of your cows!" Furth explained.

"Who is it?" they heard his wife yell.

"Superstoe and Furth," he called back to her. "Drunk."

They had a rope around her neck and were tugging her out of her stall when Foster, coat and boots pulled over his long underwear, stood in the door, shotgun pointing.

"Fun is fun," he said, "but if you take that poor pregnant cow out the door I'll shoot you."

"Pregnant?" cried Superstoe.

"We wanted a virgin," Furth said.

Superstoe grabbed Foster's lapel. "We saw him!" he whispered. "A few minutes ago!"

Foster backed away.

"We saw him! Didn't we, Lazarus?"

Furth nodded.

Foster asked, "Who?"

Superstoe looked furtively about and put his mouth to Foster's ear.

"Santa Claus!" he yelled at the top of his lungs.

They charged out the door and leaped into the truck. The engine caught. Furth threw in the clutch.

The tires whined in the snow.

"Get out and push!" Furth cried.

"He'll shoot me!"

Furth shoved. Superstoe sprawled in the snow. Getting to his knees, he looked into the barrel of the shotgun.

He plunged his head into the snow. He waited for the bullet to sear through his body.

A year passed, but he heard only the whine of the tires. He looked up. Foster was convulsed in laughter.

Superstoe sprang to his feet and grabbed his hand. "Merry Christmas, Bob, and many happy returns of the day."

Frantically the tires spun. The windows of the cab were frosted.

Foster stepped into the cab, shotgun in hand. At the same moment the truck leaped forward and skated into a snowbank.

In return for driving them home in his station wagon, they gave Foster breakfast and four bottles of whiskey.

18   At the end of January, Arthur Pall was assigned the task of feeling the pulse of the nation—as Knutson put it. He was to fly about the country and confer with party leaders, and at the same time deny that Knutson might run for the nomination.

Pall's affable, confidence-inspiring personality had already proven invaluable to Knutson. With his help, Knutson had engineered his most impressive counter-attack by leading the opposition in defeating one of the President's priority bills. Then Knutson promptly entered a bill of his own which, some said, was no different from the President's.

Pall possessed the genius—as surely as he might have possessed a genius for painting or violin playing—for winning confidence, friends, and information. He was also a natural actor.

As he traveled, he carried a black attaché case. It contained a red mustache, a black mustache, a red wig, a black wig, glasses, and make-up.

Midway in his travels, he sent word that he had become ill; he would stay with his old friend Dr. Edwin Watt, until he recuperated.

After sending the telegram, he returned to Watt's house, ate lunch, changed clothes, put on the black wig and mustache, and flew to Nashville. Posing as an FBI agent he inspected the personnel records of the Tasty Tidbit Feed and Fertilizer Corporation.

From there he flew to Fort Wayne and obtained a job at the Bumper Feed Company. He began work on a Tuesday. On Sunday he ate dinner with another employee, Ronald Pickers, and Pickers's mother.

The following Sunday he ate dinner with them again. Afterward, the three of them went to a movie. They returned home, Mrs. Pickers retired, and the two men took a leisurely stroll around the block.

Monday morning he flew back to Nashville, wearing the red wig and mustache. That evening he went to a bowling alley and chanced to meet a certain George Black, an employee at the Tasty Tidbit Feed and Fertilizer Corporation.

Tuesday evening he met Black for dinner in a small restaurant on the outskirts of town.

Thursday he dined at Black's home. The children called him Uncle George.

Friday evening the two men ate at a Howard Johnson's. Afterward they drove about for an hour in Pall's rented car.

At one the following morning Pall parked the car in the airport lot and bought a ticket to Chicago.

At the Chicago air terminal he entered a men's room, inserted a dime in one of the doors, and entered the stall. He removed his topcoat, reversed it, and put it on again. He removed the red mustache and wig. He crammed them into a pocket of the topcoat. He put on the black mustache and wig, and adjusted them in a hand mirror. He sat down.

After ten minutes he flushed the toilet, exited, and bought a ticket to Minneapolis.

At the Minneapolis airport he bought a ticket to Great Spoons.

He made a phone call from the Great Spoons airport, and half an hour later Watt picked him up and they drove to Watt's house.

The next day Pall resumed his pulse-feeling tour.

19   "But, Paxton, my friend, what do I care who is in the Kremlin? I am an American now," protested Ivan Borozov.

Superstoe looked at him carefully, trying to determine which eye to look at; he could never remember which was the glass eye. "You know, Ivan," he said, tapping the pile of mimeographed papers and pamphlets, "Ben is Senator Knutson's right-hand man. He'll be needing an expert Kremlinologist soon."

"What is that? You know my English is not so good, Paxton."

Superstoe sat at the vacant desk in Borozov's office, which he shared with an Italian who taught French and German. Borozov's students had difficulty understanding Borozov, and the Italian's students insisted the Italian's accent made *his* English incomprehensible; but the two instructors understood one another's English perfectly. If, occasionally, they found communication difficult, they spoke in Latin.

"An expert in Russian affairs, Ivan," Superstoe explained. "If Knutson is elected President ..."

"Senator Knutson is running for President?"

"Shh."

"I see. I have never understood American politics. But I am a loyal citizen. I always vote. I vote for the best man."

"That is admirable, Ivan. And if you vote for Bryan, and he is elected, I think it is quite likely that, after a time, you will be appointed ambassador to Russia. Therefore, you will have to know who is who in the Kremlin."

"I would not like to be ambassador, Paxton. If I returned to Russia, they would shoot me."

"They're not like that any more, are they?"

"Then they would send me to Siberia. Shall I exchange one North Dakota for another?"

"Don't worry, Ivan. As ambassador you will have diplomatic immunity."

"Paxton, old friend, you do not know the Russians as I know them."

"Exactly. That's why you will make a superb ambassador. You understand them. They will trust you."

"A Russian trusts no one."

"Don't you trust me?" asked Superstoe.

"Of course! I trust you because you are an American and I am an American. But as I am a Russian, I do not trust Russians."

"Good. You see? You know your countrymen. The most important qualification. Now you do your research, and don't say a word about this ..."

"You can trust me, Paxton. We are Americans."

"Correct."

"But I am very busy. I do not find time to keep up my reading in my field. Look." Borozov took a thick blue volume from a shelf. "The new Russian dictionary. They have made many changes."

"Part of the de-Stalinization program, undoubtedly."

"Maybe so. I am only now to the B's in the dictionary."

"As Knutson's expert in Russian affairs you will, of course, receive a salary." Superstoe thought for a second it was the glass eye which lit up. "After a time, Ivan, you will be famous. You will be able to be a professor at any university you want."

"Oh, Paxton, you have very clever—how do you say it?—wid?"

"Wit?"

"That's it."

Superstoe departed. But, as he left Jolligrass Hall, he had a sudden impulse. He walked to the adjacent building, took the elevator to the third floor, and walked briskly down the corridor. He stepped into the outer office, walked past the secretary, and strode into the president's office.

The president was writing. He looked up. Superstoe stared at him.

Superstoe waited.

The president's head moved slightly; he had finally recognized Superstoe.

Superstoe slowly extended his right arm. He pointed his index finger and raised his thumb.

The thumb fell. "Zap," said Superstoe. He strode from the office and down the hall, jogged down the stairs, and strolled to his jeep in the parking lot.

A ticket was slid under a windshield wiper. The jeep did not display the sticker permitting it to be parked in that lot; moreover, the jeep was parked in the space allotted to the dean.

Superstoe placed the ticket under the wiper of the president's Chrysler, returned to his jeep, and headed back to Crossbar.

20 Thanks to Pall, a $100,000 government grant was awarded to Furth, or rather to New Light Enterprises, for research on the effect of smog on cattle raising in the Midwest. Another $30,000 came from a private institute for a study of the social habits of prairie dogs at Theodore Roosevelt National Park. The money was given to Johanneson, to offset his expenditures.

The germs themselves cost little. Nor were the trucks expensive, for they were second-hand, as were the fans. But they were now supporting nine men—the six assistants, Superstoe, Furth, and Johanneson—and Pall had given George Black and Ronald Pickers each $50,000.

The ten of them—Pall came for the meeting—gathered in the Dialectic Room.

"We are beginning," Pall said, "by sabotaging the feed because once the program has begun that method will be more risky. Also because we wish to begin in the spring, and there are no crops in the spring. In addition, the area which we can cover with the trucks is limited. The infected feed will cover a large area, which is desirable for our first stage."

Five of the six assistants sat tensely. The sixth, Laurence Miller, the mathematician, sprawled lazily in his chair, even though his was the greatest sacrifice; he had agreed to shave off his goatee. The other five, and Pall, sat on two benches refashioned from those removed from the picnic tables.

Furth, a lab coat over his overalls, smoked his Christmas pipe and jotted axioms in a notebook. He was inventing a new non-Euclidean geometry, to be called Furthian geometry. Adams's chair at the head of the table was vacant.

Superstoe sat in his customary chair. He was wearing a sweatshirt bearing the face of Beethoven. The printed image had been altered so that the composer appeared to be cross-eyed. Superstoe wore a vague smile.

Johanneson was inspecting the maps he had tacked to the bookshelves—highway maps, meteorological maps, agricultural maps.

In the kitchen the dishes were stacked. They had just finished a dinner of roast pork and baked beans.

"Now," said Pall, "let's go over the checklist a final time. We can't be too careful." Silvers and Lee nodded agreement. Pall shuffled through the papers before him. "Did I give the list to you, Lazarus?" he asked. "Lazarus? Lazarus?"

Smith nudged Furth. Furth nudged him back and continued to write.

"Lazarus?" Pall called.

Johanneson pulled the cork from a bottle. That didn't work. He poured a glass and set it before Furth. Furth drank the whiskey and continued to write.

Pall searched his papers again.

"Didn't you give it to Paxton?" asked Wilson.

Superstoe threw a paper airplane at Pall. Pall unfolded it. "This is the grocery list," he said.

Furth closed the notebook. "I don't remember, Arthur," he said.

"Jesus," Pall grumbled.

"Can't you remember it?" asked Johanneson.

"It doesn't matter," said Pall. "What the hell."

"That's the spirit," said Furth.

Each truck had license plates from a different state. Each man had a forged operator's license. Each man had money for expenses.

The first team, Silvers and Miller, were to depart the following morning for the East Coast. Five days later the second team, McAllen and Wilson, would leave for the South. Eight days after that Lee and Smith would leave for the Southwest. Before each truck left, Superstoe tied a small American flag to the aerial.

PART TWO

The Epidemics

1   The Department of Agriculture advised farmers to remain calm. Vaccine was being rushed to the stricken areas.

The President declared Tennessee, Kentucky, Missouri, Illinois, Indiana, and Ohio disaster areas.

Bryan Knutson took the Senate floor. "Much to my very deep regret and, I must say, to my very deep apprehension," he said, "the President has not made available all the pertinent information concerning the swine epidemic now raging unchecked in ten states.

"In the first place," he continued, "there is not one epidemic but two. The government laboratories seem unaware of that fact. Two types of virus, closely related and producing identical symptoms, have been identified by an independent laboratory.

"In the second place, I should like to request—no, gentlemen, the situation has become too critical—I am *demanding*, as a representative of the hard-working men, women, and children of the state of North Dakota, I am demanding that the President—not an aide, but the *President himself*—reply, immediately, to the following questions ..."

President Long held an impromptu press conference. As he answered, he sipped a glass of buttermilk.

"Mr. President, Senator Knutson has charged on the Senate floor that the FBI is secretly investigating the deaths of two workers in two factories which produce feed for livestock, including swine. Senator Knutson implies that these deaths have some connection with the hog epidemics. He also implies that the preceding implies sabotage. Would you care to comment, sir?"

"I would not care to comment on that at this time. It would not be in the national interest. In the interests—in the national interest."

"What about Senator Knutson's statement that there are two viruses at large instead of just one?"

"Why, we've always known that. But since the two germs do the same thing, we did not wish to complicate matters by going into a lot of technological detail that would have confused the issue. We've always known it. From the first day. The first hour."

"The Public Health Service report states virus A began spreading on April 22 and virus B was first reported on April 26. Which virus did you know about from the first hour?"

"Yes."

"That is, Mr. President, was it virus A or ..."

"Both, goddammit, I told you, both."

2   Pall and Zorr passed out advance copies of Knutson's speech, to be delivered that afternoon in the Senate. An hour later they were seen, and joined, by two reporters as they ate lunch in a cafeteria.

"Say, you know President Long has just announced the epidemics came from contaminated feed?" one reporter said. "He's ordered both plants closed down."

"Really?" said Pall.

The other reporter spoke, tapping the advance copy of Knutson's speech. "How did you get this information, Art?" Pall drank from one of the four cartons of milk on his tray. The reporter leafed through the advance copy. He read: "Ronald Pickers, an employee at the Bumper Feed Company, and George Black, an employee at the Tasty Tidbit Feed and Fertilizer Corporation, both died suddenly on the same day: the day the epidemic began. At the time it was assumed each had a heart attack. Three days ago the FBI exhumed the bodies and attempted autopsies."

He searched for another paragraph and resumed: "You might be interested in the following information—obtained by my staff. During the two weeks previous to his death George Black completed all the payments on thirteen household appliances, his car, *and the mortgage on his house!* What's more, he paid all these debts *in cash!* And during those same two weeks he bought, *with cash,* a color television, a movie camera, a projector, and an outboard motor! The second man, Ronald Pickers, was making arrangements to buy tickets for himself and his mother for a year-long, around-the-world cruise that would have cost *three times* his yearly salary!"

Again the reporter searched and resumed. "Pickers was seen talking with an unidentified man who wore glasses and had long red hair and a red mustache. The witness recalls that the red-haired man spoke with a Spanish accent."

3   The President's press secretary related that the FBI had questioned clerks at hotels and motels in and near Nashville. As a result they investigated thirty-seven reportedly red-haired men who had registered in the area during the preceding months.

A thorough investigation revealed that six of the men wore mustaches; nineteen of them wore glasses; two of them were bald.

One man, however, the FBI was unable to trace. He had given a false address and false license numerals. The motel manager recalled that he spoke with a Russian accent. A waitress remembered a German accent. A filling-station attendant swore it was a French accent.

The man had registered at the motel under the name of George Malfeesance.

"There is absolutely no evidence," the President told the television cameras, "that the epidemics were spread by a foreign power. There is no evidence to support the charge that the epidemics were a clandestine attack of germ warfare."

"Are not forty thousand dead hogs evidence of germ warfare?" Knutson asked the nation in a televised interview. "Obviously it is the work of a foreign power. George Malfeesance affected a variety of accents in order to hide the true identity of the guilty power."

"I have ordered," said the President, "a complete investigation. The movements of all foreign nationals in the country are under constant surveillance. All radical groups within the country are being investigated."

4   "Could it be," Knutson asked reporters, "that a governmental agency, or a military clique, or a group of fanatics within the Army Chemical Corps is plotting to overthrow the government?"

"I have ordered a complete investigation," the President announced, "of every governmental agency and of the armed forces, including the Army Chemical Corps. I rest assured, however, that there is no plot to overthrow the government. I have complete confidence that every agency, every unit of the armed forces, is absolutely loyal. That includes the FBI, the CIA, and the Army Chemical Corps, which have been most frequently mentioned by individuals intent on stirring up unrest and panic and endangering the national security merely to further their own selfish ambitions."

5 Dr. Ed Watt, brown crew cut above black-framed glasses, meerschaum pipe in hand wearing tweed coat and striped tie, closed the refrigerator door. He puffed on his pipe. "I'd say you had a lot of overkill here," he mused.

Furth shrugged. "Once I'd started I couldn't stop."

"That happens."

"We won't use them all," Furth said.

"I hope not." Watt read the labels on the flasks nearest him on the table. "Salmonellosis, anthrax, Coxsackie virus infection, yaws, trachoma, infectious hepatitis, conjunctivitis . . ." Watt removed his glasses and rubbed his eyes.

"I wanted things that would spread," Furth said. "Flies carry these."

Watt replaced his glasses. "I know," he said. "These livestock diseases infect people, too."

"That's incidental."

"I was just thinking I'd better give myself some more inoculations."

Furth opened the refrigerator and handed him a can of beer.

"I'll have one from the kitchen," Watt said. Furth punctured the can and drank. "Whose idea was the feed plants?"

"Arthur's."

"I remember when he was at the university. He killed more cats than the anatomy department."

They strolled into the warm air. All about them young wheat rippled like a green sea in the breeze.

"It's best to be prepared," Furth observed.

"By all means."

They walked toward the house.

"Long should handle it better," Watt said.

"He's being strategic," Furth explained. "Ben says the military wanted him to play down the B.W. until their spies figured out which country was doing it."

They entered the house. Furth washed his hands, and then he opened the refrigerator, pushed aside several cottage-cheese cartons, and extracted a can of beer. He opened it and handed it to Watt.

Watt glanced into the refrigerator. "You must like cottage cheese," he said.

Furth closed the door. "Paxton's wild about it."

6 "Tanned and jovial, looking better than he has for months, President Long met with reporters on the porch of his vacation retreat in Colorado.

"He told reporters, 'I am gratified to see the hysteria in the country vanish. It should be obvious to everyone by now that there is not, nor has there ever been, a biological-warfare attack on the country. The only advantage a foreign power could derive from such a limited epidemic is blackmail, and we have received no threats, no challenges, from any country. Certain persons simply used these tragic but naturally occurring diseases to try to further their own political futures.'"

Superstoe laid the newspaper on the table and sipped his coffee. "I'm glad the President is feeling better," he said. "I was worried about his ulcers."

The phone rang and Furth lifted the receiver.

"How are things in Glocca Morra?" asked the voice of Arthur Pall.

"Peachy creamy," Furth answered.

"Weatherman forecasts smog."

"What's he say?" asked Superstoe.

"Smog." Furth turned to the telephone. Then he looked back at Superstoe. "What am I supposed to answer?"

"Don't you remember?"

"No."

"I don't remember either."

Furth looked into the receiver. "Lots of smog?" he asked.

"Jesus Christ," Pall said.

"Jesus Christ," Furth repeated to Superstoe.

"I don't recall that code. Maybe it's a wrong number."

"Smog and locusts," Pall said.

Furth beamed. "Roger." He hung up.

"Roger?" asked Superstoe. "Do we know a Roger?"

"Certainly. Jolly Roger."

7 Knutson pushed aside his hundred-dollar plate of cold roast beef. The introduction droned on. He smiled to himself and fingered the piece of paper just handed him by Zorr.

He allowed the applause to continue until it faltered ever so slightly; then he raised his arms to plead for silence.

"The President says there is no evidence that germ warfare is being waged against the United States. Yesterday he said the rising number of cases of fowl plague did not constitute an epidemic.

"But, ladies and gentlemen, and our guests, members of the press, I should like to disclose some rather interesting information which has just this moment been handed me.

"As you must have noticed, it is often extremely difficult to obtain information from the executive branch of the government." He paused until the laughter died.

"Here," he resumed, "is the information I have this moment received. I expect tomorrow the administration will say *they* released this information tonight. I hope some friend of the administration is here with us tonight, so he can rush over to the White House with these facts. The FBI and the CIA, it seems, have been working so hard they've taken a vacation." He paused again, smiling at the laughter.

"In the state of Texas, ladies and gentlemen," he began.

8   In the basement Superstoe lay on his back on top of the new deep freeze.

"Don't you think it's hot for July?" he asked as Furth leaped down the stairs.

"I'll say. Those damn fools nearly got arrested racing a Porsche down a Texas highway."

"Who?"

"Lee and Smith."

"I'd like to crawl inside. Did you have to fill it with steaks?"

"You don't want to be a vegetarian, do you?"

"Is it that bad?"

"Rinderpest is very infectious. All the cattle in Texas have it. And the sheep."

"Arthur says chicken is five dollars a pound in Washington."

"Today it's six."

"Is fowl plague very infectious?"

9   Even President Long had to admit something strange was going on. Unfortunately, he couldn't say what. So he fired the head of the CIA and the Secretary of Defense.

His press conferences became more infrequent. Rumor spread that his ulcers were worse.

Meetings of the National Security Council became routine exercises in futility.

A meeting would commence with an announcement of the latest tally of livestock, poultry, and human casualties. Then the acting director of the CIA would report that there was still no evidence of who was responsible.

"But there must be something," the President would insist.

"The Russians are worried," the man would reply. "They think it's the Chinese, and they're afraid they'll be hit next."

"Maybe it *is* the Chinese."

"There's no evidence."

The President would turn to the Director of the FBI. "Haven't *you* found anything?"

"Every available agent is investigating this case. In each epidemic area people are being questioned. All suspicious persons are under surveillance. Every lead is being followed up. Every ..."

"I said have you *found* anything?"

"No, sir. There were two reports of a panel truck being seen at night in Vermont ..."

"Well?"

"We discovered a panel truck belonging to a television repairman."

"Yes?"

"He admitted parking the truck in rural areas at night."

"Yes?"

"There was a mattress in the truck. He was having extramarital relations."

President Long insisted that the press and Senator Knutson were exaggerating the seriousness of the epidemics. In July he was nominated to run for a second term.

In August the other party nominated Knutson. He won the nomination on the second ballot.

He was now a national figure. His party pictured him as the nation's savior.

In his acceptance speech Knutson declared, "This nation faces an unprecedented crisis. This nation needs leadership.

"Someone is spreading these epidemics. If the FBI and the CIA cannot discover who is spreading them, there can be only two explanations. Either the FBI and the CIA, under the present administration, are abysmally incompetent and blundering—*or* the FBI and the CIA are hiding something. And if they are hiding something, then they, and others, must be involved in a plot—a blood-chilling, sinister plot—directed against the people of the United States of America."

10   "It's not fair," said Superstoe. "Ben and Isen and Arthur on the campaign trail, and I have to sit here in Crossbar stuffing envelopes."

"Every little bit helps," said Furth.

"The future President should have a more dignified job."

"We're unsung heroes."

"When I'm President they'll write songs about me."

"I wouldn't doubt it."

"Set to the scores of the Brandenburg Concertos."

"And sung by the Beatles."

"You're not serious."

Watt walked in the door. Superstoe rose and shook his hand. "Dr. Livingstone, I presume?"

"Good evening, Tarzan," Watt replied.

Superstoe crossed his arms over his bare chest. "It's abnormally hot for September. I think it's the Chinese nuclear tests."

"The times are out of joint," Watt said. "I came for a steak."

"Let's see your ration book."

"I'm in a hurry," Watt said. "I have to drive to Fargo tonight and catch a plane to Chicago."

"Medium or rare?"

"Rare."

"A bloody cow on the double!" Superstoe yelled over his shoulder.

Watt sat. "I've been appointed Knutson's personal physician."

"In that case we'll find you a steak," said Furth. He headed for the basement and returned with three sirloins. "Do you have the tranquilizers?" he asked.

Watt nodded. "Arthur convinced him he needs a dependable physician. An expert in germ warfare. Arthur persuaded him spies lurk in every corner."

Superstoe, in the corner, narrowed his eyes.

"It's a vicious campaign," Furth said.

"Long's ulcers are in terrible shape," Watt observed. "They'll have to operate someday."

"Poor man, said Superstoe. "He never should have run for re-election."

"Ben thinks he'll attack Cuba next month," said Furth.

"He has to blame someone," Watt agreed.

"Did you come all the way out here for a steak?" asked Superstoe.

"Of course. Don't you know Knutson's setting an example to the 'beleaguered nation'? He eats only vegetables and fruit."

"I know," said Furth. "Did you see the publicity when he tried to sneak a hamburger and the press got wind of it?"

11 "Presidential Nominee Bryan Knutson today implied that the livestock epidemics and the more recent blights on citrus fruits and corn were initiated by the Army Chemical Corps by order of the President.

"The thinly veiled accusation came at the conclusion of the latest 'red paper,' released today by Knutson's press secretary, Isen Zorr. The forty-seven-page report, prepared by Knutson's staff, purports to show that only a well-equipped laboratory with access to top-secret information and material could have spread the epidemics. Only the Army Chemical Corps, the report states, has access to such information and material.

"At the press briefing at which the 'red paper' was released Zorr implied that the epidemics were instigated by the President to create a crisis. Zorr said, 'Everyone knows the voters tend to re-elect an incumbent during a crisis.'"

Superstoe handed the newspaper to Furth. "Aren't you glad we decided to subscribe to the *Times?*" he asked.

The stock market continued to plummet.

News commentators looked confused. Government officials looked worried.

The President looked ill.

Then, five days before election day, the President was rushed to the hospital for emergency surgery.

12   While the others attended the late President's funeral, Superstoe, carrying a battered portmanteau, entered the East Wing of the White House. He was Special Assistant to the President-elect and Chief Liaison for Governmental Transition, and he was charged with supervising on Knutson's behalf the transfer of duties. He was assigned a small office in the White House basement. He slept on the couch in his office and supped in the now unfrequented second-floor kitchen.

After the funeral Knutson, accompanied by Watt, flew to Phoenix, Arizona, for a three-week vacation. Watt continued to administer tranquilizing drugs—under the guise of vitamin pills, vitamin injections, and immunizations. Additional drugs were administered to counter the extrapyramidal and sedative effects of the tranquilizers. Reporters remarked at how easy-going Knutson had become.

Adams rented a suite at a Washington hotel. He conferred with Superstoe, Pall, and Zorr, and they drew up the list of appointments. For the moment the only appointments they announced were those of Zorr as Presidential Press Secretary and Pall as Special Presidential Assistant for National Security Affairs and Chief Investigator into the recent epidemics.

Meanwhile Furth closed down the lab, destroyed the cultures, and discussed plans with the six assistants, Silvers, McAllen, Lee, Wilson, Miller, and Smith. Then he locked the doors, rode his motorcycle to Great Spoons, sold the motorcycle, bought a suit, and flew to Washington.

Pall leased a house in Georgetown. There he, Zorr, Furth, and Superstoe would reside. Watt found a house and brought his wife and three children.

Finally Johanneson came, by train, with his maps, and rented a small apartment.

The appointments were announced a week before the inauguration.

Adams's appointment as Secretary of State caused a little surprise. But he was an impressive-looking man, so no one doubted his ability.

No one could argue about Johanneson, either. He was a farmer, and a successful farmer, as well. Clearly he was qualified to be Secretary of Agriculture.

The other cabinet posts, except that of Secretary of Defense, were filled by sensible, well-qualified, experienced men.

The Secretary of Defense was Lazarus Furth.

At first Congress questioned Furth's qualifications. But not for long. Congressmen were amazed to learn how much he knew about the Department of Defense. They were pleased to find he was an expert not only on weapons, missiles, strategy, computers, and nuclear energy but on chemical and biological warfare as well. What's more, Furth promised Congress he would close the germ gap.

Finally it was announced that Paxton S. Superstoe would become Director of the CIA.

13   It was eleven of the morning after the inauguration. Furth and Pall entered the bedroom and looked at the quilt-covered mound in the center of the king-sized bed. The mound rose and fell regularly. A top hat lay on one of the pillows.

With a flourish Furth opened the newspaper, folded it back, folded it in half, and began to read:

"In the early-morning hours of the inauguration ball, after President Knutson had retired, the festivities were unexpectedly given new life by the new Director of the CIA, Paxton S. Superstoe.

"Displaying a vivacity and a humor quite foreign to his predecessors in that post, Superstoe began by telling anecdotes. His listeners were soon convulsed with laughter. The dancing stopped and more guests gathered around Superstoe.

"Then Superstoe, still wearing his top hat, leaped onto the bandstand and took the baton from Jerry Jones, noted society bandleader, and conducted the band through several numbers, beginning with a waltz and concluding with a watusi. Superstoe joined in the dancing on the last number, much to the delight of the guests and band members.

"The guests called for an encore. Superstoe obliged by performing a surprisingly professional soft-shoe dance to the accompaniment of 'Casey Would Waltz with the Strawberry Blonde.'"

Furth paused. The mound on the bed was motionless.

"Like a babe," said Pall.

Furth flipped to another page. "Superstoe remains an enigma," he read.

"Who says that?" asked Pall.

"The dean of Washington reporters." He resumed reading. "Superstoe's performance at the inauguration ball—which was spirited behavior but was by no means the consequence of overindulgence—is even more surprising in view of the fact that heretofore he has remained, one might even say fanatically, out of the limelight. He has sedulously avoided reporters, often fleeing into doorways and rest rooms to escape members of the press.

"Before his appointment Superstoe was an insignificant professor of linguistics, noted more for his eccentricities than for his scholarship. But a highly placed source confides that Superstoe was an individual whose talents were either not recognized or not utilized, and his natural humility prevented him from rising to a position of importance earlier in life.

"The same source asserts that President Knutson has for some time relied heavily on the advice and talents of Superstoe and that Superstoe, like Adams and Furth, has long enjoyed the role of unofficial but indispensable adviser to the new President."

"What highly placed source was that?" asked Pall.

"Wasn't it you?"

"Me!"

"It must have been Paxton."

"Where is it?" he cried, springing up and throwing back the quilt. He found the top hat and set it upon his head.

Then he noticed them. He tipped the hat, saying, *"Bonjour, mes petits. Pax vobiscum."* He blessed them.

"A rough estimate," Furth observed, "reveals that four times as many column inches in this morning's papers are devoted to CIA Director Paxton S. Superstoe as to President of the United States Bryan Knutson."

"You see?" said Superstoe. "Have faith. Genius will be recognized."

"It's not so much genius as eurhythmy," Pall said.

"Nothing," said Superstoe, "is more fundamental to wisdom than harmony."

"By the way," Furth said, turning a page, "the FBI found one of our trucks."

Superstoe and hat disappeared under the quilt.

"Shall I pack our bags?" asked Pall.

Superstoe's hat appeared. Then his eyes. "What was in the truck?" he asked.

"It had been dismantled," Furth replied.

"Did they trace it?"

"Indeed."

"We're under house arrest?"

"It was found to have been purchased in Trenton, New Jersey, by one Gerald Malpheesense."

"Where did they find it?"

"In a junk yard in Florida, surrounded by dead birds, dead rats, and dead cats."

14   "Eleven employees of the Army Chemical Corps laboratory in Maryland were found dead this morning of nerve-gas poisoning," Pall told the reporters. "The evidence is pretty clear. It was a suicide pact. They realized they would be discovered. They took the easy way out."

"What," asked a reporter, "was their motive in spreading the epidemic?"

"Subversion."

"They were in league with a foreign power?"

"That is not yet clear. You can appreciate, gentlemen, the delicate nature of this inquiry. Matters of the highest security are involved. It's impossible to release more information at this time."

The Chemical Corps was removed from Army control and placed under the direct supervision of the Special Presidential Assistant for National Security Affairs.

The mystery of the epidemics solved, everyone settled down to work.

15 The mournful howl of a dog echoed down the long corridor.

Furth opened a door and halted before an attractive secretary. She smiled and said, "Good morning." She spoke into the intercom: "Mr. Furth is here, Mr. Superstoe."

Furth leaned to one side to view her knees.

"You may go right in, Mr. Furth."

Furth entered and closed the door. "Paxton, you're working like a dog," he said to the bloodhound seated in the chair behind the desk.

The bloodhound howled.

Furth sat and crossed his legs. "You look worried," he added.

"Not in the least," Superstoe replied from behind. Furth twisted his head about. Superstoe was sitting cross-legged on the floor surrounded by papers. He wore a deerstalker on his head.

Furth stood and turned the chair. Then he sat again, crossed his legs again, and picked one of the papers off the carpet.

"I can tell at a glance your profession and what you had for breakfast," Superstoe said.

Furth looked up from the paper.

"The chemical stains on your fingertips reveal that you are by profession an undertaker. The odor of your breath, the smudge on the right lens of your glasses, and the stain on your left trouser knee indicate that you ate French toast, bacon, eggs, and coffee at breakfast."

"Wrong. I am by profession an investigator. You forgot the tomato juice."

"What do you investigate?"

"Truth."

"Truth is the most obvious entity in the world. It lies all about us, plain to see. But no one sees it."

Superstoe scrambled to his feet, leaped over the papers, and tipped his chair forward. "Down, Mother," he commanded. The bloodhound slid to the carpet and loped to the corner. Furth sat on the floor and examined the papers.

A gray-haired man who looked like a genial, successful automobile salesman entered the office. Superstoe fingered the bill of his deerstalker and said, "Sit, Thomas. I'm told you're in charge of our spy school."

Thomas sat, leaned back, smiled, placed an ankle on a knee, put an elbow on the arm of the chair, and replied, "I am. That's not the official name, but ..."

"I want a résumé of the course of instruction."

"Certainly. I'll call my girl and have it run over immediately. If your girl had told me, I would have brought it myself."

"Are all our spies the same type?" Superstoe asked cunningly.

Thomas leaned forward, both feet on the carpet. "I don't know what you mean," he said.

"The same psychological type."

"They must pass tests, psychological among others. We want well-balanced men."

Superstoe gave a short gasp. He inquired, "Do they take spying seriously?"

"I'll say they do!" Thomas assured him. "I'll arrange an inspection for you tomorrow. See for yourself."

"Are our spies eccentric?" asked Superstoe, pulling the bill of the deerstalker over his right eye.

"Oh, no. You'd never spot one in a crowd."

"An eccentric?"

"One of our boys."

"Why not?"

"They're trained to be inconspicuous."

Superstoe pulled the bill completely over both eyes. He tilted his head back to see Thomas. "Isn't that dangerous?" he asked.

"It's the only way ..."

The cap flew back and Superstoe shot forward. "There's only one way to spy?" he cried.

Thomas shifted in his chair, replaced the ankle on the knee, and adjusted his tie clasp. "Every man passes a uniform test," he began to explain.

"How long have you had your job?"

"My present position? Four years. Four and a half years."

Superstoe untied the bow on the top of his cap. The earflaps flopped down his cheeks like a bloodhound's ears. "What," asked Superstoe, "did you do before that?"

"Counterintelligence."

"You were a spy?"

"A counterspy. I worked in Vienna mainly."

Superstoe tied the earflaps under his chin. "Are you satisfied with your training program, Thomas?"

"I am indeed, Mr. Superstoe. I'm quite satisfied. Although we're continually reexamining the program, seeking to improve it. We do not stand still."

"Never?"

"Never."

From a drawer of his desk Superstoe took a pair of field glasses. Holding them reversed, he found Thomas in the lenses. "Do you," he asked, watching the tiny Thomas twins, "think I am a spy?"

Thomas clasped his hands together. His lips began a smile. He might have been watching a mildly humorous variety show.

"You are the number one spy. You're the Director, Mr. Superstoe."

Superstoe adjusted the focus. Still watching through the glasses, he asked, "I mean if you observed me in public, would you think I was a spy?"

"We've learned to suspect all types."

"Answer my question."

Thomas cleared his throat. "No," he said without smiling. "I wouldn't think you were. We've learned to watch for certain common characteristics . . ."

"Why not?"

"Excuse me?"

"Why aren't I a spy?"

"Why wouldn't I suspect you? You've been pretending to be eccentric. Odd behavior calls attention to itself. We don't . . ."

Superstoe lowered the glasses and squinted. "We'll have to change the entire training program," he said.

"Now really. This is silly. I'll get the complete résumé and explain the entire program. You'll see right away . . ."

Superstoe replaced the field glasses. His hand remained in the drawer.

"I can guess what the résumé says," Superstoe said.

"The course is a complex one. Our requirements are exceedingly high. We've had an excellent score . . ."

"I am a spy. You wouldn't have guessed. I can't allow you to train my spies," Superstoe said grimly.

Thomas relaxed. "Oh, but calling attention to yourself is too old a trick. Really."

"Do our enemies know that?"

"Yes, of course they do."

"Then they know we'd never try it, don't they?"

"Of course they . . ." Thomas closed his mouth, discomfort on his face.

"Obviously something has to be done," Superstoe said. He withdrew his hand from the drawer and pointed the black automatic at Thomas's mouth.

Disbelief, then the nervous anticipation of a joke passed across Thomas's face. Unsmiling, deadly earnest, Superstoe rested his elbow on the desk and squeezed the trigger.

Thomas blinked. His body jerked. His hands flew to his face.

Superstoe squeezed the trigger again.

Thomas lowered his red, wet hands.

"You're a lousy counterspy, Thomas," Superstoe said. "Now go and get that résumé. And don't get any red ink on it. I'll use red ink to mark it."

Thomas, wiping his eyes with his fingers, stood. "You're absolutely crazy!" he shouted.

Superstoe aimed again. "Vamoose," he said.

Thomas backed, turned, and reached for the door knob. Then he saw Furth in the corner. "Furth?" he said involuntarily.

Furth looked up. He stared at Thomas for a few seconds—he had been oblivious of the shooting. Then he shook his head, like a mother over the thousandth bloody nose, and returned to his reading. The bloodhound, in another corner, howled.

"You didn't even know the Secretary of Defense was in the room!" Superstoe shouted, standing and aiming.

Thomas swung open the door and plunged out. A woman screamed.

"God damn it—Jesus, I'm sorry . . ."

The secretary had been run down, and Thomas, tripped by the collision, lay on top of her.

She screamed again, seeing what she assumed to be blood drip onto her face.

Superstoe stood over them. As Thomas got to his feet, Superstoe warned, "I'll say nothing this time. But the next time you try to rape Miss Cunningham in my office ..." He glanced at Miss Cunningham's thighs.

She watched Thomas depart, looked at Superstoe, pulled her skirt down, and attempted to get to her feet gracefully. Gallantly Superstoe gave her a hand.

Then she saw the gun and screamed again.

"Nothing to worry about," said Superstoe, putting the barrel to his temple and pulling the trigger.

16   Superstoe wandered in and out of offices. He asked questions. He looked in desks, files, and wastebaskets. He offered suggestions.

Stories circulated, but most of the employees found him a pleasant commander. He demanded accuracy and he rewarded imagination. He inquired after wives and children, shifted persons to duties more congenial to them, and illuminated the gloom of seriousness that hung over the modern offices.

But many of the officials at the higher levels resisted his ways. A clique formed against him. They thought he was incompetent, unprofessional, and cracked.

A bus boy in the cafeteria told him about the insurrection.

That night he ate alone, preparing himself sardine and onion sandwiches, a salad of tomatoes and artichoke hearts, and a fruit salad. Then he ate half of the apple pie he had bought on his way home. (Meat and eggs, as well as citrus fruits, were still exorbitant, if they could be found at all.)

As he washed his dishes he heard Zorr enter downstairs. He heard the voice of a girl. A door closed. He heard nothing more. Thoughtfully he resumed washing the dishes. (Zorr lived on the first floor, Furth and Superstoe on the second, and Pall on the third. But recently Pall had been sleeping at the apartment of the sister of a senator's wife.)

As Superstoe dried his hands Furth entered. He opened the refrigerator. "Hungry?" asked Superstoe.

Furth closed the door. "No. Habit."

"Life would be chaos without it."

"Too much is deadly."

"Moderation in all things."

"More or less." Furth yawned and started for his bedroom. "Early to bed and early to rise," he yawned again, "makes a man sleepy."

When he had gone, Superstoe made several telephone calls. Then he went to bed.

Three days later Thomas had been transferred to the American embassy in Togo. Two other members of the clique were transferred to minor positions in the Post Office Department. Four others were given posts in Afghanistan, Dahomey, Libya, and Iceland. The eighth member of the clique was arrested two weeks later by members of the Washington vice squad.

17   As Secretary of Defense, Furth was blunt, demanding, and uncompromising.

His comments on memos were succinct:

No
Yes
BS
Think, knucklehead
Jolly clever of you

When he received reports that exhibited inaccuracy, bias, stupidity, or bad diction, he ripped them in half and sent them back.

He took books to committee meetings and read while the others argued.

He hired a former classmate at MIT to be his administrative assistant.

He angered military officials.

But the generals feared him, for it soon became clear that he was a better tactician and strategist than they, and, moreover, he could hold his own against the war games computer.

To Congress he was a brilliant, shrewd, slightly odd Secretary of Defense.

They thought he was odd because he doodled at mysterious mathematical problems during hearings. They knew he was brilliant because be knew everything. They thought he was shrewd because he never said more than he had to.

He got along surprisingly well with members of Congress. He seldom argued with them. (He agreed to their suggestions; then, back at the Pentagon, he did as he pleased.) He seemed impervious to their needling, if not ignorant of it. (He was aware of it, but he was above it.) And he was, they agreed, dedicated to maintaining a strong defense.

Actually be didn't give a damn about defense. That is, when in Crossbar he didn't care if the nation had one ICBM or a million. But Superstoe had his plans, and it was Furth's job to prepare for those plans.

Thus he began stockpiling foodstuffs and having them crated for parachuting.

He spoke with the Commissioner of the Internal Revenue Service. Moonshine whiskey would not be poured down the drain when seized but shipped to Defense Department warehouses.

Narcotics seized by government agents would also be stockpiled.

Bombers were transferred from SAC to Far Eastern bases and their nuclear bombs removed.

A small, dependable staff, consisting of Furth, Superstoe, Pall, and Johanneson, drew up top-secret plans. Sealed orders were sent to certain bases; the orders were to be opened only on a designated signal from Furth. Not even the Chiefs of Staff knew of these plans, which went by the name of Operation Happy Surprise.

Secret, but known to select congressmen and Defense officials, were accelerated preparations for biological warfare. After the epidemics of the preceding year Congress enthusiastically voted the funds. Research was expanded. More inoculations were given to military personnel. The nuclear warheads were removed from some missiles and replaced by germ warheads. Germ bombs were produced and stockpiled. Satellites, which at a signal would descend from the sky onto a preselected target, were launched into orbit. The satellites contained bacteria or viruses. The satellites had been in the developmental stage during the previous administration.

To meet the demand for expanded research, development, and production of germs and vaccines, pharmaceutical companies expanded and new ones were established. One new company became in a few months a serious competitor to the older corporations; its growth was attributed to the number of defense contracts awarded it by virtue of the company's original and important contributions to the field.

Soon the company, which was first housed in unused railway warehouses in Great Spoons and later in new, modern buildings near Crossbar, entered the domestic market,

producing a new brand of aspirin, several varieties of tranquilizers, and various contraceptives.

The company, Manichean Laboratories, was founded by
six young men: David Silvers, Robert McAllen, John Lee,
Fritz Wilson, Laurence Miller, and Jack Smith.

18

18 Adams's most important innovation as Secretary of
State was his institution of regular dinner meetings with
foreign ambassadors. He invited two or three at a time to
his suite for dinner, wine (unless the diplomats were strict
Moslems), and conversation. Sometimes Superstoe, Furth,
Pall, or Johanneson joined him at these intimate dinner dialectics (as Superstoe called them).

The foreign diplomats liked Adams. He spoke to many of
them in their own languages; if he didn't know their language, he knew their history, customs, and etiquette. Yet a
few diplomats were discomfited by his disdain for polite
circumlocution.

Congressmen hated him. Unlike Furth, he argued with
them. He berated their stupidity and scorned their pet projects.

His relations with the press were even worse. He would
not tolerate their idiotic questions.

One reporter accosted him as he was entering his hotel.
"Why do you hate reporters?" the reporter asked breath-
lessly. (The reporter had been running.)

"I don't hate reporters. I hate inane questions."

"What do you consider inane questions, Mr. Secretary?"

19

19 April came.

Bryan Knutson waded out of the surf, took a towel from
a Secret Service agent, and sat in the chair beneath the huge

umbrella. A pitcher of lemonade and two glasses sat on the table through which the umbrella's pole was mounted.

Watt, also in swimming trunks, poured a glass and handed it to Knutson. He held the AMA *Journal* open on his lap.

The reporter sat facing them. The shade from the umbrella did not reach him. He had to hold his hand over his eyes to look at them. A notebook lay on his lap.

"You're certainly looking fine, Mr. President," the reporter said.

Knutson rubbed the towel over his chest. "Never felt better in my life."

"You seem to have learned from your predecessor."

"How's that?" Knutson asked.

"Not to allow the burdens of responsibility to lie too heavily on your shoulders," the reporter said.

"No, no. What's the use of worrying? You've got a job to do, you do it. Ulcers don't solve any problems."

"Are you enjoying your vacation, sir?"

"Oh, yes. Yes, indeed. Of course it's not really a vacation."

"Of course not."

"I'm on the phone every day with my advisers, with the cabinet. Reports to read, so forth. Where'd I put that magazine, Ed?"

Watt handed him the *Playboy.*

"How much longer do you expect to stay in Florida, Mr. President?"

"A few days."

"Three weeks in all, then?"

"That's right."

The reporter tried to edge his chair into the shade. The chair was driven deeper into the sand. Squinting in the glare, he asked, "Could I ask you a few questions?"

"I'd be awfully damned surprised if you didn't."

The reporter smiled to acknowledge the wit. He was known in the trade as an old hand. A less-experienced man would have laughed; Bob Bingen was required only to smile. He had played tennis with one President and poker with another.

"A few rumors have been going around," Bingen began offhandedly, "and I wondered if you might not want to quiet them down." He wet his lips and glanced involuntarily at the glass pitcher, speckled with cool beads of perspiration.

Watt refilled Knutson's glass. Ice cubes clinked against the sides of the pitcher and one plopped into the glass.

Bingen took a handkerchief from his pocket and wiped his forehead. His perspiration had stained his notebook. He flipped to a clean page.

"Rumors are always flying," Knutson said, smacking his lips. "That's damn good lemonade. Sure I can't have some gin in it?" he asked Watt.

Watt merely smiled and drew on his pipe.

"There have been a few comments on Dr. Watt," Bingen began. "Isn't it unusual to have a doctor in constant attendance? Since you're healthy, that is."

"It's always been done," Knutson said. "Every President. Press exaggerates as usual." He looked up from the magazine. "This is off the record, Bob, but I don't think we've heard the last of germ warfare. That plot we uncovered—it was just a symptom. There are fanatics everywhere, in the country and outside. Germs that get you like that." He tried to snap his fingers, wiped his hand on the towel, and then snapped them successfully. "It's necessary to have a trained man by me every moment. You should see the shots I get, the pills I have to take ..."

Watt cleared his throat but did not look up from the journal. Knutson drank his lemonade.

"You used to drink socially, Mr. President ..."

Watt spoke. "A President has more responsibilities than a senator."

"Could I ask what injections, what pills …?"

Watt smiled and shook his head.

Bingen began again. "There's always speculation about just who makes what decisions, Mr. President. At first it appeared that you yourself were shaping policy. All important announcements came from your office. Then word got around that a few of your appointees were actually the authors of policy." He paused.

Knutson turned a page and said nothing. Bingen could see on the page a photograph of a blonde arranging a vase of flowers. Behind the roses she was nude.

Bingen resumed. "Congressmen and various officials have mentioned receiving directives from Zorr or Superstoe or Pall. A State Department official said that foreign policy was determined by Secretary Adams's daily moods."

Knutson turned another page and moved the magazine closer to his eyes. Bingen couldn't see the page. Getting no response, he wet his lips and added, "A cabinet member said he was told to take orders from Adams, Furth, or Superstoe. That you would never contradict their orders."

Knutson carefully extracted a fold-out from the magazine. Shielding his eyes, Bingen thought he saw Knutson's pupils dilate.

Watt sipped his lemonade.

Bingen looked down to avoid the glare and noticed the notebook again stained with his perspiration.

"Look at this, Ed," Knutson said, holding up the fold-out. Watt glanced over and nodded approval. "Janet Jumper," Knutson read.

Watt looked at the picture more closely. "Real name's Bernice Beckwith," he said. "A colleague of mine mentioned her at a conference recently."

Knutson leaned across the table towards Watt. "What'd he say?"

"He's been treating her," Watt said.

"What for?"

"Hemorrhoids."

"What're they?"

"Piles."

Knutson looked at the photo in disbelief. The girl was lying on a couch. "Her fanny looks all right to me," he said. "She's on her stomach because she has a scar," Watt said. "Caesarean."

"No!"

Watt emptied the pitcher into the two glasses.

Bingen, his voice cracking from dryness, leaned forward and asked, "Have you heard the story that's going around? A senator calls the White House and asks for the commander in chief. The operator asks, 'Is it a social or a business call?' 'What difference does that make?' the senator asks. 'If it's a social call, I'll ring the President,' she says. 'If it's business, I'll ring Mr. Superstoe.'"

Knutson stared at the fold-out, then turned back a page. "Maybe you're right," he said.

"Hmm?" Watt inquired, his pipe in his mouth.

"The flowers cover her stomach. But you can see her tits and part of her pussy."

"They say the firing code to launch a nuclear attack doesn't follow the President around any more," Bingen blurted in desperation. "They say it's kept in Furth's office."

Knutson looked at Bingen. "What, Bob?"

Bingen tried to speak, but only a croak came out.

"Rumors, rumors," Knutson said, looking at the photo. "Everyone hates the President. One of the drawbacks of high office—malicious talebearers. Right, Ed?"

Watt nodded, studying a photograph of a heart operation.

Bingen whispered, "Is that an ice cube still in the pitcher?"

"Are you thirsty, Bob?" Knutson asked with concern.

Bingen smiled wanly. "It's a hot day."

"You should wear sunglasses," Knutson said. Watt raised an arm. A Secret Service agent rushed up. "Lemonade,"

Knutson said, "and another glass. Put gin in the glass. You like gin, Bob?"

"Just a glass of water, anything," Bingen rasped.

"People are jealous," Knutson observed, closing the magazine. "Envious of success. Reporters—excepting you, Bob—have to print something. Something bad. Good news—nobody will read it. So they make up stories. They're jealous of me, because I was elected so quickly. Only been a senator a few years, hadn't gone very far in the Senate. Other senators are jealous. Jealous of my staff. My boys work wonders. Absolutely trustworthy, loyal, brilliant, sharp as tacks, keen as razors. Even I didn't know it at first. Gold buried in the ground, that's what they were. It takes genius to discover genius, you know that, Bob. Not everyone could have discovered Adams, Furth, Superstoe, Zorr, Pall. A leader's as success-ful as his staff. Every general knows that. Every good gen-eral. It's a complex world, Bob. The whole world's like a computer. Can you run a computer? Neither can I. But Furth can."

"Furth used to be ..."

"Adams is a philosopher," Knutson continued. "You can't have an executive or a banker making foreign policy. Government's not a day-to-day affair. We have to think centuries ahead of time. I'll admit I never used to have much faith in intellectuals, except to do studies. But these men are practical. The way they uncovered those epi-demics for me—why, they put everybody to shame, CIA, FBI, reporters ..."

"You've known Adams a long time?"

"Oh, yes."

"And the others?"

Knutson rummaged beneath the table and extracted a magazine with a picture of a brunette on the cover. She was wearing black hose, nothing more. "What others?" asked Knutson.

"Furth, Superstoe ..." Bingen's voice cracked.

"Fine men. Couldn't do without them." He opened the magazine.

The lemonade and glass arrived. Bingen gulped it down and coughed.

"Enough gin?" asked Knutson.

Bingen nodded, hand on throat.

"All the stories don't worry you, then?" he asked after a moment.

"I never read the stories. I just look at the pictures." Knutson flipped a page.

"The rumors, Mr. President, do you worry ..."

"Worry?" asked Knutson, looking up. "Why?"

"As a senator, you seemed to worry about a lot of things. And during the campaign, the first part of the campaign, especially ..."

"I don't know why people worry. I see them rushing around, bothered, worried. They're nuts. Things work out. Life goes on. What's all the fuss about?"

"Some critics have said you take your responsibilities too lightly."

Knutson brushed away a fly. "Well, what does it matter what critics say? What does it matter? I do my job, they do theirs. Live and let live. Right, Ed?"

Watt nodded.

20   During President Long's term, before the epidemics began, Congress passed a constitutional amendment providing that if the office of Vice President became vacant the President was empowered to appoint a Vice President to serve the remainder of the term, the appointment being subject to Congressional approval. In early May the amendment was ratified and became effective.

The following day, while in a private briefing with Arthur Pall, the Vice President succumbed to a fatal heart attack.

21   That evening Adams was summoned to the office of the Secretary of Defense.

He opened the door without knocking—the staff in the outer offices had all left—and looked into the darkness. "Lazarus?" he inquired.

"Knock and it shall be opened," Superstoe's voice came from the blackness.

"I didn't have to knock. Where are the lights?"

"Close the door and come in," Furth said. "I think better in the dark."

Adams closed the door and took a step, cracking his knee against a chair. He swore.

"It is better to light just one little candle," Superstoe advised.

Adams sat carefully in the chair. "This blackout isn't a new economy measure, is it?" he asked.

"Shit, we're the wealthiest nation in the world," Furth said. "You think I'd worry about a few kilowatt hours?"

"Then what are you thinking about?"

"Paxton brought me a new Russian code. His experts can't crack it."

"You think you can?"

"I nearly squared the circle in grade school. This should be easier than that."

"All adolescents are filled with ambitious dreams," Adams observed, striking a match. Abruptly his face broke the darkness. Lit by the tiny flame, carved in flickering shadows, his eyes, his nostrils, his mustache, his chin glowed cannily.

"That's what has saved us," Superstoe said. "We're perpetual adolescents."

The match went out. The glow of Adams's cigar brightened and dulled as he puffed. The pungent smell filled the room.

"We were just discussing, Ben," Furth said, "if we shouldn't expurgate Bryan immediately. Paxton thinks the shock would assist us."

The orange-red spot glowed more brightly. Then it faded. "I intended to ask," Adams said, "who decided to expurgate Vice President Doberman."

"Who?" Furth repeated.

"Weren't you there?" asked Superstoe.

"Where?" asked Adams.

"When we decided."

"Who?"

"Us."

"You two?"

"And Arthur, Isen, and Ed. Weren't you there?" asked Superstoe.

"I think not," Adams replied.

"Think hard."

"I always do."

"When did you return from Lima?"

"Tuesday."

"Oh, well, that explains it," Superstoe explained.

"You see," Furth explained, "we thought it might look suspicious if the V.P., the Speaker, and the President of the Senate all caught fatal infections."

"The amendment merely simplifies our plans," Superstoe added.

"And a heart attack the day after the amendment went into effect is such a coincidence it has to be a coincidence," Furth said.

"So," Superstoe proceeded, "Bryan will appoint you V.P., and we'll ..."

"I do not intend to be Vice President."

"It won't be for long," Superstoe said.

"I don't intend to be President, either."

"Well, we assumed—it's your prerogative, you're our patriarch, our leader of dialectics, white-haired and venerable, the Nestor of Crossbar and Washington ..."

"Thus I am not Agamemnon, Achilles, or Odysseus."

Bored, Furth interjected, "We'd better decide on someone or Bryan'll appoint his own veep."

"Ben, you really must be more cooperative. You said you wouldn't join Knutson's staff, too."

The tip of the cigar brightened and faded. "I will not be President." The orange-red spot glowed again. "You or Lazarus can be President."

No one spoke.

Then Furth: "Obviously it has to be one of us."

Silence.

"Paxton?" asked Furth.

"What?"

"What are you thinking?"

"What are *you* thinking?"

"I asked first."

"I think you want to be President," Superstoe said.

"Of course I want to be President. Everybody wants to be President except Ben."

"Then go ahead," said Superstoe.

"Really?" asked Furth.

"I don't mind. You've worked hard."

"We'll take turns."

"Certainly," Superstoe replied. "Of course you're much younger than I. I might die before it's my turn. But don't worry about that. You go ahead."

"Oh, Paxton."

"No, no. I can go back to Crossbar and teach. If I'm not needed, then ..."

"Oh, Jesus Christ."

"I won't harbor a grudge."

"Take the fucking office, Paxton."

"No, it's all right, Lazarus."

Silence.

"It was Paxton's idea," Adams observed.

"Paxton's?" asked Furth.

"Whose did you think?" asked Superstoe.

"I thought it was everyone's. A meeting of minds, as at a Quaker meeting."

"It was Paxton's," Adams repeated. "On a Saturday morning, just before dawn."

"I don't recall that," Furth said.

"I do," said Superstoe.

"You don't remember," Adams said, "because you were snoring. You were on the floor. Paxton tripped over your legs."

"I don't remember that," said Superstoe.

"Okay, Paxton becomes President first," Furth agreed.

"No, don't mind me," Superstoe said.

"Oh, for Chrisake," Furth growled.

"Shall we put it to the gods?" asked Superstoe.

"Do you think we can find a bull in Washington?" Furth asked.

"We'll draw straws."

Furth sighed. "Okay. We'll draw straws."

They heard Adams move. "I have matches," he said. He lit one and blew it out. "He who takes the unburnt match wins." He held both matches in his hand and stood. Superstoe and Furth approached the glow of the cigar.

"Who's going first?" Adams asked.

"You go first," said Superstoe.

"No, you," Furth said.

"After *you*."

"I insist."

"*I* insist."

"Paxton, goddammit ..."

"I'm thinking of a number," Adams said, "between one and infinity."

"One," Superstoe said instantly.

"Infinity minus one," Furth said.

"Two," said Adams.

Superstoe's fingers felt for the matchsticks. He pulled one out.

Furth took the other.

"Give me the box," said Superstoe.

The match scratched the abrasive and spat into flame. It illumined Superstoe's wide grin and boyish eyes. He held the match aloft. *"In hoc signum vincimus,"* he proclaimed.

Adams and Furth smiled.

The flame descended the matchstick.

"Ouch."

Superstoe dropped the match and rubbed his finger against his thumb. Furth stepped on the flame.

22   Four days after Vice President Doberman's funeral Superstoe was sworn in.

Some senators had expressed doubt about the wisdom of the appointment; they said Superstoe had had little experience in government. On the other hand, they had to admit that he had done a remarkable job with the CIA. The agency seemed to be making fewer mistakes, to be more efficient, to be able to predict events with more certainty. And there was really nothing they could find wrong with him, except his innocent obscurity previous to Knutson's election. There were the rumors, but before the Senate committee he had evidenced no sign of eccentricity. No one could find fault with his whistling "America, the Beautiful" as he entered the hearing room.

So the Senate confirmed his appointment, 85 to 7.

The swearing-in ceremony was simple and brief. There was no celebration. It was quite businesslike. Superstoe repeated the oath clearly and modestly. He appeared serious, purposeful, and humble.

Knutson, reporters observed, appeared slightly fatigued.

Pall was named Director of the CIA.

23   The following week Knutson met not at all with reporters. Aides confided that for the first time since the election he seemed irritable, fatigued, restless, depressed.

Saturday morning Knutson, accompanied by Watt and a senator—Senator Lionel Evans, an old friend of Knutson's—flew to the President's hunting lodge deep in the forests of Minnesota for a scheduled five-day vacation. Mrs. Knutson remained in Washington.

The President's party reached the lodge by seaplane, the President, Senator Evans, and Watt arriving in one plane and Secret Service agents in a second. Other agents were already on the scene; they had inspected the lodge and its environs, cleaned the lodge, launched the boats, repaired the dock, and readied the fishing tackle. They declared the area perfectly secure.

Watt cooked dinner. Later Senator Evans was to recall that Knutson ate little.

During the night Knutson knocked at Watt's door. He explained he was not sleeping well and requested a sedative. Watt gave him two capsules.

In the morning Knutson complained of a fitful night, despite the sedative. He recalled having distressing nightmares.

After breakfast the three men went fishing. Knutson was unusually silent and reflective. After lunch—Evans fried the fish; he had caught three, Watt two, the President none—Knutson went for a walk, alone. He returned at dusk, looking haggard and slightly disoriented.

After supper the three men played poker. Knutson found it difficult to concentrate. He tried to look at a magazine but soon threw it aside. Watt loaned him a detective novel, *The Green Garter,* by Raphael Diké, but he was unable to read more than the first page.

Finally he retired, and Evans and Watt retired shortly after.

The bedrooms were located on the second floor of the lodge. The stairs from the first floor led to the hall which ran the length of the lodge and terminated at the bathroom. There were two bedrooms of average size on the east side of the hall. Watt slept in one and Evans in the other. On the west side there were also two rooms, one larger, one smaller. The Secret Service agents slept in the smaller; Knutson was in the larger.

Knutson's room contained one of his guns, a twelve-gauge shotgun. It hung on the wall. Beneath it there stood a bureau, and in the bureau there was a box of shells.

A Secret Service agent was on duty outside Knutson's door. Another was on duty at the head of the stairs. A third stood guard beneath his window. Two more patrolled the grounds.

Knutson emerged from his room at about 1:30 A.M. He went to the bathroom, and then he returned to his room. The agent outside his door observed that he looked as if he had not slept. The agent asked if there was anything he wanted. Knutson did not reply. He closed the door and locked it.

The agents outside the house observed the light in Knutson's room go off, then go on again, ten minutes later. (A generator supplied electricity.) It burned, they said, for nearly an hour, and then went off.

At 3:30 A.M. in Washington Superstoe, wearing red, blue, green, and white checked pajamas, looked into the lighted New Dialectic Room. He saw Furth, wearing a paisley robe, seated at the table with papers spread before him and a pencil in his hand.

"What are you doing?"

Furth looked up. "Working out Furthian numbers," he said.

"What are they?"

"I'm inventing them."

"What are they for?"

"I don't know. Nothing, maybe. I can't sleep."

"Has Isen come in?"

"Hours ago."

"Arthur?"

"No. Why are you up?" Furth asked.

"Had to piss," Superstoe replied. He stared at the papers. "I rather liked Bryan," he said. Then he padded barefoot down the hall, entered his room, climbed into bed, pulled up the covers, closed his eyes, and fell asleep.

24   Furth answered the phone at the first ring. It was 6:17 A.M. in Washington, 5:17 in Minnesota. He woke Superstoe.

Superstoe listened to the voice of the Secret Service agent. He gave instructions, hung up, and began to dress. Zorr entered the room in his undershorts. "Call the Chief Justice," Superstoe commanded. "Then dress. Then call the President of the Senate, the Senate Majority Leader, the Senate Minority Leader, and the Speaker of the House. When you get to the White House, inform the press."

The phone rang again. It was the Chief of the Secret Service, calling from his Washington home. He advised that a detail of agents was on its way to Superstoe's house to escort him to the White House.

Superstoe arrived at the White House at 7:07. He asked to see Mrs. Knutson. The maid said she was asleep; she never rose before eight.

"Wake her," Superstoe ordered.

As he waited the Army doctor arrived. Solemnly Superstoe shook hands with him. "I was afraid she might need a sedative," he said. "I wanted a doctor on hand."

"She doesn't know yet?"

"I'm going to tell her now. I thought I should bear the burden of telling her."

25   At 7:39 Zorr met with reporters. By 7:41 the news of President Knutson's suicide appeared on radio and television.

The Chief Justice arrived at 7:31. At 8:16, when the four congressional leaders had arrived, they, the Chief Justice, and Superstoe stepped into the press room and Superstoe repeated the oath of office.

At 8:45 Superstoe appeared on radio and television. He bespoke the shock felt by the nation and assured the populace of an orderly transition of power.

During the day he met with forty-seven congressional leaders, with the Cabinet, with reporters, with the Russian Ambassador, with numerous aides and officials, met the presidential jet on its return from Minnesota and, without further comment to the press, escorted Mrs. Knutson back to the White House and spent the following hour with her, her son and daughter, and her sister.

Senator Evans gave a brief news conference at the airport, assuring reporters that it had been, without a doubt, suicide.

Watt, meanwhile, accompanied the body to the hospital and supervised the autopsy. Pall met him at the hospital and observed the autopsy.

Watt had substituted depressants for tranquilizers.

Experiments at the Army Chemical Corps lab, the CIA Special Effects Laboratory, and Manichean Laboratories had indicated that under the circumstances suicide was a strong probability, if not inevitable.

With Pall's assistance, the hospital laboratory found no trace of drugs in the tissues sent by Watt from the autopsy for analysis.

PART THREE

The Crises

1   As Superstoe had expected, the nation was shocked, amazed, and frightened. Accordingly, the nation looked, with doubt, hope, faith, charity, and passion, to him for leadership.

He was, as the news analysts said, an unknown quantity; his intentions were obscure; he had not been tested; the future was misty.

But he was the President.

He had taken charge.

He acted, as all could see, with authority and confidence.

The day after the suicide the stock market began to recover the losses of the previous day.

But not even Superstoe could anticipate everything.

He did not expect the call at 8:32 on the morning of the funeral which reported explosions and gunfire in Sacramento, California.

Superstoe tried to phone the Governor, but the line seemed to be disconnected. It was impossible to reach an operator at the Sacramento telephone exchange.

Superstoe called Furth. "I don't know what it is," he told him, "but we'll not take any chances."

Furth dispatched two helicopters to investigate and ordered paratroopers to load up and the planes to take off as soon as possible and head for Sacramento; they would receive further orders in flight. Infantry troops at Fort Ord boarded trucks, and the trucks moved toward Sacramento.

Superstoe federalized the California National Guard but couldn't reach the commander, who lived in Sacramento.

Zorr assured the press that everything was under control.

At 9:03 the California Highway Patrol reported that five cars which had been sent to investigate were pinned down by machine-gun fire near the state capitol building.

Furth alerted troops in Nevada and ordered them to Sacramento.

Zorr announced that President Superstoe was taking personal charge of the "incident."

A Highway Patrol car was destroyed by bazookas.

The line connecting Superstoe's, Furth's, and Zorr's offices was held open. Zorr was watching the teletype and listening on a phone connected with a San Francisco newspaper office where radios were tuned to the Sacramento stations, waiting for them to return to the air. Furth was talking to the Highway Patrol commander in San Francisco, advising him to rendezvous with the Army convoy from Fort Ord.

Superstoe was chewing the eraser on a pencil and staring out the window. It was his first crisis as President.

His telephone console buzzed. It was Adams. "What the hell's going on?"

"I really can't say, Ben. Someone has lots of guns."

"It can't be a foreign invasion."

"I shouldn't think so."

"What ..."

Zorr yelled over the other line.

"Hold on, Ben," said Superstoe.

A Sacramento radio station had returned to the air. A voice was nervously reading a statement to the effect that the city was now under the authority of the "Patriots' Militia, an organization, civilian and military, dedicated to the preservation and strengthening of the traditional American ideas of liberty, free enterprise, patriotism, anti-communism, anti-socialism, and God."

The statement proceeded to explain the reason for the Patriots' Militia's action. The national government, it said, had been captured by traitors, murderers, one worlders. President Knutson did not commit suicide; he was murdered.

The Patriots' Militia called upon every red-blooded American man, woman, and child to rise up with them and throw off the yoke of tyranny before it was too late. Loyal patriots should take up arms in every town and city across the nation and should not put them down until the traitors were removed from office.

At that moment Superstoe's telephone console buzzed again. The operator said, "A General Clemens calling from Sacramento. He says he's the commander of the Patriots' Militia."

Superstoe's face brightened. "How nice," he replied. "Now, Lois—is this Lois?"

"Yes, sir."

"Now, Lois, you connect this call with Lazarus, and with Isen's office, and with Ben, so they all can hear. Then put General Clemens on."

"Yes, sir."

Superstoe swirled back and forth in his swivel chair, the phone to his ear, and whistled "From the Halls of Montezuma to the Shores of Tripoli."

Pall entered the oval office, dressed in morning coat and striped trousers. He was smiling. "I thought we were going to Knutson's funeral this morning," he said, "but maybe it's ours."

"It is exciting," Superstoe agreed.

"What's happening now?"

"The commander of the rebels is on the phone."

"Well. Anything else?"

"Paratroopers should be in the air soon."

"What's the public think?"

"Oh, no one believes these fanatics. They've cried wolf too often."

"Everything's ready, Mr. President," the operator announced.

Superstoe flipped the switch sending his caller's voice through the speaker on the console, so Pall could hear. Then he turned on the tape recorder.

"Good morning. This is Superstoe."

A heavy breathing came from the speaker. A throat was cleared. In the background they could hear excited voices and, faintly, sporadic gunfire.

"Who is it, please?" urged Superstoe.

There was a cough and then a gravelly voice saying, "Superstoe?"

"Yes, good morning, this is Superstoe. Who are you?"

"Superstoe, this is General Clemens, Supreme Commander of the American Patriots' Militia."

"Flemens?"

"Clemens, Clemens."

"Clemens."

"Right, Clemens. Supreme Commander ..."

"Yes, I understood that."

"Superstoe, I am in complete control of Sacramento, the city of Sacramento. I ..."

"Are you?"

"Yes, I am. I have ..."

"Is that gunfire I hear?"

"It is. Indeed it is. Superstoe, listen carefully. I have ..."

"I'm listening carefully, General Flemens."

"Clemens!"

"Clemens, yes."

"I have ..."

"Where are you calling from?"

"The Governor's mansion. I'm holding the Governor and his family hostage. My men also have the Lieutenant Governor and his family, the Mayor and his family, and five thousand other hostages. We are in control of the capitol building, the radio stations, the telephone exchange, the power company, the police station, Highway Patrol Headquarters, and the National Guard Armory. I ..."

"You've been busy."

"Listen carefully, Superstoe. We're announcing our conditions on the radio now. I'm giving you ten minutes to resign your office. We demand your immediate resignation, as well as Adams's, Furth's, and Pall's. You must ..."

"Don't you want Isen to resign too?"

"Who?"

"Isen. Isen Timothy Zorr."

"Zorr?"

"Yes."

"Yes, Zorr too. You must all come on television in ten minutes and publicly resign. The Speaker of the House must be sworn in as President. If you refuse, we'll kill all our hostages, including the Governor and his family. He has three little girls."

Superstoe was doodling as he listened. He was drawing diminishing concentric circles. Now he printed the name FLEMENS, boxed it, and filled it with cross-hatches until the name was obliterated. He said, "Well, General Clemens, it looks as if I don't have any choice."

"That's right."

"But it's quite impossible to get on television in ten minutes."

"Ten minutes, Superstoe, or five thousand people die. Five thousand deaths on your hands."

Superstoe held a palm out before him and examined it. He said, "Then I'm afraid you'll just have to kill them,

Clemens. Because I can't possibly arrange for television on such short notice. I have to contact Furth and Adams and Pall—God knows where they are or how long it will take. And I have to contact the Speaker of the House. The television cameras have to be set up, the airwaves cleared. I have to find a justice to swear him in. It's quite impossible in ten minutes. It will take at least two hours."

"I'll give you half an hour, Superstoe."

"Well, I'm terribly sorry, you'll just have to kill them. It's quite impossible. Perhaps I could do it in an hour and a half."

"One hour. That's the limit."

Superstoe had printed the name CLEMENS on his memo pad and was drowning it in concentric circles. "I'll tell you what I'll do. I'll try my best to do it in an hour. But it might take a few minutes longer. You mustn't be impatient. Say an hour to an hour and a half."

"If you're not on television in one hour everybody dies."

"All right, Flemens. An hour to an hour and a quarter."

"One hour, Superstoe. And listen. If ..."

"I'm listening."

"If there's any sign of troops or airplanes or anything, all the hostages get it. Understand?"

"Yes, yes."

"And we must have a general amnesty."

"Yes, of course."

"You'll cooperate with us?".

"I don't have any choice, do I?"

"That's right. You don't."

"But, Clemens," Superstoe added, "if you kill those hostages before I appear on television, I'll simply send in the troops."

"Don't worry. You resign. We won't harm the hostages."

"All right. I'm going to hang up now to arrange for the television. What time do you have there?"

"Six-forty."

"I have 9:37. Eastern time."

"All right."

"You watch your television now. You have one, don't you?"

"I've got one. Don't you worry about that."

"You're sure it works?"

"Don't worry, Superstoe. You just get on it and resign."

"Be sure and watch then. Goodbye."

"Goodbye."

Superstoe switched off the line. "Lazarus?" he said.

An aide answered, "The Secretary is on another line giving orders."

Zorr entered the office.

"Isen," Superstoe said, "notify the networks I'll make a statement in approximately an hour. Have it announced immediately that I'll address the nation in an hour." He tapped the pencil against his chin. "They'll have announced their demands. To the rebels it must appear that I will resign. To the populace it must appear that I won't."

"Isen is good at Delphic statements," Pall observed. "Knutson was always making them."

"Announce that I shall do everything necessary to avoid bloodshed and restore order," Superstoe added.

"Speaking of Knutson," Zorr said, "they're wondering if the funeral will go on as scheduled."

Superstoe looked at him in surprise. "Of course," he answered. "Why not?"

Zorr departed and Superstoe chewed the eraser. In a moment Furth's voice came over the telephone. "Paxton?"

"Yes?"

"It will be over an hour before the paratroopers get there. Three hours for the convoy from Fort Ord. Longer for the convoy from Nevada."

"How much over an hour?"

"Maybe two hours."

"Oh, dear. Can you drop incapacitating gases from planes or helicopters?"

"We don't have any gas in the area."

Superstoe drew a parachute on his pad. "Don't they have tear gas in San Francisco? The police?"

"I suppose," Furth replied.

"Isn't there a carrier docked at Alameda?"

"Probably."

"I wonder how long it would take to get the tear gas to Alameda, the carrier's planes to take off and drop it on the Governor's mansion and other sites?"

There was silence for a few moments. Superstoe heard Furth talking to someone. He returned to the phone. "Maybe forty minutes. But how the hell will they ever find the Governor's mansion?"

"Don't they have maps?"

Furth sighed. "Paxton ..."

"Do the best you can."

"Of course."

"Let me know when things happen. Time the gas to hit just before the paratroopers drop."

He switched off the phone and pursed his lips. A few seconds later Adams was on the phone. "I had to talk to a couple of ambassadors and assure them you wouldn't resign," he said. "What are you doing now?"

"Why, I was just going to have a cup of coffee. What's new with you?"

"Ivan arrived in Moscow," Adams replied.

"Well, then. Everything's dandy." He switched off the phone.

His secretary entered and placed a cup and a cardboard box on his desk. Superstoe opened the box. He looked inside. He reached inside. He pulled out a doughnut, bit, and was immersed in a fog of powdered sugar.

Zorr returned. Superstoe began writing on the memo pad. "These are instructions for the television technicians, Isen," he said. "I'll come on in about an hour or so. At the same time announce that the Speaker of the House has just been killed in an automobile accident. Then we'll go off TV for a few minutes and try to contact Clemens and see who else he'd like as President. A little later I'll come back on and begin a statement. Then the audio will go off due to technical difficulties. We can have it come on again for a second, then off again. Have a Supreme Court justice on the screen with a Bible. Then, when we get word from Lazarus that the paratroopers have dropped, turn on the audio and I'll announce that the city is in government hands, infantry entering the city, et cetera, et cetera." He tore off the sheet and handed it to Zorr. Zorr started out the door.

"Oh, and Isen," Superstoe called. Zorr stopped and turned. "When you get a chance, later in the day, announce the appointments of Ivan Borozov as ambassador to Russia and Edwin Watt as Secretary of Health, Education, and Welfare. And that I'm appointing Lazarus Vice President, but for the time being he'll retain his post as Secretary of Defense."

2 Only Furth was absent from the funeral, which took place, with great ceremony, as scheduled.

Unfortunately Operation Squelch—as Furth named it—did not proceed as smoothly as hoped.

The paratroopers arrived before the tear gas; some of the paratroopers had abandoned their gas masks; many of the rebels *had* masks; two Navy helicopters collided and crashed.

The paratroopers easily took the telephone and power stations. The rebels surrendered at the first sight of them.

But the paratroopers were unable to find the Governor's mansion. And the two squads that formed and moved toward the National Guard Armory were pinned down by rifle and mortar fire.

Furth, who was in the War Room and in direct contact with the commander on the scene, was informed of each event. He ordered the squads pinned down around the armory to retreat and advance on the capitol building.

They started out but got lost and radioed for instructions. Then the commander's radio malfunctioned and Furth was cut off. The Army Chief of Staff was sitting beside him. Furth tapped the four stars on the general's shoulder. "Heads," Furth said through his teeth, "will roll."

But not all went amiss. The lost paratroopers commandeered a taxi to lead them to the capitol building. They found it occupied by twenty-four frightened rebels who, upon seeing the paratroopers, gratefully surrendered their arms. They were holding eighteen office workers captive.

They had heard Superstoe's announcement that the city was in the hands of federal troops, but they had seen no troops nor received any orders from General Clemens.

The paratroopers released the captives and disarmed the rebels, including the four who were stuck in an elevator.

At one in the afternoon the convoy from Fort Ord arrived. The troops deployed, guided by city policemen who could find the Governor's mansion and Lieutenant Governor's and Mayor's homes.

They found the Lieutenant Governor's house abandoned by the rebels; the Lieutenant Governor, his wife, and his son were tied and gagged in the basement, unharmed.

The Mayor's house had also been abandoned, but the Mayor was unconscious, and his wife and daughter had been raped and were suffering from shock.

At the Governor's mansion they were met by gunfire. A voice yelled that unless the troops dispersed the Governor and his family would die. The troop commander demanded to hear the Governor's voice. General Clemens refused. The commander radioed the Pentagon War Room.

"If they won't show you the Governor it means they've already killed him," Furth said. "Take them. But try not to kill them. We'll want to try them."

The troops fired tear gas but the fire from the mansion continued; evidently the rebels had masks. The troops kept up their fire until reinforcements arrived, then threw down a smoke screen and stormed the mansion. For the first minute or two they had to shoot their way from room to room, being met by determined fire and two grenades. Then the firing stopped.

They took six rebels prisoner and counted seven dead and five wounded.

They found General Clemens. He had committed suicide.

They found the Governor and his wife dead; but the three girls, locked in the nursery, were unharmed.

The nation was aghast at the insurrection and slaughter.

Superstoe was praised for acting firmly and shrewdly.

Superstoe called in the Director of the FBI and ordered all units of the Patriots' Militia disarmed and arrested. The Director explained that his bureau did not know the identities or whereabouts of all the Militia members. Superstoe fired him and named Laurence Miller Director of the FBI.

Congress promised the President bipartisan support.

3   To the Europeans it appeared that America was in a state of anarchy. Newspapers bannered conflicting rumors: Superstoe had resigned; Superstoe had not resigned; General Clemens was President; Superstoe had committed suicide; Furth had joined the troops in Sacramento and been killed.

Taking advantage, therefore, of the apparent chaos, East German guards closed all three autobahns, shot down a U.S. Air Force jet, and moved more troops into East Berlin.

President Superstoe heard the report and lifted the telephone. He gave a brief order, sat back, and waited.

A few minutes later Adams entered the oval office, sat in a chair, and blew a series of smoke rings.

"You'd think," said Superstoe, "that in these modern times a telephone call would be a simple matter."

"The difficulty is diplomatic rather than electronic," Adams replied. "It's an innovation."

"It's time for a few innovations."

"I expect to see quite a few in the next few days." Adams pulled at the right handle of his mustache—a sign of slight nervousness or excitement.

Finally the phone buzzed. "East Berlin," the operator said. "The Premier."

Superstoe lifted the receiver, whispering to Adams, "I'm afraid my German's a little rusty."

"He'll get the message."

Superstoe smiled warmly into the receiver and began to speak in German. "Good day! Friedrich?" A pause. "Friedrich? Is it you? Good! Paxton here!" Pause. "Paxton! Superstoe!" Pause. "Yes, it really is! You can't believe it? Well, it is, sure enough. Say, Friedrich, about the autobahns and airplanes ..."

Superstoe looked at Adams and placed his palm over the mouthpiece. "What's he saying, Ben? He's talking so fast ..."

"Propaganda," Adams replied.

Superstoe gave a nod and looked sternly into the mouthpiece. He shouted, "Friedrich, you son of a whore!"

The torrent from the loudspeaker ceased. Superstoe continued. "Can that crap and listen to me. I'm going to send convoys through the autobahns. I'm going—will you shut your mouth and listen? I'm also sending a fighter squadron into the air. If—" Pause. "No, you listen to me, Friedrich. And if you shoot at my planes—if you so much as aim at my planes, or if you shoot at my convoys—you'll find exactly five Polaris missiles landing in your backyard." Pause. "In your backyard." Pause. "In your country. What's more, I'm going to tell you precisely where those five missiles are aimed." He read from a list on the desk.

He listened a moment and then interrupted. "I am not bluffing, Fred."

The East German Premier resumed his outburst. Superstoe whispered across the desk, "He seems an unstable chap, doesn't he?" Adams nodded and blew another series of smoke rings. When the Premier paused to catch his breath, Superstoe said, "Another thing, Friedrich. I've spoken with Moscow on the hot line. They've promised not to defend you. They don't really like you, you know."

Superstoe hung up.

His secretary entered and placed a cardboard carton on the desk. Superstoe opened it and licked the lid. "Would you like one, Ben?" he asked.

"What?"

"Vanilla malt."

Adams teeth chopped firmly on the cigar. The secretary departed and returned, placing a glass and a bottle of John Jameson before him.

"Now I'd better get something off on the hot line," Superstoe said. "It's the first time it's been used in a crisis, isn't it?"

"I believe so."

"It's time we used it."

"I'll cable Ivan to see Soznolopak," Adams said, filling his glass.

"I imagine he was happy to be going back to Mother Russia."

"Yes. A little afraid, however, they'd arrest him. But he said anything was better than making out another set of semester exams. He'd just started typing the stencils."

"They're having exams at the university?"

Adams nodded.

Superstoe giggled gleefully. He drank the malt. He pulled a blue-and-purple-bordered handkerchief from a side pocket and erased his white mustache.

"Ivan will handle it," he said. "Ivan is a genius. You're a genius. I'm a genius. We're all geniuses. The country is in good hands. Finally. Where's my pencil?"

4 Superstoe waited.

He waited until the cable came saying Borozov had left the embassy for his appointment with the Premier and Chairman of the Central Committee, Alexei Soznolopak. He waited until the report came from West Germany saying the thunderstorm had passed and the fighter squadron could take off.

Meanwhile his ultimatum to East Germany was announced to the press.

Adams called from his State Department office. "A very hasty note from Bonn," he said. "The ambassador's in my office now. They say you've given *de facto* recognition to East Germany."

Superstoe had missed his afternoon nap. He was a little testy. "Tell him," he said, "that if he bothers me again with such trivia I'll *give* Berlin to Friedrich. It's more trouble than it's worth."

The Army convoys, each led by tanks, were refused admittance to the autobahns. Following orders, the tanks rammed through the blockades. The East German guards fired. The American troops deployed on the western side of the boundary, dug in, and waited. American jets screamed over East Germany. They were attacked. One American plane and one East German plane were shot down.

Superstoe picked up the red phone. The order was relayed to the nuclear submarine stationed in the Mediterranean.

5 Ivan Borozov strode jovially down the Moscow boulevard. He had thought he would never return to the land of his birth. He hated the Communists, who had shot his father, but he loved Russia.

He was ushered into the office of the Premier and Chairman. They talked for an hour. Soznolopak reiterated that he was pledged to stand behind Germany. Borozov reaffirmed the resolution of the American government. Finally the Premier rose to dismiss him.

Borozov remained in his chair and threw his hands out before him. "Ah, comrade, comrade," he cried. "Here we sit talking of bombs, of East and West. I must return and submit my report. But, before I go, I do not forget that I, too, am Russian. Whatever happens, let us be friends, you and I, Alexei Mikhailovich, for we were both born in Mother Russia. Let us drink a toast to Mother Russia, Russian to Russian, what do you say?"

Soznolopak, a lean, ascetic man, replied sternly, "You are an American, Mr. Ambassador. And I am working. I do not drink while I am working."

Ivan Borozov leaped to his feet. He slammed his fist to the desk. "Son of a bourgeois imperialist!" he cried. "You refuse to drink to Mother Russia?" Borozov cried to the aides. "Who is the better Russian, he or I? I am an American citizen, it is true! But I love Russia more than Comrade Alexei Mikhailovich!"

"No man loves Russia more than I!" Soznolopak screamed. "Bring a bottle of vodka!"

An hour later Soznolopak wept. "Ivan Alexandrovich," he sighed, "where have the good old days gone? The days of fervor and excitement?"

"Comrade," said Borozov as he refilled their glasses, "I say the same thing. War is a stupid business."

"Of course it is. But I have these bloodthirsty generals on my back."

"Comrade, these are new times. They call for new thought. You are a Russian. I am Russian. We understand one another. Don't we?"

"We do, comrade. Do you realize, no one calls me comrade any more? It's out of fashion."

"Comrade," said Borozov, what is Germany to us? What is China to us? We are for Russia. Aren't we? Let us drink again to Mother Russia."

"To Mother Russia!"

"Let us fall on our knees and kiss the earth of Russia, watered by the blood of generations of patriots."

"To the beautiful soil of Russia!"

"Let us drink to the beautiful wheatfields of Russia!"

"And to the barren steppes!"

"To the Russian potatoes!"

"To the Russian potatoes!"

"To pure Russian vodka!"

"To pure Russian vodka!"

"To Russian women!"

"To the beautiful Russian women!"

"The Russian woman is the, hope of the future. The Russian mother, the Russian girl!"

"The hope of the future!" Soznolopak echoed.

"American women are stupid and skinny. Again to the Russian woman!"

"Again to the Russian woman!"

"Ah, Comrade Alexei Mikhailovich, which is the mightiest nation on the earth?"

"I wish I knew, Comrade Ivan. It is America or Russia, but truly I do not know which. I wish I knew."

"Then we know which are the two mightiest nations."

"Yes, we know, dear Ivan."

"Then are we to fight one another? We are brothers! Are we to fight, are brothers to fight, over a whore of a German and a whore of a Chinese?"

"That would be stupid, little Ivan. Very very stupid."

"Then let my friend Paxton come to see you."

"My generals would not like it."

"Are your generals Chairman of the Central Committee?"

"No!"

"My friend Paxton loves Russia as much as you and I."

"I do not believe it."

"You do not believe me, your friend and brother, your countryman!"

"I would love to believe you, little Ivan."

"Our friend Paxton will come, and we will drink vodka, and we will toast Mother Russia, and we will toast brotherhood. To brotherhood!"

"To brotherhood! To sisterhood!"

"To sisterhood!" Borozov cried. "And do you know, Alyosha, that Paxton even speaks Russian?"

"No!"

"Yes!"

"To the grand Russian language!" cried Soznolopak.

"To the grand Russian language! He does not speak it as well as we, to be sure, comrade. He only speaks a little. But he has learned Russian—he has learned it in fact from me, Ivan Alexandrovich."

"No!"

"I swear it on the Russian flag behind you."

"To our friend Paxton!" Soznolopak toasted. He swung his arm into the air, lost his balance, and started to fall out of his chair. Borozov grabbed his arm and pushed him back into the chair. He leaned close to him and whispered into his ear.

"Do you know, Alyosha dear, that I have taught ignorant farm boys in North Dakota the great mother tongue of the great Russian people?"

"No!"

"I have."

"To the North—what was it?"

"Dakota."

"To the North Dakota farm boys who speak the great Russian tongue under the tutelage of my brother Ivan Alexandrovich!"

"They are not very smart, these Americans, comrade, but I had one student who learned to speak Russian better than he spoke English."

"Long live the glorious Russian language!"

"In all your schools you teach English, do you not?" asked Borozov.

"We do."

"And in America we teach Russian. What does that mean, Comrade Alyosha?"

"I do not know. What does it mean, Comrade Ivan?"

"It means we have always known that America and Russia are brothers."

"We have. We have always known it."

"And the Germans. What are the Germans?"

"Dogs."

"How much has East Germany cost you?"

"Do not remind me of unpleasant thoughts, dear Ivan."

"How many millions of rubles will it cost you next year, brother Alyosha?"

"I have nightmares of such things, little Ivan."

"Then I will tell you what we shall do. Shall I tell you, brother?"

"Tell me, brother Ivan."

"We shall give Germany to the Germans. Let West Germany pay for East Germany."

"Impossible, brother. We have our pride."

"We do! We have our pride, brother Alyosha! We have our beautiful Russian pride! And so this is what we shall do! Shall I tell you what we shall do, dear brother?"

"Tell me, dear brother Ivan Alexandrovich."

"We shall give you China."

"Brother Ivan, I do not want China. I wish China were a dream. I would like to wake up in the morning and find that China had been a bad dream."

"China is a wolf, brother. A hungry wolf."

"He is."

"Is he your friend?"

"He is not."

"He is not my friend either. Soon he will try to eat you."

"He will not succeed."

"Of course he will not. But let us kill the Chinese wolf together. We will help you. Then, when he is dead, the dirty Stalinist Chinese wolf, you will form the government. It will be Russia's victory."

"I think China would be another Germany, dear Ivan. More rubles down the drain."

"America will pay for China! America is rich!"

"I wish dear Russia were as rich."

"We are brothers! The rich brother will help the less rich. Soon we will all be like the nobles of old times. We will lie around and drink and talk. Computers will be our peasants. The state will wither away ..."

"You talk foolishness, Ivan. The state will never wither away. It will only get bigger and bigger. Are you an idiot?"

"Exactly, my Alyosha. You are a wise man. We are both wise men. We know what the world is like. Don't we?"

"I hope we do, Ivan."

"Then we know America and Russia must not fight. Wise men do not fight each other, do they?"

"They do not."

"To Russian wisdom, Comrade Alyosha!"

"To Russian wisdom, Comrade Ivan. To American wisdom!" He tipped his glass. He tipped it higher. "My glass is empty, Ivan," he said.

Borozov reached for a bottle. Carefully Soznolopak focused on it. "That bottle too is empty, Ivan."

Borozov inspected the entire row of bottles. "They are all empty, Alyosha," he said sadly.

"We must get another bottle. What are we toasting, Ivan?"

A man rushed in. "The Americans ...!" he began. He recognized Borozov. His face filled with horror.

"Speak, speak, or close your mouth!" Soznolopak yelled.

The man, staring dumbly at the row of vodka bottles, announced, "The German Socialist Republic shot down an American plane."

"Oh, well," murmured Soznolopak.

"Five Polaris missiles were fired on East Germany."

Soznolopak stopped breathing in the middle of an inhalation. Then he finished the inhalation and exhaled slowly, cautiously. His eyes flicked to Borozov. Borozov watched the eyes shift, as Soznolopak tried to remember which was the glass eye. He could not remember. One eye looked at him, the other at an empty bottle.

"The generals are waiting," the man said.

"Ivan," Soznolopak whispered wearily.

"Sir," the man urged.

"In a minute! Out!" Soznolopak shouted.

Sadly, resignedly, Borozov lit an American cigarette. He offered one to Soznolopak. "I do not smoke," Soznolopak said, taking one. Borozov lit it.

"Alexei Mikhailovich," Borozov said, "my friend Paxton warned them. I told you he was not bluffing."

Soznolopak puffed on the cigarette; he did not inhale it. "You told me, Ivan Alexandrovich. I warned those German fools."

"Let them stew in their own juices."

"It will serve them right," Soznolopak agreed.

The man was in the room again. "The generals ..."

"Fuck the generals! Out!"

The door slammed. Soznolopak leaned across the desk and said softly, "The generals, Ivan, will demand war."

"We must not have war. It would be foolish. If we fight a war, let us fight on the same side."

"I agree, Ivan. But I must do something with my generals."

"Let Paxton come. He will come as a pledge of our friendship. He will come and you can discuss what to do with Germany."

6   In the newspapers, in the diplomatic channels, in the United Nations, it appeared that the world was leaping off the precipice of doom. Or, as some expressed it, the United States had leaped and was dragging the rest of the world with it. Or, as still others put it, "Is Superstoe crazy, or what?"

Two Polaris missiles had destroyed two East German Army camps, and with them most of the reserve troops. (The East German Premier had assumed Superstoe's list of targets had been a trick. When Superstoe promised to destroy the two camps, the Premier concluded Superstoe would expect the troops to be moved; therefore, the Premier ordered the troops to remain in their barracks, as Superstoe had anticipated.) The other three missiles destroyed airfields, reducing the East German Air Force by two-thirds. (The Premier had massed planes at the three designated airfields, presuming those would be the only safe ones.)

Shots were exchanged across the border and in Berlin, but neither side began an attack.

American planes did not attempt to enter the air corridors. American troops did not try to enter the autobahns.

The East German government promised all-out war.

The Russian government promised to support East Germany to the bitter end.

The White House announced that any aggression by East Germany would bring ten more Polaris missiles onto East German territory. The ten target sites were listed in the announcement.

France and Great Britain denounced the missile attack. They protested they had not been informed.

But behind the scenes it was different.

In East Berlin the Premier was being castigated by the members of his Central Committee. They debated deposing him for incompetence.

In his State Department office Adams met with ambassadors from NATO nations. He served wine and passed round cigars.

At the White House Furth, Zorr, and Pall met with congressmen. They served cocktails.

In Moscow Soznolopak met with his Central Committee. They demanded action. He replied, "But you know, gentlemen, if we help attack West Germany, or even West Berlin, this crazy man Superstoe will fire all his missiles."

"Then we will fire ours!" a general said.

"But you know," Soznolopak reminded, "if it comes to an all-out war, we will lose."

The debate continued. After a time Soznolopak left the meeting room and was driven quickly to the airport.

Meanwhile in America and—via satellite—in Europe, Superstoe appeared on television. He repeated his address three times, speaking in English, French, German, and—less fluently—in Russian.

He said the United States had not attacked East Germany; it had merely fulfilled its obligations and, in doing so, been obliged to conduct a "limited punitive action."

The television address was taped. As it was broadcast, Superstoe was flying over the North Pole in Air Force I.

In the rear of the plane translators were translating into Russian and stenographers were typing copies of the treaty Superstoe had dictated as the plane flew over Canada.

Forward, in his office, Superstoe studied an English-Russian dictionary.

7   Borozov and Soznolopak stood waiting at the Moscow airport. It was summer, early summer, but Moscow was still chilly.

Borozov, his one eye twinkling, eyed a stewardess. He looked as if he might have been a prince, before the revolution, overseeing his estate. Soznolopak stared glumly at the cement.

"Your Paxton is a brave man," Soznolopak muttered. "I could kill him now."

"He is a brave man, comrade," said Borozov. "And if you killed him, do you think our two thousand five hundred missiles would rust in their barrels?"

"Two thousand four hundred and ninety-five," Soznolopak corrected.

"Those five have been replaced by now."

"These are bad times, Ivan."

"It is the beginning of good times, Alexei. A new era."

"I am not sure of that."

"It is cold. Let us have a vodka. The Russian heart is always confident."

"I had to leave a meeting of the Central Committee to come here. Even in a socialist state we have democracy. If the committee votes to fire me, I am fired. I think we are even more democratic than America. In America your President is sure of four years. I am not sure of four days."

"Do not worry, Alexei. They will not fire you."

"They are very angry that we have not responded to those missiles."

"They are fools. You are the smartest man in Russia."

"Perhaps I am. But the fools always have the majority."

"Did you tell them we will help you fight the Chinese wolf?"

"They do not trust you."

Borozov put his arm about his comrade's shoulders. "Brother," he said, "your committee is angry because they are sober."

"You think vodka is the answer to everything."

The plane landed. They walked forward. The door opened. The President of the United States descended the steps.

He hugged Soznolopak and greeted him in Russian. "And the Mrs.?" asked Superstoe. "How is she?"

"I think she is well."

"Your sons? Are they well?"

"I hope they are, Mr. Superstoe."

"Call me Paxton. Guess what I have in the airplane for you, Alexei."

Soznolopak grimaced. "An intercontinental ballistic missile?"

Superstoe whispered into his ear. "Five giant American deep freezes. Each filled with steaks, chops, and frozen peas."

Soznolopak's eyes widened.

"I also brought you a movie projector and fifty Hollywood spectaculars, several crates of fruit, and a complete Brooks Brothers wardrobe."

"Mother of God," Soznolopak murmured.

8 The Central Committee had not been told of Superstoe's coming. Only a few of the members looked at him as he followed Soznolopak into the meeting room.

Then one member recognized him. He said, "Superstoe!"

Superstoe smiled and nodded.

Others looked up from their papers. The member who had been speaking stopped, bewildered. The name flew around the table. The Russians were incredulous. They argued back and forth whether it was really Superstoe.

Soznolopak took his chair at the head of the table. The man at his left asked, "Who is this?"

A bit uneasily, but with valiant nonchalance, Soznolopak replied softly, "Superstoe."

"SUPERSTOE!" The members were shouting, asking what it meant. One member cried, "He has sold out. The Americans have conquered." Those who heard him leaped to their feet. Chairs were overturned.

Superstoe raised his voice above the commotion. He waved his arms. After a moment the hubbub died. He was singing the Russian national anthem.

The members stared at Superstoe and at Borozov, who was standing beside Superstoe, singing the bass to Superstoe's tenor.

At the second verse Soznolopak joined them, but he sang so softly no one could hear him.

At the third verse a few of the members joined in.

At the conclusion of the anthem the member who had suggested the Americans had conquered wondered if Soznolopak had kidnapped Superstoe. The members applauded Soznolopak and rushed to congratulate him. Borozov took advantage of the situation and passed around glasses of vodka. Toasts were proposed. Even the generals looked happy.

Then someone asked Soznolopak how he had done it. Soznolopak replied with an apologetic smile, "I'm afraid you misunderstood, gentlemen. President Superstoe is here voluntarily. To discuss a treaty."

Someone threw a glass against the wall. Shouts of "Treason!" "Traitor!" "Sell-out!" "Bolshevik!" filled the room. Frantically Borozov tried to refill the glasses. Soznolopak looked worried.

Superstoe raised his glass and cried, "I drink to Lenin!" The shouting died. The Russians eyed him coldly. Borozov, unable to find his glass, raised a bottle. "I drink to Lenin!" he said.

No one spoke.

Borozov's eye coldly swept from face to face. The glass eye watched the huge picture of Lenin on the wall. "Does anyone," he asked threateningly, "wish to drink to Lenin?"

Reluctantly the members raised their glasses and muttered. "To Lenin."

Finally, dubiously, they agreed to listen to Superstoe's proposals.

Superstoe pushed aside his glass and an empty vodka bottle. He placed a sheaf of papers on the desk before him. Borozov moved around the table distributing copies of the proposals and at the same time refilling the glasses.

A servant entered bearing a huge tray of tidbits—pickled herring, pickles, crackers, small sandwiches.

One member asked, "Is this a party or a meeting?"

Superstoe merely smiled and popped a slice of herring into his mouth. He rubbed his hands together and began in Russian, pronounced with a slight Midwestern American accent.

"First I will explain what I would be pleased if the Soviet government would do. Then I will enumerate the numerous concessions I—the American bourgeois capitalistic government—am pleased to make in exchange."

A Russian nearby muttered, "He expects us to sell out."

"This is stupid, Alexei," another said.

A general cried, "I propose we immediately attack the capitalist warmongers! We have their President hostage. They will not dare attack."

Borozov's fist crashed on the table. He shouted. He pounded the table again. The blood rushed to his face. His eyes—even the glass eye—gleamed fiercely.

The harangue lasted five minutes. He talked so fast Superstoe had difficulty understanding him, but he perceived the gist of Borozov's torrent of words, which consisted of a denunciation of the committee's collective stupidity and ill manners.

As Borozov raged on, Superstoe leaned to one side and whispered into Soznolopak's ear, "I've never seen Ivan so angry."

Soznolopak answered, "We Russians think we are supposed to be emotional, that is all. Ivan is only pretending. Ivan Alexandrovich is a true Russian."

Borozov flung his arms into the air and ceased his tirade. He weaved slightly back and forth. He grabbed a glass and cried, "To Marx!"

Gently Soznolopak placed a hand on Borozov's arm. "Let us hear first Paxton's words, Ivan Alexandrovich."

Borozov gasped. "You will not drink to Karl Marx?"

"Later, Ivan," Superstoe said in English.

"*Comment?*" asked Borozov. When he was drunk he had difficulty distinguishing one language from another.

Superstoe cleared his throat and clasped his hands before him. "As I was saying, comrades," he began.

"Who is he, calling us comrades?" someone asked.

Superstoe pounded the table. "If you interrupt me once more, BOOM!" he shouted. He added a short harangue, ending, inadvertently, in several Polish curses he had learned from Adams.

"How was that?" he asked Borozov in English.

"Very Russian," Borozov replied in German.

Superstoe fortified himself with a small sandwich. "Now," he began again, "I propose—" he chewed and swallowed. "By the way, Alexei, these are very good. Remind me to get the recipe."

Soznolopak held his head in his hands.

"Are you ill?" asked Superstoe.

Soznolopak nodded.

"Would you like an aspirin?"

Soznolopak waved a tired hand at the sheaf of papers before Superstoe. "Please, Paxton," he murmured, "continue."

"Certainly." He turned to the others. One was refilling his glass. "Here's what I want," he said. "I want you to agree to my plans for reorganizing the United Nations. This reorganization—described more fully in the papers before you—consists essentially of the creation of an inspection service to oversee disarmament and prevent secret construction of bombs, missiles, or germs and the creation of an international police force to enforce compliance with the international laws we shall all agree on."

The Russians began muttering and talking. Superstoe raised his hand. Soznolopak pleaded for silence.

Superstoe resumed. "The purpose of the reorganization is simply the prevention of war. It will free us to compete economically rather than militarily. Why should we fight? We have more to gain by peace than by war."

A general cried, "Never coexistence! World Communism . . . !"

Superstoe said calmly, "Be careful, General. The era of Stalinism has passed. Are you a reactionary, by chance? A sympathizer with the Chinese? Isn't it true you are in secret correspondence with the Chinese government?"

The general's face went white.

"Impossible," Soznolopak said. "Secrets are impossible in the socialist state."

Superstoe raised his eyebrows significantly. Soznolopak looked at the general and made a note on the pad at his elbow.

"And until the UN reorganization is effected," Superstoe continued, "I propose a nonaggression understanding. Specifically, you will not give any aid to East Germany. In return—" he shouted over the eruption of noise—"I will give you West Berlin."

Silence fell.

"If you honor our agreement," Superstoe went on, "and restrain East Germany, and if you refrain from helping China—it is possible China will attack America hoping you will join her—then, when the UN has been reorganized, you will permit us to remove all the citizens of West Berlin to West Germany. Then the entire city will become a part of East Germany, and the air corridors and the autobahns can go to hell."

"But we must permit the West Berliners to leave," Soznolopak said.

"Of course. And they must be able to take their money and movable possessions with them. On the other hand, all the industrial plants, et cetera, will remain, undamaged."

"Hmm," Soznolopak said.

"You agree not to interfere in our dealings with East Germany and China," Superstoe said, "and you agree to the UN proposal, and we will give you West Berlin and ..."

"*What* dealings with China?" asked Soznolopak.

"Any that might crop up," Superstoe blandly replied.

"What have you in your mind, Paxton?"

"Well, I've merely thought that China might become more aggressive. But, whatever happens, I would not attempt to change the socialist character of China. I don't care if China is a Communist state. I would only hope she became more friendly, like our brothers, the Russians."

Soznolopak started to speak, but Superstoe rushed on. "Let me finish my proposals. In exchange for your cooperation I will give you the following." He snatched another slice of herring and a cracker. "A shipload of vaccines, in case China or Albania tries a germ attack on you."

"*Albania?*" someone echoed.

"Plus," Superstoe continued, "agricultural experts, free fertilizer, and a thousand new tractors."

"Bah."

"Make it five thousand," Superstoe said. "A billion-dollar grant for the building of Soviet schools and universities and medical colleges, a hundred-million-dollar grant for the building of television stations, and a million free television sets."

"He will corrupt us with the television," someone said. "America is already corrupted."

Superstoe blinked innocently. "All to be given over a ten-year period." He sipped his vodka. "How does that strike you?" he asked.

The Russians looked at one another. One said, "He must be lying."

"Superstoe," said Superstoe, "does not lie to his Russian brothers."

"He talks capitalistic propaganda," someone said.

"Trotskyite!" Superstoe shouted. Then, calmly, "Does it seem a fair bargain?"

"We would lose prestige," a general said.

"Another thing," Superstoe said. "I suggest we cooperate in space exploration. The first men on the moon will be a Russian and an American."

"Two Russians," Soznolopak said.

"Ah, no," replied Superstoe. "We too have our pride."

Soznolopak nodded understandingly.

"Of course we'll be making friendly trade agreements, expanded student and teacher exchanges," Superstoe said.

"That is possible," Soznolopak agreed.

"Another sort of exchange occurred to me," Superstoe said, "that would further friendly relations."

"Wives?" asked someone.

"Government officials," Superstoe said. "For example, Ben Adams becomes your Foreign Minister for, say, six months, and your Foreign Minister takes over as my Secretary of State. That way we'd get to know each other's problems."

"He is crazy, the American," someone said. "Completely."

Superstoe winked at him.

"We'd get to know each other's secrets as well," Soznolopak replied.

"That's fair, isn't it?" asked Superstoe.

"We have more secrets than you."

Superstoe spread his arms. "I have no secrets," he explained. He leaned over the table. "What about exchanging propaganda ministers?" he asked. "*That* would increase understanding incalculably."

The Propaganda Minister shook his head violently.

Superstoe grabbed Soznolopak's wrist. "We could exchange generals!" he whispered.

Soznolopak considered for a moment. He looked interested.

Someone said, "A very important question has not been asked, Alexei Mikhailovich."

"Yes?" asked Soznolopak.

"What if we don't agree to Superstoe's proposals?"

Superstoe looked pained. The Russians waited. "What," asked Superstoe, "bothers you, comrade? I'm sure we can reach an amiable agreement."

"No, no," the man protested. "Tell me: what if we come to East Germany's aid?"

Sadly Superstoe sighed. He held out his hands, palms up. He shook his head. "What *could* I do, comrade? I would have to drop nuclear missiles and germs on beautiful Russia."

"And we would do the same to America!" the man shouted.

"And there we'd be," said Superstoe. "For what? That way we both lose. My way, we both win. Is it so difficult a decision?"

"How do we know he will keep his word?" a general asked.

"I'll tell you what," Superstoe said happily. "I'll remain here, in your hands, at your mercy, a hostage, until everything is satisfactorily arranged."

"There can be no doubt," the Propaganda Minister said. "He is quite mad."

Superstoe stood. "Perhaps you'd like to discuss this in private," he said. "Ivan and I will wait in another room. Come, Ivan."

Borozov, who had been drinking steadily, rose, swayed, and wove heavy-footed in the direction of the door. Superstoe shut the door behind them.

Soznolopak opened his mouth to speak, but the door flew open and Superstoe's head appeared. "One other thing, Alexei," he said.

Soznolopak shuddered. He held his breath.

Superstoe glanced around the table. The Russians were expectant, tense. Now, they thought, comes the truth. Of course—the American concessions were unbelievable. Superstoe will demand more.

"I would like," said Superstoe, "dinner. I'm terribly hungry. Could you arrange it, Alexei?"

Soznolopak looked extremely tired. He nodded his head.

"I'd love some borsch," Superstoe added.

Soznolopak lifted the receiver at his elbow.

"An authentic Russian dinner!" Superstoe explained.

Soznolopak repeated, "An authentic Russian dinner."

"Thanks, Alexei." The door closed.

Superstoe pulled Ivan from the wall against which he had been leaning and gently guided him down the gloomy hall. Borozov mumbled something.

"What, Ivan?" asked Superstoe.

"I said," said Borozov, "that personally I have never cared for borsch."

9 Three and a half hours later Soznolopak left the meeting room. His last words were: "So. It is decided. We will agree to the treaty. We will not begin war. But we will insist on West Berlin *before* the UN reorganization. And we will ignore the treaty whenever we wish."

He found Superstoe at the table in a lounge. A great pile of dirty dishes and goblets rose before him. Across from him sat two waiters, laughing hysterically, tears rolling down their cheeks. Superstoe was just refilling their snifters with a rare cognac Soznolopak recognized as coming from his private stock. Superstoe was telling dirty stories in Russian.

When the waiters saw Soznolopak, one fainted and fell to the floor, but the other, more sanguine from the cognac, waved at Soznolopak and, grinning, yelled, "Comrade Alexei Mikhailoshit, you sour-faced revisionist, come have a glass of your own bourgeois brandy, you slave driver, you!" The waiter collapsed into laughter.

Superstoe poured a snifter and handed it to Soznolopak. "Sit down, Alexei," he said soberly but cheerfully, "and tell me the news. And you mustn't be hard on the waiters. It's all my fault."

Soznolopak drifted into the chair beside Superstoe. He looked at Superstoe. Then he looked at the stack of dishes.

He looked at the waiter lying on the floor. He looked at the other waiter, whose laughter had subsided into a steady, self-hypnotic chuckle and who would obviously be asleep in another few seconds. He looked behind him at Borozov asleep in a stuffed chair.

"I believe you, Paxton," Soznolopak replied. He set the snifter of cognac on the table without touching it.

"A toast to brotherhood," Superstoe said, putting the snifter back into Soznolopak's hand.

Gently, resolutely, Soznolopak returned the snifter to the table. "I have had enough toasting today," he said wearily.

"Well?" asked Superstoe. "You accept my proposals?"

Soznolopak mustered a smile and nodded. "Yes," he said. "Congratulations, Mr. President." He shook Superstoe's hand.

Superstoe waggled his finger at Soznolopak. "Now, now, Alexei, you needn't pretend with me. You agree—but you will stall and change your mind when it suits you. All right. But remember: you are dealing with me, now. With Superstoe." Superstoe sniffed, sipped, and swallowed the cognac. "Exquisite bouquet," he whispered.

Soznolopak absently picked up his snifter and sniffed. "Yes," he said, half to himself. Then to Superstoe, "But you know, Paxton, you are very lucky. History is a strange story. Fate is an unpredictable, whimsical force." He sipped. "You are very lucky," he repeated.

"Why do you say so?" asked Superstoe.

"Why," replied Soznolopak, "if it were not for the epidemics begun by your traitors, that man Knutson would not have been elected. Then if his Vice President, Doberman, had not had the heart attack, you would not have been made Vice President. And *then*, if Knutson had not gone crazy and blown his head off ..."

Superstoe touched Soznolopak's arm. "But, Alexei," he said quietly, "that was not luck."

Soznolopak, sniffing, was smiling a little and seemed not to have heard. He swallowed a few drops of the cognac and asked, "How do you mean, Paxton?"

"We"—tapping his chest with his forefinger—"started the epidemics so Knutson would be elected."

Soznolopak smiled more broadly. He is ever the joker, he was thinking.

"We"—he tapped the table—"killed Doberman. We caused Knutson to commit suicide." He spoke matter-of-factly, the way he would have corrected a translation from Caesar back at Crossbar High School.

Soznolopak set his snifter on the table. His fingers rested on the edge of the table. "Mother of God," he whispered. He stared at Superstoe.

Superstoe grinned like a boy after his first sexual intercourse. "You see, I'm quite ruthless," he said.

Soznolopak refilled his snifter. That was when he noticed the other bottle of the rare cognac, empty. He smashed the empty bottle against the floor and looked ready to cry. "My God, Superstoe!" he cried. "Enough is enough! These are the last two bottles in the country! There are only another dozen bottles in existence!"

Superstoe patted Soznolopak's knee. "I have one of those bottles, Alexei. I will give it to you. I will have my CIA agents steal another five or six bottles and send them to you." He lifted his snifter and clinked it against Soznolopak's. "Cheers."

Soznolopak drank and wiped the perspiration from his forehead. "Paxton," he said, "tell me. Tell me truly. What are you after? What is your goal? Let us be honest with one another."

"Certainly. My goal, so far as you are concerned, is permanent peace. That's why I want the UN reorganized. I want every country to abide by international law, I want disarmament—so I can spend my money on other things than missiles and guns—and I want peace and law guaranteed by impartial inspectors and an international police force. That's all."

"Your goal, so far as *I* am concerned," Soznolopak repeated. "What is your goal so far as I am not concerned?"

"To create the Good Life in America. Of course I expect other countries to follow my lead eventually. But I am not concerned with that. I am merely concerned with ending international greed and foolishness, so I can get about my work of reforming America."

"Do you have a cigarette?"

"I don't smoke. But Ivan does." He found Borozov's cigarettes and handed the pack to Soznolopak. He lit the cigarette with Borozov's lighter. Then he leaned closer and said softly, urgently. "Between us, Alexei, we can reform the world. The rest of the world causes us problems only because we are enemies. But, if we are friends, if we act together, for our mutual interests"—he straightened his back, his eyes gleamed—"we can put the world in order in a month, stop spending billions on defense, and spend it on worthier enterprises." He sipped his cognac.

"But to accomplish this you are willing to risk all-out war."

"Yes."

"You would destroy both our countries."

"If necessary. Because *afterward* I think the world would see the necessity for a strong UN."

"But, Paxton, it is likely that in fifty, in a hundred years, your goal will be accomplished anyway, without the risk of war."

"It is just as likely there will be war before then."

"Well, that is a gamble."

"So are my plans."

"Wouldn't it be better to wait?"

"No. I cannot wait. I spent most of my life waiting."

Soznolopak mopped his forehead. Superstoe lifted the bottle. "Empty," he observed. "There's only one thing to do. We must have a party to celebrate our treaty. We'll all go to the American embassy. Your entire Central Committee." He stood. "Come. You get your comrades together, I'll call the embassy."

"Paxton, it is four in the morning."

"Where's a phone?"

"The committee are tired. I am tired. I am very tired. Ivan is asleep."

"Ivan's only drunk. Come. It is for Soviet-American brotherhood."

10   Borozov awoke in the limousine as it sped through the dark, deserted Moscow streets. He looked into the night. "I knew it," he said. "Siberia. Well ..."

"We're going to a party," Superstoe said.

"A farewell party they call it in American movies, Paxton. I should not have come. Thank God I left my wife in America."

"No, no, Ivan. A party at the embassy. To celebrate. They agreed to the treaty."

"That means they are stalling."

"Of course. But sufficient unto the day is the evil thereof. Is there plenty of champagne at the embassy?"

"How would I know? I just arrived. I can't remember where my office is."

"It's the one with the secret listening device behind the wall."

"They're in all the walls, Paxton. There's even one in my shower."

"Then Alexei will know if we have any champagne."

Superstoe hopped from the car and leapt up the steps. The door was locked; the building was dark. He leaned his shoulder against the buzzer and remained there four minutes until the door was opened by a blinking young man with sleep creases across his cheek.

Superstoe shoved the young man aside and strode inside, followed by Borozov. Superstoe switched on the lights. "Didn't you get my call?" he demanded. "Turn on the lights! Break out the bottles! Find the corkscrews! Fry bacon and eggs!"

The young man watched Superstoe stride down the hall, flipping light switches. He turned to Borozov. "Who the hell is that?" he asked. He was drugged with sleep and seemed to have put off his customary diplomacy when he had put on his yellow-and-black-checked pajamas.

"Superstoe," Borozov answered.

Without thinking the young man said, "Bullshit."

Borozov slapped him smartly on the cheek. "Capitalistic warmonger!" he shouted. "Doesn't the ambassador know who the President is?"

"I'm not even sure you're the ambassador!" the young man shouted back. "Christ knows *who's* President! I can't keep track of them!"

Superstoe was back. He gave a tug at the string of the young man's pajamas. They fell to the floor.

"Watch your tongue, my boy," said Superstoe. "You're lucky I'm a reasonable man. Now pull up your pants and put on a tie."

The young man lunged after his pajama pants. Borozov whistled and pinched a buttock.

Superstoe nudged Borozov. "I'll tell your wife," he said.

"Tell this man's wife. He shamelessly exposes to me his ass."

The young man, twisting his elbows and torso, had his pajamas back to his waist. He clutched them with both hands. "Listen!" he cried, like a schoolboy set upon by bullies. "What's going on? Huh? Just what's going on?"

Superstoe grabbed the young man's elbow. "Here now," he said, like a teacher separating squabbling boys, "what's your name?"

The hand was firm on his elbow. The young man looked more closely at the bald chubby man below him. "You *look* like Superstoe," he said.

"There's a good reason for that. Now what's your name?"

"Merrill. Lou Merrill."

"How do you do, Lou," said Superstoe, extending his hand and squeezing.

Lou Merrill gave a short yelp and leaped away.

"Oh, dear," said Superstoe. "I'm terribly sorry."

Lou Merrill twisted at his pajamas and did several quick shallow knee bends. "Careful!" said Superstoe. He watched concernedly. "Back in?" he asked.

Lou Merrill fled up the stairs.

"Merrill!" Superstoe called.

Merrill stopped and looked back.

"Oh, my goodness!" said Superstoe.

Merrill fled.

Superstoe turned to Borozov. "Did you see . . .?"

Carefully Borozov winked his glass eye.

Behind them they heard footsteps. They turned. The Central Committee, sullen and weary, were crowding through the door, Soznolopak in the lead.

"Make yourselves at home!" Superstoe cried. "I'll get the glasses!"

He jogged up the stairs, crying, "Party! Party! Everybody up! Reveille! Ta-ta-tatata ta ta tatata!"

He reached the fourth floor and hurried down a dimly lit corridor. He opened a door. The room was dark. He reached for a switch. The light came on, and a woman sat up in the bed and screamed.

"Who are you?" asked Superstoe.

"Who the hell are *you?*"

"Can you tell me where the communications room is?"

"It's in the basement."

"I thought it was on the top floor."

"What do you want?"

"The communications room."

"I thought you said the rest room."

"No, the ..."

"Next floor up."

"I thought this was the top floor."

"No."

"Who are you?" asked Superstoe.

The woman pulled the sheet higher, to her neck. "Mrs. Peabody."

"Where's Mr. Peabody?"

"I wish I knew."

"Would you like to meet some nice Russians, Mrs. Peabody?"

"What?"

"Throw on a robe and go downstairs. We're having a party."

"*What?*"

"Are you hard of hearing, dear?"

"Who the hell *are* you?"

"Superstoe," said Superstoe, closing the door and bounding up the next flight of stairs.

Two men were in the communications room. Superstoe sat beside one, picked up a pencil and note pad, and said, "Send this right away, top priority, straight to Adams."

"Are you Mr. Borozov?" the man asked.

"No, I'm Superstoe. Now here's the message."

"Sure you are. And I'm Furth. Now look ..."

"Son, it's these little things that make my job so difficult. The world problems I can handle, but ..."

"He looks like Superstoe," the other man said. "But it's impossible ..."

"With Superstoe all things are possible," said Superstoe. "Send this: *BenLaz: Go No. 1. Pax vobiscum.* Got that? Immediately."

The man looked at the message, then at Superstoe. He looked at the other man, and then back to Superstoe. "Yes, sir," he said. "I'll code it."

"It's already coded. Send it as it is."

"I'm not allowed ..."

Superstoe sprang to his feet, cursing in Russian. He stood over the teletype machine. "How do you work this?" he asked.

"Right away, sir. As it is, sir."

Superstoe waited until he saw the message typed out. "When an answer comes, tell me, I'll be downstairs. At the party."

An hour and fifteen minutes later the reply came. It read:

"O.K." Superstoe was sitting on a couch beside a general, who was telling the story of his World War II campaigns. Outside, the ruddy sun cast a pink glow over Moscow.

11 On its return from Moscow the presidential jet landed not in Washington but in New York.

Superstoe slid into the limousine. Beside him he found Pall, grinning. "Morning," said Pall.

"Good morning, Arthur," said Superstoe.

"Good news," said Pall.

"Chariot's coming?"

"It's come."

Superstoe crossed his legs and relaxed.

"The Russian delegate received instructions to be 'interested but noncommittal,'" Pall went on.

"So I expected. Alexei told me the delegate would have instructions to be enthusiastic."

"So he does, now."

"Good boy."

"And France."

At the United Nations Superstoe first spoke privately with the Polish delegate and promised him compensation for the fallout from the Polaris missiles. Then he strode to the podium and presented his plan for the reorganization of the UN.

Many of the delegates were pleasantly surprised by Superstoe's speech; but they were skeptical of his plan; they knew the other big powers would never agree to it.

So when the Russian delegate promised unequivocal support of the Superstoe Plan and said Superstoe would go down in history along with Marx and Lenin, the other delegates examined their earphones and wondered if the translators had misunderstood.

But that was nothing compared to their surprise when the French delegate, looking a little uneasy, vowed that France would be the first nation to sign the new charter as outlined by Superstoe.

12 The following morning the newspapers were filled with the Superstoe Plan and the reactions to it.

Congress, as Superstoe expected, denounced the plan. They said it was a surrender of national sovereignty. What's more, they wanted to know why they weren't consulted first.

There were also strange reports of diplomatic cables being tampered with.

—

Superstoe invited congressional leaders to dinner to convince them of the wisdom of his plan. But, before he attended the dinner, he called Furth.

"Lazarus?" he said.

"Yes, Paxton."

"Operation Happy Surprise. Tonight."

"Righto."

Superstoe replaced the receiver, straightened his bow tie, patted his white dinner jacket, entered the dining room, nodded, sat, and tasted his shrimp cocktail.

Meanwhile American planes thundered off Far Eastern airfields—from carriers, from South Vietnam, from South Korea, from Formosa, from Guam. They headed for the Chinese mainland. It was the largest airlift in history.

Some of the bombers were met by Chinese jet fighters. American jet fighters, flying escort, engaged in battle. Other bombers were downed by ground-to-air missiles. But most of them completed their mission, returned to their bases, loaded up, and took off again.

Over their targets the bombers dropped wooden crates attached to parachutes.

The crates contained rice, flour, powdered eggs, powdered milk, canned meat, nylon hose, toys, alcohol, narcotics, and chocolate bars.

The crates also contained counterfeit Chinese currency and propaganda in the form of comic books printed in Chinese.

On the crates the words GIFT OF THE PEOPLE OF THE UNITED STATES OF AMERICA were stenciled in red, white, and blue in English and in Chinese.

13   Operation Happy Surprise—or, as it came to be called later, Operation Fillbelly—continued for ten days.

By the third day no more fighters were sent to intercept the bombers, and ground-to-air missiles ceased.

At first the Chinese government said the crates contained germs and poison gas. Then they announced the crates were being dropped by the Chinese government itself, and the labels were stenciled on the crates by capitalistic saboteurs and the comic books had been planted by Russian spies.

Not everything, however, went as planned. Some of the crates which were dropped on North Vietnam, in hopes of improving that tiresome, drawn-out war, were blown off target and landed among South Vietnamese troops. One company deserted en masse. Two other companies, after eating, drinking, and smoking to satiety, blithely surrendered to the Vietcong. The Vietcong confiscated what was left of the airdropped supplies. That evening the two companies of South Vietnamese and the platoon of Vietcong which captured them swaggered arm in arm, singing and laughing, to the Vietcong base.

Again Superstoe invited congressional leaders to dinner.

One senator, over after-dinner brandy, expressed his colleagues' thoughts. "Mr. President," he said, "just what the hell are you doing?"

"Why, I'm solving our problems," replied Superstoe. "The Chinese people are not our enemies. Besides, the press was not informed of *all* the contents of the crates. In addition to food and clothing, they contained booze, pot, and counterfeit bread."

The congressmen were speechless.

"Don't you think it's time we took the initiative in international relations?" asked Superstoe.

"But what's the point?" asked the senator.

"The point?" asked Superstoe, placing a palm over his mouth. He waited a second until the eructation came, and hen he resumed. "The point is, the government will fall and will be replaced by a less belligerent government."

"What makes you think so?"

"Wait and see," said Superstoe.

That was on the third day of Operation Happy Surprise. The next four days were busy, but nothing new occurred. Congressmen and editors denounced Operation Happy Surprise as useless and foolish and scoffed at the Superstoe Plan before the UN as utopian, premature, and cowardly. Meanwhile they were still discussing the Polaris attack on East Germany, calling it foolhardy and reckless.

Superstoe was pleased. Congress and the press had so many things to complain about that they found it difficult to concentrate on any one issue.

Then at the UN the French delegate again reversed himself and, with a puzzled look on his face, endorsed the Superstoe Plan for the second time, having bitterly denounced it the day before.

The next day he was recalled to Paris and replaced by the Foreign Minister, who took the floor and asserted that the Superstoe Plan was the height of idiocy.

Again France protested that her diplomatic cables were being tampered with.

Superstoe gave an informal press conference.

He sat in the rose garden wearing bright red shorts. Tom Collinses were passed among the reporters.

One reporter observed, "We have so much news we don't know what to headline."

Superstoe looked concerned. "How confusing," he said.

He was asked about the French charges.

"France is our friend. France has always been our friend. Would *we* spy on France? How would we know their diplomatic codes?"

"But the alleged false cables directed the delegate to support your plan. You must admit it looks suspicious."

Superstoe removed his sunglasses. "Have you ever read Plato, son?" he asked.

"Not for some years," the reporter answered. "Not since college."

"I recommend him," said Superstoe. "You must learn to distinguish between appearances and reality." He paused. "Possibly the charge of espionage is merely to cover up the confusion and vacillation in the French government."

They asked about the UN plan and congressional opposition.

"The thirteen colonies were not eager to join a national federation, either," Superstoe replied. "But really, you can see for yourselves, only narrow, selfish minds could oppose the plan."

"How long," someone asked, "will Operation Happy Surprise continue?"

"A few more days."

"What do you expect to gain from it, sir?"

Superstoe looked surprised. "Why, in the first place, it indicates the basic character of this administration. It indicates our unselfishness, our good will, and our desire for peace. The Polaris missiles on East Germany were necessary—we are friendly, but we are not cowardly—but they might be misinterpreted as aggressive. We are not an aggressive nation."

"Mr. President, during the German crisis, for some hours after the missiles were dropped on East Germany, you were not seen, and the presidential jet was reported to have taken off for an unknown destination. There are rumors that you flew to a secret bomb shelter in case we were attacked by Russia."

"There are?"

"Yes, sir, there are."

"That's unkind." Superstoe replaced his sunglasses.

"Would you care to say where you were, Mr. President?"

"I don't mind. I was on the plane. Then I was in Moscow, talking things over with the Central Committee."

The reporters dropped their drinks and rushed to the telephones.

On the sixth day of Operation Happy Surprise Superstoe received a call from Pall.

"Operation Decameron has begun," Pall said.

"Thank you, Arthur," said Superstoe.

He looked at the clock. It was 10:35 in the morning. He looked at the empty cardboard box on his desk. He contemplated for a moment, and then he stepped into his secretary's office. She was at her desk, typing.

Superstoe stared down the top of her blouse.

She looked up and smiled. "Yes, Mr. President?"

Superstoe did not reply.

"May I do something for you?" she asked.

"Yes," he said thoughtfully. "I'd like another doughnut."

She handed him a box.

"These are glazed," he said.

"I'm sorry. I bought them for myself. I don't have any others. I'll call ..."

"Don't bother."

"You may have these."

"No, no, they're yours."

"Really, I've had all I want. Please have them."

"You've had all you want?"

"Oh, yes."

"You're sure?"

"Yes, I'm sure."

Superstoe touched the box. "Absolutely sure?"

"Yes, sir."

He bit off half the doughnut. "Thank you, Judy."

"That's quite all right."

"That's a pretty blouse."

"Thank you, sir."

Superstoe hurried back to his office.

14   On the seventh day of Operation Happy Surprise, at 11:38 A.M., fourteen cases of bubonic plague were reported in Los Angeles.

On the tenth and last day of Operation Happy Surprise seventy-nine persons had been hospitalized with the plague in Los Angeles.

"Yes," Zorr told reporters, "it looks like clandestine germ warfare."

Sternly Superstoe addressed the nation. "The aggressors will be found," he said, "and they will be punished."

Pall and Superstoe gave a joint news conference.

Pall said, "Five crew members from a British ship docked at Los Angeles are missing. The five men are Chinese, from Hong Kong. It has been impossible to trace them further, but it seems likely they were, and are, employed by a foreign government."

Superstoe said, "I have no intention of plunging the world into nuclear war. But I assure you, gentlemen, the perpetrators of this plague will be punished—in an appropriate manner."

"You mean," asked a reporter, "the five Chinese who are missing from the ..."

"I mean," Superstoe interrupted, "the government who employed those five men."

"When will you attack?" asked another.

"I did not say I would attack. I said I would punish."

"Then when ..."

"When I choose."

"If," Pall added, "it *is* China which is responsible, then it indicates the fragility of the Chinese government. Operation Happy Surprise was too much for them."

—

After the news conference Pall and Superstoe returned to the oval office. There they met Adams, Furth, and Zorr.

Superstoe picked up a peanut-butter sandwich from the tray on his desk. "Now," he said, "our next step"—he bit into the sandwich—"is"—he chewed—"Isen!"

"Yes?"

Superstoe chewed, swallowed, and ran his tongue around his gums. "I said crunchy."

"Half are crunchy," Zorr replied. "I like smooth."

Superstoe eyed him. "I am the President, Isen," he said evenly.

"Yes, sir."

Superstoe inserted the sandwich into Zorr's mouth and turned to the tray. He exposed three sandwiches before he found one spread with crunchy. He replaced the top layer of bread and ate. A frosted mug of beer sat on his desk. When he had finished the sandwich and drunk the beer, he asked, "Where was I?"

"The next step," Pall reminded.

"Yes. Ben, what's the word from Ivan?"

"He's playing chess every Sunday afternoon with Soznolopak."

"Is he winning?"

"One out of three. He says Soznolopak is rather expert."

"He mustn't disgrace his country.

"Which one?"

"America."

"He says Soznolopak is rather vain about his chess skill."

Superstoe nodded. "I see."

"He says," Adams continued, "Soznolopak is worried about what we'll do with China. He says if we attack China he'll have to come in on their side. He let us get away with East Germany, but ..." Adams drew on his cigar.

"Of course," said Superstoe. He turned to Pall. "All the government leaders are in Peking, Arthur?"

"So far as we know."

"Can't you be more certain?"

"No."

Superstoe sighed. "It's not the best of all possible worlds. However"—he turned to Furth—"drop the germs in Peking."

"Done," said Furth, picking up the phone.

"Do you think it will work?" asked Zorr.

Furth shrugged his shoulders.

"The germs in the satellites are very fast working?" asked Superstoe.

"Very fast," Furth replied.

"They won't be able to get away?"

"I hope not."

Adams reached for his beer. "Ivan says Soznolopak thinks we planted the plague in L.A. to give us an excuse to attack China," he said.

"Alexei is a shrewd devil," Superstoe observed.

15 Eight thousand seven hundred and forty-one persons were hospitalized with bubonic plague in Los Angeles.

Then—accidentally—the plague began in Las Vegas. People rushed to the casinos that they might be quarantined within rather than without the premises.

Elsewhere the populace was frightened.

Newspapers and Congress demanded that Superstoe do something.

Then typhoid broke out in West Berlin.

It was a Sunday morning, and Watt was in Superstoe's office.

"Nobody tells me anything," Watt said.

"What do you mean?" asked Superstoe.

"Why have you planted typhoid in West Berlin?"

"I haven't."

Watt sat down. "Who did?"

Superstoe spread his hands. "Beats me," he said. He began folding a piece of paper. "East Germany might have done it out of spite," he went on. "West Germany might have done it, assuming we'd think it *was* the East and would launch an all-out and reunify the two sectors. France might have done it—who knows why France does anything? Russia might have done it to placate the generals. There are so many spies and saboteurs in Berlin there's no knowing who did it. There we are," he concluded, holding up the cunningly folded paper.

"What have you done?"

"Made a cootie catcher."

"About West Berlin?"

"I'm going to have a swim." He set the cootie catcher atop Watt's crew cut. "Join me?"

Watt sat on the edge, dangling his feet in the water. He was nude. "I wonder how it will end?" he asked.

Superstoe, in red trunks, bounced on the diving board. "What?" he asked. "The Yankees' winning streak?"

"B.W."

"Arthur says the U.A.R. is thinking of slipping germs into Israel," Superstoe remarked.

"It's becoming a fad," Watt agreed.

"Which means, if they do, Israel will slip some into Egypt."

"Of course."

"Arthur reports India and Pakistan have set up B.W. labs."

Watt splashed his legs in the warm green water. "It's easy enough to do. We proved that."

"It's a fearful weapon, said Superstoe, bouncing higher. "We must"—bounce—"see"—bounce—"that it's"—very high bounce—"outlawed." He sprang, spread his arms, glided out and downward, a plump, red-tailed swan, and entered the water with a minimum of splash.

Watt shook his head. "I don't know how he does it," he said to Furth, who was floating in an inner tube. Furth had taken swimming lessons since he was five years of age. He still couldn't swim.

"He has a natural grace," Furth explained.

"He does," Watt agreed, nodding his head.

Superstoe emerged with a snort near the inner tube and swam about. Then he submerged.

Furth jumped, rocked, clung to the inner tube.

Superstoe surfaced, honking.

"It's an ugly goose," Furth said.

"He can't sublimate everything," Watt said.

"Strange," said Furth, trying to wipe the spots of water from his glasses.

"You're rather strange yourself, young man," said Superstoe, bouncing the tube.

"We've received no response from Peking. The incubation period was over yesterday. People should be dropping in the streets today. Shame about Tientsin."

Watt slid into the water and turned on his back.

"Tientsin?" he asked.

Furth nodded.

"Nobody tells me a thing," Watt explained.

"I haven't been sending out memos."

"The first germ satellite missed," Superstoe explained. "Landed in Tientsin."

"Never did figure out where the second landed," Furth added.

"But the third one," Superstoe began.

Furth smiled, showed his slightly yellow teeth (he had never had a cavity). "A charm," he said. "Right down the chimney of the Premier's mistress's house."

"Aha!" Superstoe exclaimed. He swam rapidly to the side and hauled himself up. He ran to the corner of the pool where a bamboo pole was lodged in the ladder. "I have a bite!"

He had stocked the pool with bass, trout, and bluegills.

16   It was the following Monday evening. Superstoe was showering. He was singing "We Shall Overcome."

Someone pounded frantically at the frosted glass door.

Superstoe opened the door. The Secret Service agent jumped backward to escape the spray. "The red line!" he cried.

Superstoe stepped carefully onto the tiled floor, out of the bathroom and into the bedroom. "Would you throw me that towel?" he called behind him as he lifted the phone.

"Towel?" asked the voice on the phone.

"Yes," said Superstoe.

"Mr. President?" asked the voice.

"Who else?"

"General Jaspers, Mr. President," the voice said anxiously. "A nuclear device has been dropped on Taipei by an aircraft from the Chinese mainland. Another craft of the same origin was intercepted heading toward Manila. It was shot down."

"I see," said Superstoe, watching the puddle form beneath his feet on the maroon carpet. He took the towel and wiped his head. "Notify Furth and Pall. Stand by for orders."

"I've put all commands on red alert."

"Dandy." Superstoe hung up. To the agent he said, "See if you can get Ben in New York. And then Isen. He should be in the White House somewhere."

He dried and put on shorts, undershirt, blue dress shirt, trousers, tie, socks, and shoes.

The red line buzzed again.

"General Jaspers, sir. Another aircraft intercepted approaching Saigon. Exploded in the air. Another nuclear device."

"The nuclear device exploded?"

"Correct, sir."

"Stand by, Jaspers."

He stood thoughtfully by the small desk with the three telephones—one red, one white, and one blue. The blue one buzzed. He let it buzz three times, and then he lifted the receiver. He said, "Lazarus, I've been thinking."

"So."

"Let's drop the germs on the troop concentrations."

"Done."

"But then ..."

"Hold on," said Furth. He returned in a minute. "They've started an offensive in Korea and are landing on Formosa."

"They're desperate."

"It appears so."

"They want to pull Russia in."

"I don't doubt it," Furth said.

"I hope Alexei trusts us."

Furth merely cleared his throat.

"Are you getting a cold?" asked Superstoe.

"I hope not."

"You don't think it's a germ?"

"Please, Paxton."

Pall came on the line. "There's no word yet on what's happening to the Peking government," he informed them.

"Lazarus?" said Superstoe.

"Yes, Paxton."

"We'll drive them back to the Yalu River. No farther."

"We'll be lucky to get that far."

"We'll use the nerve gas."

"I intend to."

"Send the Marines."

"Still, it might take a couple of weeks."

"I don't expect miracles. And drive them off Formosa. That shouldn't be too hard."

"They seem to be bombing ..."

"Just a second, Lazarus. Red line again." Superstoe put the red receiver to his other ear. A few seconds later he replaced it and said into the blue one, "Seoul. They didn't catch it in time."

"Sounds messy," Pall commented.

"Probably a dirty bomb," Furth said. "The Chinese have no delicacy."

"Well," said Superstoe, "we can't stand for too much. The Polaris subs in the Pacific, Lazarus ..."

"Yes."

"Take out the Chinese airfields, military industries, troop concentrations you might not get with the germ satellites."

"Done."

Adams's voice came onto the line. "What's going on?"

Superstoe told him. Then he said, "Hop over to the UN, Ben, and tell them. Explain we won't invade China. We're just putting its war machine out of commission. For everybody's good."

"All right." Adams did not sound enthused. Then he said "Soznolopak?"

"Yes?"

"I think he'll be nervous."

"I'll put a call through to him."

"Wonderful." Adams said it dryly.

"And so," said Superstoe, "until our next get-together—oh, Ben, another thing."

"Yes, Paxton."

"Do you think it would help if I addressed the UN again?"

"I doubt if anything will help. I'll let you know."

"Good show, me lad. *Adiós.*"

He hung up the blue phone and picked up the white. "Get me the Kremlin," he said. He hung up. He looked around the room. "I wonder where Isen is?" he said to himself. He picked up the white phone again. "Get me the embassy in Moscow. And send a man up here from the hot line." He hung up. "In case the call doesn't get through," he said to himself.

Zorr appeared in the doorway. He looked as if he had dressed hurriedly.

"It's about time," said Superstoe.

"Something wrong?" asked Zorr.

"Possibly. Where have you been?"

"In my room."

"Yes?"

"Yes."

"Doing?"

"Remember the secretary to the ambassador from Nigeria? With the long hair and the long legs? Marjorie ..."

Superstoe slipped on his coat. "I'll be addressing the nation soon," he said quickly. "Until then, tell the press that everything's under control." He hurried out the door. "Tell them Superstoe's at the helm, and the ship of state is heading for calm waters." He was hurrying down the hall.

"Shall I quote you?" Zorr yelled.

He hopped down the stairs. "Yes, of course," he yelled back.

17   In his office, some minutes later, he received a call from Adams. "Ivan's on his way to the Kremlin," Adams said.

A few minutes later Soznolopak was on the line. "I understand," Soznolopak said, "that you are having some difficulty in the Far East."

"A little, Alexei. I wanted you to know ..."

"Yes, yes. You want me to sit on my ass while you take over China. You said, Paxton ..."

"Alexei, I don't want China. I can't possibly occupy China. *You* may occupy China. China is all yours."

"I don't want China."

"Well, all I'm doing is destroying the armies, planes, ships, munitions plants, nuclear reactors, and things. That's all. It will be for your benefit, too."

"I know that, Paxton."

"Why don't you send some missiles to China? Let's be allies."

"It is not good propaganda for socialist nations to be at war with one another."

"Then you mustn't go to war with me, Alexei. We have social security and medicare."

"You are not a socialist state."

"I have propaganda problems too."

"Paxton, my committee thinks we must do something."

"Don't do anything rash."

"I'll do my best. You are lucky, Paxton."

"Yes, I know." Superstoe drew a four-leaf clover on his sketch pad.

"You are lucky," Soznolopak continued, "I am Chairman and Premier."

"Oh my goodness," Superstoe said, "I know! I know, Alexei! If it weren't for you—but we understand each other."

"I hope so."

Superstoe drew a horseshoe. "I'm lucky you're as shrewd as you are," he said. "You handle your committee marvelously. I wish I could handle Congress as well."

"You have difficulty with your Congress?"

"Yes, indeed. They are against my UN plan. I get them behind me only when there's a crisis."

"So you have been having many crises."

"I've been trying to straighten things out."

"Like China."

"Alexei, you're a shrewd man. We'll both be better off when China is out of our hair."

"I know that, Paxton. My committee doesn't. They're afraid of you."

"Oh ... "

"I admit I am afraid of you."

"*Alexei.*"

"Well?"

"Look here, Alexei. You know you can trust me. You know my aims."

"Some of them. But my committee ..."

"Screw your committee. Listen, Alexei. Shall I fly over again? Remain as your hostage to prove my good intentions?"

"Good God no! Not again!"

"Aren't you an atheist?"

"Certainly!"

"Just wondered."

"Atheists can swear," Soznolopak said hotly.

"Swearing seems decadent and bourgeois, doesn't it?"

"And you, Paxton? Do you believe in God?"

"I know what I know," Superstoe said. "By the way, the first shipment of tractors is on its way."

"I know."

"Could you use some gold?"

"What?"

"I thought perhaps your committee might have more faith in me if I sent you some gold bullion."

Soznolopak was silent a moment. Then he said, "It might help."

"Good. Then goodbye for now, Alexei."

"Goodbye, Paxton."

"Give my regards to your wife."

"Thank you, Paxton."

"Goodbye."

But Soznolopak had hung up.

"He sounded tired," Superstoe said to himself. "I wonder if he's been sleeping well."

18 A few minutes later Zorr entered the office. "The Civil Defense Director wants the cities evacuated," he said.

"Fire him," said Superstoe.

"People are beginning to panic."

"Didn't you give them my message?"

"Yes."

Superstoe was silent.

"Alexei wouldn't attack us, would he?" asked Zorr.

"It's always possible Alexei will be deposed and a new premier order an attack. Ah, here we are."

His secretary entered and handed him a chocolate ice cream cone.

The red line buzzed.

Zorr caught his breath.

"Nervous?" asked Superstoe, licking.

"Me?"

Calmly Superstoe lifted the receiver. "Superstoe," he said.

"Gen—General Jaspers, sir. We have objects on the radar coming over the North Pole. So far unidentified." He sounded nervous.

"Well, identify them," said Superstoe and hung up.

The line buzzed again.

"Yes?"

Jaspers's voice was strained. "I thought you should know about anything that occurred, sir. In view of things. In view of the crisis. Sir."

"What crisis?" Superstoe hung up.

Five minutes passed, and then the blue phone buzzed. Superstoe picked it up. "Yes, Lazarus?"

"I don't understand what's going on," Furth said.

"Well," said Superstoe.

The line was silent for a few seconds. Then Furth resumed. "I just received a strange call from Jaspers. He was incoherent. Then another man came on, a Colonel Magazine, and said, 'We've lost Jaspers.' What's going on?"

"I can't imagine, Lazarus."

"And why call me to tell me that?"

"It does seem unusual."

"Jaspers started apologizing for calling me," Furth went on. "He said he'd notified you of a meteor shower, and you had told him to fire off a Minuteman, and that it wasn't a meteor of Russians after all but a gaggle of geese from Goosebay and Greatneck. Is there some new code in effect?"

"Probably," said Superstoe.

"No news from Russia?" Furth asked incidentally.

"No. Why don't you have dinner with me?"

"I was thinking of it."

"Bye."

"So long."

Superstoe called his cook to suggest a menu.

19   Publicly Russia threatened war; but nothing happened. American aid was rushed to the Far East to clean up after the nuclear blasts. Aid was sent to Japan, too; considerable fallout had drifted over that country.

The Chinese military machine was destroyed. Reports indicated that the government leaders were dead. Several factions were struggling for control of the government.

A shipload of fertilizer, six shiploads of wheat, and a shipment of gold bullion headed toward the Soviet Union.

Debate in the UN on the Superstoe Plan bogged down.

Rift Valley fever, cholera, and typhoid epidemics began in Israel.

Two weeks later cholera, typhoid, glanders, and malaria commenced in the United Arab Republic.

Superstoe addressed the United Nations.

He told the delegates that until the Superstoe Plan was effected he would be forced to punish aggression himself. If there were any further instances of biological warfare, he said, he would ask the CIA to identify the aggressor nation, and then he would destroy that nation's military capacity with nuclear weapons.

"However," he concluded, "when the United Nations has been reorganized, and when an international inspection corps and an international police force are operative, the United States will disarm as speedily as any other nation and will comply wholeheartedly with the decisions of the United Nations and the World Court."

That evening, after his address, the United States government invited all the delegates to a lavish twelve-course dinner. The dinner was preceded by an Indian raga, designed to soothe the nerves and calm the mind.

A dance followed the dinner. Superstoe performed Russian, Chinese, Greek, Turkish, Arab, and Israeli folk dances.

Adams attended, but he did not dance. He talked with delegates, while Superstoe, Fall, and Zorr danced with their wives.

At one point Superstoe suggested to Zorr that he should not take the daughter of the Hungarian ambassador onto the balcony again and that he should wipe the lipstick off his face.

Furth, Johanneson, and Watt were there as well, but they mostly talked, although Watt danced one waltz with his wife.

And, at about four in the morning, Furth executed, to everyone's amazement, an intricate Zulu war dance.

20   Still the United Nations was reluctant to adopt Superstoe's reforms.

Many nations, as well as the United States Congress, were shocked by the proposal for evacuating the citizens of West Berlin and turning the city over to East Germany.

Congress talked of impeaching Superstoe.

Some Congressmen said he was autocratic. Others said he was nuts.

Meanwhile a civil war raged in China. Russia took advantage of the chaos to adjust the Russian-Chinese border in several places.

Nationalist China attempted an invasion of the mainland but was restrained by American ships and planes, which were forced to destroy several landing craft and one airfield—built some years before by America.

Gloom, pessimism, and instability pervaded the country and the world. The feeling grew that the only answer to things was violence.

The gloom extended even to the Cabinet Room of the White House.

The table was spread with bottles, glasses, and sandwiches, but only Superstoe ate and drank. The others—Adams, Furth, Pall, Zorr, Watt, Johanneson, and Borozov—stared into space or at one another.

Finally Furth spoke. "Everything's fucked up," he said. They considered that for a while.

Watt smiled and observed, "We live in a decadent age."

"That's why there's hope," said Superstoe. "After decadence comes rebirth."

Adams flicked an ash into his sterling-silver chamber pot—a gift from Superstoe.

After a few moments Watt said, "You're a dispirited group." He pulled a bottle of pills from his pocket. "Have a Librium."

Superstoe reached for another ham sandwich.

"I hope Congress doesn't impeach us," Zorr said, puffing on his cheroot.

"Don't worry," said Pall. "If they try it, we'll impeach them first."

Again there was silence.

Suddenly Adams slammed his fist on the table. "Damn it, Paxton ...!"

"Me?" cried Superstoe. "What have I done?"

Adams looked at the ceiling.

Then the phone rang. Superstoe answered it, listened, and hung up without a word. He looked around the table. "Riot in Harlem," he said.

Zorr relaxed. "With this weather it was inevitable," he said.

"It's quite out of hand," Superstoe said, shoving aside glasses, bottles, and plates. "The governor's sending the National Guard. Machine guns—he'll likely send tanks, too. Federalize it, Lazarus. Ed, round up vaccines."

"Vaccines?"

"They've had a rash of measles and chicken pox the last few weeks ..."

"Nothing unusual," Watt said.

"No. But with germ warfare going on everywhere, there's been talk that the measles and chicken pox ..."

"Yes, yes, I know," said Watt.

"Then this afternoon," Superstoe continued, "the police caught two men introducing poliomyelitis virus into a Harlem water main." He paused and drummed his fingers on the table top. "The word spread. Now they're burning, looting, talking of marching into white areas. The police are trying to seal off the area. Streets blocked, subways stopped."

Superstoe stood. "So, Ed," he said, "get vaccines to New York. Lazarus, collect doctors, nurses, and ambulance men; we'll send them into Harlem and set up inoculation centers."

"Do you think those rioters will stand around while doctors walk in?" asked Watt.

"We'll drop tear gas first," said Furth.

"That's not likely to inspire trust," Superstoe said. "You see, those two men they caught were FBI agents. They said they were acting on orders."

They stared at him.

"That's impossible," said Zorr.

"But it's not enough to merely deny it. Announce we're sending doctors and vaccine. We're not sending troops." He started for the door.

"But, Paxton," Watt said, "there aren't enough facilities. Where are we going to set up these inoculation centers? On the streets?"

Superstoe, in the doorway, thought for a second. "In the bars."

"In the *bars?*"

"Everyone goes to the bar."

"Are you crazy?"

"I wish people would stop asking me that." He disappeared.

21   The government's plan was announced, but the rioting continued.

One ambulance, filled with vaccines, started through the police blockade and was stopped by a Molotov cocktail. Another tried to enter on a nearby street. The driver was shot. That was at six in the evening of the following day.

Superstoe received the report at 6:14.

"Well," he said, "I'll have to go myself. Isen, order the helicopter, et cetera. Announce it to the press."

"Right," said Zorr. "Will you direct it from City Hall?"

"Direct what? I'm going to Harlem."

"Not *in?*"

"Yes, of course."

As he stepped onto the lawn—stepped from the conditioned coolness of the White House into the suffocating, intolerably stifling night—the Chief of the Secret Service accosted him.

"You can't!" he cried.

"I am," Superstoe said, smiling.

"We can't possibly protect you!"

"Fine," said Superstoe, strolling toward the helicopter. "I resign. I can't be responsible."

"Now don't be peevish, Bob. See you in the morning."

"You're crazy!"

Superstoe sighed.

"Goddammit, you'll be killed!"

Superstoe had a foot on the step and a hand on the doorway of the helicopter. "If I am, Lazarus and Ben can do my job as well as I. Or nearly as well," he added as he hopped inside.

22   Preceded by howling motorcycles the limousine sped across the Triborough Bridge. At the barricades it pulled up amidst police cars, fire engines, and two Army ambulances. The police, in helmets and short sleeves, carried rifles and machine guns. The wooden barricades were reinforced with sandbags.

Superstoe stepped from the limousine. He motioned to the two Negro doctors, said, "Follow me," pushed a policeman to one side, saying, "Out of my way, Buster," climbed up the sandbags and leaped off the other side. The doctors, carrying medical bags, followed. It was ten minutes before midnight.

Gunfire could be heard a few streets away. But at this intersection, where he was expected, it was quiet.

A huge crowd was massed in the street. Dark faces filled the windows of the buildings. Harsh, white searchlights lit the scene.

Superstoe strolled up to the crowd. The front row was composed mainly of men, many in undershirts, all of them sweating. Superstoe was sweating.

He said, "Excuse me, please," and pushed between two men and snuggled into the crowd. The hot, wet, malodorous arms and chests and backs pressed against him, though they tried to make room. He touched a short, thin man on the chest. "Can you tell me," he asked, "where the nearest tavern is?"

The man, a look of fright in his face, slipped into the crowd. Superstoe found himself facing a middle-aged woman who was staring at him in disbelief. "The nearest bar?" he inquired of her. "I'd like a beer."

"Are you Superstoe?" a man beside her asked.

"Yes. Will you join me for a beer?"

The man did not answer. Then Superstoe's eye caught a green-and-pink neon sign. It said HOT SPOT TAVERN. He smiled involuntarily, cynically, and shouldered toward the sign.

The tavern was empty, but the crowd followed him in and he was shoved against the bar, between two stools. He craned his neck, trying to see the doorway. "Let the doctors through, please," he called. He climbed onto a stool. He saw the crowd shift near the door. Finally one of the doctors, perspiring and unsmiling, appeared by his side.

He turned to the bartender. "Set 'em up," he ordered loudly. "Beer for everyone."

The bartender stared at him.

"Come come come," Superstoe said impatiently. He threw a fifty-dollar bill on the bar.

The bartender drew beer until the bar was lined with glasses four deep.

Superstoe tried to gesture, but the crowd pressed so tightly he could not raise his arm. The doctor looked as if he were going to be sick.

"Drink!" cried Superstoe. "Refresh yourself! They're on me."

The crowd shuffled, muttered. A couple of hands reached for glasses but withdrew, empty. A voice said, "He's likely poisoned 'em."

On Superstoe's left stood a teenage boy with a fresh scar across his forehead and dilated pupils. Superstoe handed him a glass. "Have a beer," he urged.

The boy looked him in the eye without expression and drained the glass.

A gun was fired outside. Superstoe spilled some of his beer. He heard shouts. There was a commotion at the door. He winked at the deadpan teenager and took a swallow.

An authoritative voice came from the door. The crowd thinned, and Superstoe, taking a deep breath from the less-packed room, looked up at a tall, mustached Negro. The man was impeccably dressed and looked impossibly cool; yet there were beads of perspiration on his forehead. He extended his hand and Superstoe took it.

"I'm Superstoe," said Superstoe.

The man almost smiled. "I'm Washington," he said.

"Ambrose Washington?" asked Superstoe. "Have a beer."

"Your health, Mr. President." Washington took a swallow and set the glass on the bar. "I urge you to leave immediately."

"I have to straighten this business out first," Superstoe said. "Those FBI agents were hired by somebody. I don't know who yet; I'll find out. I have forty ambulances out there filled with vaccine. Sabin vaccine, typhoid, smallpox. Let them in.

"They say the vaccines are germs."

"You know that isn't true."

"You can't sweet-talk them."

"Tear gas and guns won't help."

"You better leave."

"We'll put a doctor in every bar, and every adult who gets inoculated gets all the beer he can drink. On me. Candy for the kids."

"Go to hell," said Washington.

"All right," said Superstoe. "I'll walk out into that street. I'll walk from one side of Harlem to the other until somebody shoots me. I'm white, and I'm the President. I can stand for everything you hate."

"Don't fool with me, man!"

"I'm not fooling."

"That's all we'd need."

"You stop the rioting and let the ambulances in or I'll do it."

"Nobody can stop them."

"I'll finish this beer, and then I'll go. That way." He pointed toward the interior of Harlem.

"Send the Army."

Superstoe drank.

"You goddamn fool!"

Superstoe finished his beer.

Washington whirled around and talked with five men standing nearby. They argued. Then they hurried out, and Washington returned to the bar. He drew a packet of cigarettes from his pocket and offered them to Superstoe. Superstoe shook his head. Washington extracted one and lit it with a lighter, inhaling deeply.

"You know I can't stop them now, in the middle of the night," he said.

Superstoe reached into his coat pocket and withdrew half a dozen typed pages, folded once lengthwise. He unfolded them and handed them to Washington. "I sketched this out on the plane," he said. "I'll see that the Mayor and Governor carry it through."

Washington glanced through the papers, one hip on a stool, smoking and sipping a beer. At the last page, looking up, he said, "They won't do it."

"If they don't, they won't get federal funds for anything. And I'll see that they're never re-elected."

Three shots were fired nearby; glass shattered. People shouted. A woman screamed in pain.

Washington flipped his cigarette to the floor. "Do me two favors, Mr. Superstoe. Wait till morning. And don't go out in that street. Toward morning they'll get tired. Send the ambulances in the morning; everybody'll be asleep."

"All right. I'll stay till morning."

The glass door was shattered by a rock. And then the plate-glass window.

Washington lit another cigarette. "Would you mind staying someplace else, Mr. President? A friend of mine has a nice apartment; we'll go there."

"All right," said Superstoe, slipping off the bar stool.

"We'll go out the back," Washington said as the lights went off.

"Lead the way."

"We'll have a little party while we wait for the dawn," Washington said dryly.

Someone was at the back with a flashlight. Superstoe, holding Washington's arm, followed him through the darkness.

23   At 6:45 A.M. Superstoe appeared at the barricades. He began pulling down sandbags. "Take these down," he ordered. "Send in the ambulances."

The police leaped onto their cycles and into their squad cars. Superstoe grabbed a captain. "No cops," he ordered.

"Mr. President . . ."

"Right. Now shut up." He saw his limousine and headed toward it, humming, snapping his fingers, and twisting his hips. He was in his shirt sleeves. He had forgotten his coat.

The Mayor rushed up. "Thank God!" the Mayor cried. "Mr. President—my God, we thought ..."

"Cool it, man," said Superstoe. He hopped into the limousine.

A reporter appeared at the car window. "Mr. President, tell me ..."

Superstoe hiccupped. "We had a little party," he said, "at the Baby Grand." He motioned to the Mayor. "Get in here, George, I want to talk to you." He turned to the reporter. "You know what Mohammed Ali T told me? He said I had a natural sense of rhythm."

The Mayor was in the car. "Good God," he muttered, "what the hell"—a microphone was thrust before his lips. He saw a television camera. He smiled. "The people of New York," he said loudly, "the people of America, I speak for them all when I say we cannot express our gratitude, we cannot express the magnitude of your courage, your heroism, your unprecedented ..."

Superstoe tapped the shoulder of the driver, a Negro Secret Service agent. "Let's cool it, man," he said.

Expertly the driver gunned it. The tires screeched. The microphone shot out the window. Men yelled and cursed. The limousine slipped around a corner and darted between a squad car and a fire engine and narrowly missed the police chief.

As they neared the Triborough Bridge the motorcycles caught up with them. Across the bridge and out on the parkway to La Guardia, Superstoe explained his plan to the Mayor.

The Mayor shook his head. "Impossible," he muttered, "impossible, impossible."

Superstoe put his mouth near the Mayor's ear. It was difficult to talk above the sirens. "You know," said Superstoe, "being President is not much different from being a high-school Latin teacher. Every day one is confronted by idiots who refuse to do their assignments." He paused. "I think there's a copy of my plans on the plane. I left the other copy with Ambrose. Or was it with Mohammed?"

"Oh, Lord."

"I'll let you announce the plan, George. We'll pretend it was your idea."

"No!"

"It will help your re-election."

"I'm sure."

"I'll pay for everything, of course."

The Mayor gazed blankly before him.

"All right?" asked Superstoe.

"What can I do? If I say no, you'll take away federal funds. And then you'll crucify me."

"Oh dear. Am I becoming that predictable?"

The Mayor did not reply.

"And I want you to appoint Mohammed Ali T Commissioner of Housing."

"What?" The Mayor jerked upright.

"It will keep him out of trouble."

"I have a Commissioner of Housing."

"I'll find something for him to do."

"Why don't you appoint Ambrose Washington Commissioner of Housing?" the Mayor shouted, completely demoralized.

"No," said Superstoe. "I'm appointing Ambrose ambassador to the United Nations."

He leaped from the car and bounded up the steps and into the plane. He was met by the radioman. "Call from Mr. Furth, Mr. President."

"Now what?" said Superstoe. He took the phone. "Lazarus?"

"Paxton?"

"Yes?" replied Superstoe.

"Is it really you?"

"I believe so. Where are you?"

"At the White House."

"My goodness, what are you doing there?"

"It seemed likely I would become President tonight."

"I'm sorry to disappoint you."

"It's good to hear your voice."

"Thank you, Lazarus."

"Everyone was sure you'd be shot."

"I rather expected it myself. Where's Isen?"

"On the floor."

"Is he hurt?"

"He fell asleep on the couch and rolled off. He never woke up."

"It's a soft carpet. If you can wake him, Lazarus, have him call the governors of New York, New Jersey, and Connecticut. And the mayors of—Judy will tell him which mayors. I want them at the White House tonight for a conference."

"Okay."

"We're going to take off now. See you later."

"You straightened things out in Harlem?"

"We had a grand party. You should see Ambrose Washington's wife. She's a beauty."

Superstoe slept. The plane landed. Superstoe slept on.

When he awoke, he showered, shaved, and put on a fresh shirt, tie, and suit. Then he stepped into the doorway and blinked in the sunlight.

A roar sprang from the crowd that heaved against the fences. Superstoe hesitated at the top of the landing stairs. "What's going on?" he asked.

Below him the pilot called up. "They're cheering you, Mr. President."

His secretary stood behind him, just inside the door. "You're a hero, Mr. Superstoe."

Superstoe twisted his head around. "Really?"

"It's larger than the crowd that came to welcome the Beatles."

"My my," said Superstoe. "How nice." He lifted his arms high in the air. The cheering swelled. It was deafening.

Superstoe waved his arms.

The fence collapsed and the crowd hurtled onto the airfield.

"Run for it, Judy," cried Superstoe, skipping down the steps, still waving his arms.

They raced to the helicopter, leaped inside, and rose into the air. He hung out the window, waving and blowing kisses.

As the airport disappeared, his secretary handed him a box. "Here you are, Mr. Superstoe."

Superstoe lifted the lid and extracted a doughnut.

24 The helicopter dropped to the lawn. Superstoe emerged, dusted the powdered sugar from his hands and trousers, gave the Chief of the Secret Service a fond pat on the head, and ventured into his oval office.

Zorr, seated at the desk, jumped up guiltily. A stack of newspapers lay on the desk blotter. "Have you seen the papers?" he asked.

Superstoe gave the chair a blow with the palm of his hand. He watched it spin. Expertly he calculated and leaped.

Zorr helped him off the floor and righted the chair. Superstoe spun it again. He watched. He calculated. He closed his eyes and jumped.

The chair creaked, teetered, regained its equilibrium, and gradually slowed its revolutions, with President Superstoe snug within, heels on the seat, hands clasped over his shins. A serene smile formed on his face. "What papers?" he asked.

"The newspapers."

"Do they know anything I don't know?"

"They say you're foolhardy, reckless, immature, fearless, courageous, and indefatigable."

"Naturally. I was a Boy Scout in my youth. A Life Scout, as I recall. I don't know why I never became an Eagle. I was shamefully lax not to be an Eagle." He shoved off from the desk and spun a few more times. "Once upon a time I was a scoutmaster. Did you know that, Isen?"

"I would never have guessed."

"I suggested new merit badges to headquarters, but they were never approved. I don't know why." The chair stopped in mid-revolution. His back was to Zorr. "I suggested a merit badge in Indo-European word roots, and one in sex."

"Sex?"

The chair revolved until he faced Zorr. "Well, at the camporees that's all the lads talked about. They seemed very knowledgeable, and I thought knowledge should be rewarded."

Zorr picked up a paper. "At any rate," he said, "your image has begun to improve. Someone writes about the 'unconventionally brilliant insight that dwells behind the façade of recklessness.'"

Superstoe slid the newspapers into the wastebasket. "One's image isn't important," he said. "How could I be true to myself if I listened to the erraticisms of public opinion? The true representative of humanity ignores the crowd: the crowd is mindless. The true representative understands that he is everyman; thus he acts for mankind. He acts wisely by virtue of his uniqueness. Where's the Grapevine?"

"Here," said Zorr, fishing the daily CIA report from the wastebasket.

"Who's Director of the Budget?"

"John Albright."

"I want to see him. We'll have to juggle funds. Big outlay to rebuild Harlem and create new communities in the suburbs so Harlem won't be so crowded. Nice-looking buildings, free rent for the first year, free vocational guidance, schools, a new university ..." He scratched the fringe of gray hair above his ear. "We'll take the money from Defense and space travel. And, Isen ..."

"Yes?"

"Announce the appointment of Ambrose Washington as ambassador to the United Nations."

"Are you crazy?"

Superstoe sighed. "Someday," he said, "I shall write a monograph on insanity. There's a lot of loose talk going around."

"Last week Ambrose Washington called you a nincompoop."

"He didn't know me then."

At the press conference that afternoon—held on the steps of the White House, Superstoe seated on the top step—he outlined the Harlem and East Coast Redevelopment Plan. (Mohammed Ali T had announced the plan that morning.)

Then he reviewed the world situation.

Then he answered questions.

"Do you think it wise, Mr. President," one reporter inquired, "to risk your life as you did last night?"

Superstoe finished chewing the bite of toasted cheese sandwich, took a swallow of vanilla milkshake, and said, "Yes."

There was a moment of silence. Then the reporter asked, "Could you elaborate that statement?"

"I don't know," Superstoe replied thoughtfully.

"I mean, sir ..."

"We must remember, Jerry, exactly what constitutes wisdom and what constitutes foolishness. There are times when it is wise to risk one's life. Sometimes life is meaningful only if we are willing to lose it. That is true for the President as it is for every man. The President is a man, too. Ultimately every man is dispensable. We know that, because every man is mortal. Wisdom consists, in part, of knowing what is worth dying for. Now stopping last night's particular riot was not in itself worth the President's life. But the riot was a symbol of something else. And risking my life was, in turn, a sign of what I stand for."

25 Superstoe adjourned the meeting of governors and mayors at two in the morning.

He climbed the steps to the second floor. The hall was still and dark.

He entered the kitchen. The Negro cook was sitting on a stool, studying the copy of *The Republic* Superstoe had given him.

"Evening, Jonathan," said Superstoe.

"Good evening, Mr. Superstoe."

Superstoe had engaged him. He had previously cooked in a New York delicatessen.

"You seem fatigued," Jonathan said.

"Someone said I've had three hours' sleep since night before last. I'm not sure."

Jonathan stabbed the open book with his index finger. "I want to talk to you about this sometime, Mr. Superstoe. There are things here I don't agree with."

"Good," said Superstoe.

He put on his pajamas and, seated in bed, ate a fried egg and onion on whole wheat, a hot pastrami with mustard on rye, two kosher dills, three deviled eggs, a dish of peach cobbler, and drank a liter of Châteauneuf-du-Pape.

As he ate, he scanned a stack of notes and reports.

Ambrose Washington had arrived at Adams's suite in New York and was being briefed by Adams and U.S. representatives to the UN. Zorr had noted that the press and Congress had expressed "surprise, concern, and incredulity" at the appointment.

In China there were indications that a stable government might finally be forming.

Borozov had had a duel with a Soviet general and had shot the general through the heart.

An abortive revolution had occurred in South America.

Indonesia was threatening biological warfare against Malaysia.

There were riots in Ghana.

Superstoe set the tray on a table and looked about for a pad of paper on which to jot memos. Unable to find one, he disengaged the roll of toilet paper from the bathroom wall, took a red pen from the pocket of his coat hanging in the closet, and settled himself in bed.

On the first square he wrote: "Isen—Find two American Indians. One to be Commissioner of Indian Affairs, the other to be Secretary of Interior."

On the second square he wrote: "Ben—Re: new ambassadors: a naturalized American, a Hindu, originally from India, to be ambassador to India. A Moslem to be ambassador to Pakistan. Other Moslems to be ambassadors to Arab states. Remember the Iranian economist at the university? What about him? And *cetera.*"

On the next square: "John Albright—I noticed a mistake in addition on p. 3 of Section 11A. PSS."

In the next: "Draw up Cong. bills—(1) System of federal colleges per Ben's instructions. (2) Rush plans for conversion to peacetime economy. (3) Mention tax cut."

On the next: "Invite Supreme Court to dinner."

On the next: "Judy—Jelly-filled doughnuts for a change, please. P."

He placed the roll on the bedside table, switched off the light, pulled up the sheet, curled on his side, and slept.

26 The following afternoon, as he discussed budget difficulties with Albright, Zorr entered and placed a bulletin on his desk.

Approximately four hundred white men had sealed off a Negro community in Mississippi. Several Negroes had been killed or wounded. The white men, many from neighboring states, demanded that Superstoe enter the town alone and settle grievances, as he had done in Harlem.

As he read the last line Superstoe lifted the direct line to Furth's office. "Lazarus, have you seen this Mississippi thing?"

"What Mississippi thing? Hold on a minute."

The phone at his ear, Superstoe resumed his conversation with Albright.

Furth came back on the line. He said, "Well."

"Let's do this, Lazarus. Send a big flight of jets over one end of the town to distract them. Send a band down the street, followed by a limousine. Then, from the other end of the town, drop incapacitating gases. Followed up by troops to capture those chaps."

"Every time the sun rises it's another miracle," Furth said.

"Shalom," said Superstoe.

"Shalom."

When the action was completed, Superstoe made a brief television appearance. He said, "I did not become President to play games."

27 The new Chinese government appeared permanent. It had lasted ten days. On the eleventh it sent a representative to confer with Superstoe.

The representative demanded full reparation for the American nuclear and biological attack on China and withdrawal of American troops from Korea and Vietnam.

The translator repeated the demand in English.

Superstoe blinked at the Chinese and made a "tsk tsk tsk" sound. He seemed mildly affronted. "Tell Mr. Chan," he said to the interpreter, "that his government has two alternatives. On the one hand it can complete its disarmament, demobilize the remainder of its troops, join the UN, adhere to the charter, and admit inspection teams—in which case the United States will provide economic and medical aid and will negotiate trade agreements, loans, and so forth."

The translator rendered the first alternative into Chinese.

Superstoe resumed. "Or, on the other hand, if the Chinese government rejects that alternative, I will order another attack on China, employing conventional weapons, gas weapons, chemical weapons, and biological weapons, and the attack will not cease until China is a graveyard."

The translator rendered the second alternative into Chinese. Mr. Chan burst into speech, beat on the desk, gesticulated wildly.

As he raved, the translator said to Superstoe, "Generally it's about world opinion. World opinion won't stand for what you threaten."

Mr. Chan raged on.

Superstoe stood, placed both hands on his desk, and leaned forward until Mr. Chan's breath was hot on his face. At the top of his lungs Superstoe yelled, "Bullshit!"

Mr. Chan's mouth snapped shut.

Superstoe poked Mr. Chan's silk tie with his forefinger. Mr. Chan retreated, but Superstoe sprang over the desk and poked him into the far wall, saying, at one word for every hard jab, "My opinion is that world opinion is my opinion and you can stick world opinion *up your fizzle-watsit!*"

Diffidently the translator followed to the other side of the room, racking his brain for a translation.

"Furthermore," Superstoe cried, ignoring the translator, "I'll give your government one hour to decide, you will call them from this office, and if they decide on war, I will personally, at that moment, in this office, with my own hands, slice off your ears, nose, and tongue, and hang you by your hair from that chandelier and *skin you alive!*"

He ended on an unrestrained shriek of rage, slicing, as he ended, Mr. Chan's throat from ear to ear with his forefinger. Then he turned on his heel, padded to the desk, lifted a phone, and extended it to Mr. Chan, who still stood flat against the opposite wall.

The translator cleared his throat.

"He knows English," Superstoe said.

Mr. Chan massaged his sliced throat, adjusted his tie, smoothed his coat, and sullenly, but with dignity, strode to the telephone and said, in Oxford English, "Long distance, please."

PART FOUR

The Reforms

1   As a delicate snow settled gently over Manhattan on a Saturday in December—as children whispered to Santa Clauses and parents tinkered with toys and Saks Fifth Avenue sang "Hark! the Herald Angels" and skaters spun beneath the giant tree in Rockefeller Center—the United Nations General Assembly approved the Superstoe Plan, signed the new charter, and admitted China to membership. Many heads of state were present, including Superstoe and Alexei Soznolopak, whose hair had turned from black to gray.

The nations agreed to disarm, to submit disputes to arbitration or to the World Court, to contribute men, money, and material to the United Nations Inspection Service, or UNIS, and to the United Nations Police Force, or UNPF.

The UNIS would be allowed to move freely in any country. It would supervise and guarantee disarmament, and it would continually inspect factories, nuclear reactors, laboratories, and pharmaceutical companies.

The UNPF would be made up of troops donated by the several nations and would be armed with conventional weapons and incapacitating gases. It would be composed of an Army, a Navy, and an Air Force.

Armed hostilities between states or hindrance of the duties of the IS would be punished by economic sanctions or by the PF, or by both.

At the airport Superstoe took Soznolopak's hand and wished him a smooth flight home. "Your Senate will ratify the new charter?" Soznolopak asked.

"What else *can* they do?" asked Superstoe, handing him a stick of brandy-flavored gum.

2   "We can stop it, and we will!" the Honorable Gideon Shiloh Geaseman cried.

The Senate had adjourned for the holidays; reporters had to scatter to pick up senatorial reaction. But they quickly reassembled in Nashville, Tennessee, where the flames of nationalism were being frantically fanned. It was there that Senator Geaseman, long-time intimate of the unfortunate President Long, long-time detractor of the even more unfortunate President Knutson, and short-time but dedicated foe of President Superstoe, was spending a quiet Christmas with his sister's family. "We'll see who runs this country, Superstoe or the people," Geaseman told reporters.

The Senate was scheduled to reconvene January 16. On New Year's Eve Superstoe called a meeting of his advisers.

3   "I'll see that Geaseman has a coronary," Pall advised.

"Geaseman is only the loudest," Watt said.

"Then I'll knock off ten or twenty. That should give us two-thirds."

Superstoe intervened. "That stage of our endeavors is, I hope, over, Arthur. Opinion is growing in our favor. We have but to ride the tide."

"The Senate's caught in an undertow," Furth said.

"That is typical," said Superstoe.

"I'll make them sick," Pall suggested.

"You already have," said Watt.

"So," Pall went on, "they'd be in the hospital the day of the voting."

"That might look suspicious," Zorr said.

"Everything about us looks suspicious," Furth said.

"Funk will stall it in the Foreign Relations Committee," Adams warned. Harvey Funk was the senior senator from California.

"I wonder who would be chairman if something happened to Funk?" Superstoe inquired.

"Ringlemeir," Pall said. "He's in our pocket."

"Ringlemeir has a mind of his own," Superstoe corrected. "A sound mind."

4 The Senate convened. Harvey Funk lay in a Los Angeles hospital, where his strange malady remained undiagnosed.

But Geaseman, a tall, full-bodied man with thin silver hair, a stomach gone to pot, and a rich oratorical voice that had the resonance of an Offenhauser wanting a tuneup, had not been idle. He had told his colleagues it was not a question of war or peace, as Superstoe said; it was a question of re-election. "Tariffs will vanish, the markets will be flooded, immigrants will swarm in, prices will fall. Your constituents won't like that."

Big business and the American Legion agreed.

"It's us or Superstoe," Geaseman told the caucus.

"We must have time to rally the people," Superstoe told Zorr.

Zorr told Ringlemeir. But Ringlemeir, a man with a mind of his own, thought it ought to be thrashed out on the Senate floor.

Geaseman rubbed his hands and predicted victory.

Ringlemeir had second thoughts and promised to filibuster.

Geaseman tried closure but lost: 51 for, 48 against. Ringlemeir spoke on. It was a Friday evening.

5   Superstoe clacked his chopsticks together, captured an egg roll, and ate it. He said, "We must not lose now."

"I'm surprised we got this far," Watt said.

"Paxton has great politics," Borozov confirmed.

They fell silent and consumed the dinner: bird's-nest soup, egg rolls, egg foo yung, fried wonton, black-mushroom chop suey, sweet and sour duck, steamed rice, and other, less familiar, dishes.

The plates were cleared away, and a fresh pot of tea and a basket of fortune cookies were placed on the table.

"I wonder what we should do?" Superstoe said to the slant-eyed waiter. The waiter smiled and left the room.

"Inscrutable," said Zorr.

Superstoe broke open a fortune cookie. "No problem is inscrutable," he said.

Furth added cognac to the teapot and poured. Watt lit a calabash. Superstoe invaded a second fortune cookie.

"We could consult the *I Ching*," Furth suggested.

"Nonsense," said Superstoe, taking another cookie.

Adams, who had been complaining recently of headaches, insomnia, and heartburn, said, "That last dish was deliciously unusual. I prefer not to ask what was in it, but where did you get it?"

"Mr. Chan's cook," Superstoe replied, crumbling the fourth cookie.

"I suppose you're bosom pals now," said Furth.

"The cook's a little standoffish," Superstoe replied.

"I mean Mr. Chan."

"Not exactly." He closed his eyes and drew a fifth cookie from the basket. "But I mentioned one day I was a connoisseur of Chinese cuisine. He offered to supply me with recipes, and then he sent me his cook. I loaned him Jonathan"—he opened a sixth—"and gave him my recipe for peach cobbler." He took another. "It was my mother's recipe."

He spread the strips of paper on the table before him and arranged them neatly in a column. "Would someone like the remains of these cookies?" he asked. "I don't like fortune cookies."

Furth gathered the pieces of the seven cookies in his hand and swept them before him.

"Now," said Superstoe, "let's see." He studied the seven strips of paper.

Finally Furth asked, "Well?"

"Shall I read them?" asked Superstoe.

"By all means," said Furth.

"Well then," said Superstoe.

You may expect good fortune in the near future.

He smiled with satisfaction. Then he read:

It is the wise man who distinguishes between the important and the unimportant.

Almost imperceptibly he nodded his head.

Someone who loves you is nearby.

Superstoe glanced suspiciously around the table.

The way out is through the door.

For a few seconds he contemplated.

Although beset by difficulties, the wise man attains his goal.

Without pausing he read the next one:

Remain calm. The storm will pass soon.

Superstoe scratched his head.

The way out is through the door.

Silently they sipped their tea.

Twenty minutes passed.

Finally Adams asked, "Is this a discussion or a Quaker meeting?"

"That depends," said Superstoe. "Did your inner spirit move you to ask that question?"

"It did."

"Then it's a Quaker meeting. You're the clerk."

"I'd like to know what the shit we're going to do about the Senate," Furth blurted.

Superstoe tapped a chopstick on his cranium.

The silence continued some minutes while Superstoe chewed the end of the chopstick. Eventually he rose, walked to the door, and stood before it, contemplating it.

The others fell silent and watched him. More minutes passed.

Furth broke the silence. "Watching the naked formation of policy is a fascinating experience." He watched Superstoe's back, which was hunched under a scarlet kimono emblazoned with a green dragon.

Superstoe stood motionless.

They talked awhile of disarmament schedules and plans for conversion to a peacetime economy. They seemed to have forgotten Superstoe, standing before the door.

Then slowly, ever so slowly, Superstoe extended his right hand.

Very, very carefully he twisted the knob.

The latch clicked.

Gently, gently the arm pushed, and the door eased open, millimeter by millimeter.

The other room was in darkness. Superstoe looked into the darkness, and then, suddenly, he leaped through the doorway and disappeared.

The others watched the black doorway. A minute passed. Another minute passed.

Adams's mouth was open, ready to resume the discussion, when Superstoe hopped into the room and slid into his chair. "Alert the Secret Service," he said. "I'm walking over to the capitol. I'm going to talk to the senators."

"You're going to address the Senate?" asked Zorr. "Tonight?"

"A private little chat with each senator individually. With all but two," he added. "Tonight. Isen, you visit editors and publishers and impress upon them the importance of the new charter."

"When?" asked Zorr.

"Now."

"Which publishers and editors?"

"All of them."

"But I have impressed upon them."

"Do it again, Isen. Prepare more copy. Get pictures of the ravages of germ warfare. Explain that it's either more of that, or the UN revisions."

"But they know that already."

"Yes, but they've not stressed it enough. When I've seen all the senators, I'll appear on radio and television and carry, as they say, my message to the people. Meanwhile"—he sipped his cold tea and cognac—"Lazarus, have your generals make speeches in favor of the charter."

"They don't favor the charter," Furth said.

"Explain to them," Superstoe patiently explained, "that they'll have wonderful new jobs in the UNPF and UNIS. The IS will require a huge staff. An army of people. Guarantee them plush jobs."

Furth shook his head and downed a cup of straight cognac.

"Then," Superstoe resumed, "we'll deluge the press with reports that approval of the charter is assured. We'll publish polls showing ninety percent of the populace in favor of the charter. The key thing is to convince everyone that the charter will be approved. Then even those who are against it will decide passage is inevitable."

"And therefore they'll feel free to vote against it, and it won't pass," Adams said.

"Furthermore," Superstoe continued, "let it be known that, should it not pass, I and my cabinet will resign."

He looked around the table. "How does that grab you?"

Adams deliberately sipped his cognac and then returned the cup to the table. He studied the contents of the cup. "I would think," he said, "that such a threat might backfire. What's more, it might appear irresponsible."

"That occurred to me," Superstoe admitted. "But I thought if we threatened a mass suicide that would appear even more irresponsible."

"I would suggest," Furth kindly interjected, "that under no conditions would there be a *mass* suicide."

"I mean just us," said Superstoe.

"That's what I mean," said Furth.

"Well," sighed Superstoe, "then when I announce that we will resign if the charter is rejected, I will do my utmost to appear responsible."

6   In response to Superstoe's appeal to the people, Gease-man persuaded the Senate to call in the television crews. "Let the people *see!*" he roared. "Let them see who their defenders are! Are they us, or are they Superstoe?"

Superstoe announced that not only would he and his Cabinet resign if the Senate failed to ratify the charter, but he would not eat or sleep until it was ratified.
And he didn't.

Geaseman gestured to the camera and demanded of the Senate, "Shall we hand our lands, our factories, our secrets, to every Tong, Dimitri, and Harim that comes along? Did we give our lives for this soil only to have it spread like a red carpet for hungry, ignorant, overpopulated strangers? What flag will fly from the White House tomorrow? The red, white, and blue? Or a foreign flag?"
The television camera's telephoto lens watched Superstoe pull the chain that raised the American flag over the White House.
Then, from a chair in the snow-covered rose garden—he was too weak to stand any longer—he spoke quietly and with determination to the American people, and shivered in the wind.

The vote was called.
Superstoe, propped up in bed and sipping sugar water through a bent straw, watched the count on television.
Harvey Funk was flown to Washington and carried into the Senate chambers on a litter. But, as the secretary called the name of Senator Fullerston, Funk lost consciousness for the final time.

The charter was ratified, 66 to 33.

7   Superstoe sipped his chicken broth. "Now," he said, "we can get down to business. Take these bills over to Congress, Isen."

"Yes, sir."

"And tell the networks that for the next few weeks I will give a little talk on Friday evenings, in prime time, explaining these bills to the people. They'll be informal little chats."

"You'll wear a sweatshirt?"

"Perhaps, Isen."

8   Had it not been for Superstoe, the effects of disarmament on the American economy would have been catastrophic.

Nearly every industry was affected, from watchmakers, who supplied the military with wrist watches, to the clothing industry, which supplied uniforms.

Under the UN Disarmament Schedule the United States, like other nations, was permitted to retain a small army sufficient to maintain domestic order—one percent of the population, or about 200,000 men. That meant the uniform industry would not go out of business. But it would be severely damaged.

Some industries would continue to exist on contracts with the UNPF and UNIS; but those industries were the more sophisticated—those which produced electronic equipment, computers, and detection devices—and heavy industries—especially airplane manufacturers.

Furth, whom Superstoe had designated Chief Co-ordinator for Economic Conversion, formed committees and asked for suggestions.

After two months he dismissed most of the committees in disgust.

One official had suggested that to compensate the clothing industries all government employees should be required to wear uniforms, as he had read government officials did in Czarist Russia. A subchairman had ordered the suggestion followed up, a chairman had given the go-ahead, and one morning Furth found a scrapbook on his desk containing 582 pages of proposed styles, colors, and insignia, for both male and female employees.

So it was up to Superstoe. Many of his ideas came one morning in the Cabinet Room.

Furth was present, and Albright, and Zorr and Johanneson, as well as several other officials. (Adams was in Hawaii, recuperating.) Papers, pencils, coffee cups, coffeepots, and boxes of doughnuts were scattered over the table, which was not as smooth and unblemished as it had once been. (Superstoe refused to order a new table. He said he liked a table that looked as if it had been worked on.)

Superstoe did not refer to notes. As he talked he glanced out the window, or chewed a doughnut, or sipped coffee, or folded a paper airplane, or strolled about the room, dropping crumbs on Albright's head, sipping the Commerce Secretary's coffee, adjusting the picture of John Adams on the wall, or arranging the bouquet of red and white carnations. It was as if he were back in Crossbar, lecturing on participles and gerunds.

"We shall commence," he began, "a massive building program. We shall build new communities—communities in which no two houses are alike. There will be no cars in these communities. One will park his car in a garage some distance away and be ferried, as it were, to his house by a small, silent, electric monorail, suspended in the air to avoid its hitting anyone. The monorail will have a maximum speed of ten miles an hour—perhaps five—so that one will relax; one will not be jolted from an eighty-mile-per-hour freeway to a zero-mile-per-hour home. Most likely, however, one will walk the mile to his home. One will walk on gravel paths under oak trees and maple trees and pine trees. Birds will be singing. Squirrels and rabbits and children and puppies and kittens will be frolicking and gamboling on the cool green grass beneath the arboreal canopy."

Superstoe glanced covertly around the table. Furth's chin rested in his palm; he seemed to be falling asleep. Zorr was reading a newspaper, and Johanneson was reading the Congressional Record. But the Assistant Secretary of Labor wore a dazed look; he smiled sweetly, and his eyes brimmed with tears.

Superstoe took a doughnut and went on. "Gradually we'll rebuild the entire nightmare of urbia and suburbia. Have peace and quiet for a change." He bit into the doughnut and continued talking.

"Excuse me, Mr. President," the stenographer interrupted, "I didn't catch that."

Superstoe swallowed and began again. "The UNIS staff stationed about the country will require housing."

"Now," he said in a new tone, "electronics will not be affected by peace. We'll conduct scientific exploration: exploration of space, in conjunction with the Russians—make a note, Judy, that all astronauts will have to learn Russian—exploration of the earth and of the deeps of the oceans.

"Makers of guns, munitions, et cetera, will have to close down or convert to other products. Sweden's supplying the UNPF with guns and tanks; Russia has a contract for planes; Britain, ships . . ."

"What should they convert to?" asked Zorr.

Superstoe looked at him. Then he waved his arms. "I can't do *everything*." He strolled to the window, saying, "New colleges will be built. Theatres, concert halls. New primary and secondary schools. The government will sponsor repertory companies, orchestras, ballet companies." He thought for a moment. "Maybe even opera companies."

He swerved away from the window and faced his audience. "What shall we do with all our planes, ships, and submarines?" he asked.

The Secretary of the Treasury started to speak, but Superstoe surged on. "We shall convert the bombers to passenger planes." He spread his hands to describe a billboard. "Fly to Europe on a SAC bomber. Sit where a hydrogen bomb once sat." He paused, as if listening for the effect.

"The ships—carriers, cruisers, destroyers will be converted to low-cost passenger ships. Nuclear submarines will be converted to high-cost passenger subs. Think of cruising around the world in a nuclear submarine! They will be deluxe transport! They should appeal to the jet set. Or rather the sub set." He chuckled.

"Then we have those eight hundred ICBM silos. What shall we do with them?"

"Fill 'em with wheat," said Johanneson.

"No ..."

"Then plough 'em under."

"No," said Superstoe, "we shall make them into hotels."

The Commerce Secretary choked on his coffee, spewing it on Johanneson's *Record.* Albright pounded the Secretary on the back. The Secretary knocked over his cup.

"Remove the missiles and construct rooms," Superstoe calmly continued. "Other rooms will be in the underground control areas. We'll disconnect the controls but leave the panels in place. People will love to play with them. Countdown, ten, nine ..."

"I think the view from those rooms will leave something to be desired," said Furth.

"Anything's better than those flat fields," said Zorr.

"Above ground," Superstoe said, "we'll build cabins, parks, swimming pools, ice rinks, gymnasiums." He meditated a moment and sniffed a carnation. Then he said, "As for the makers of submarines, I have another idea."

Albright winced.

"You know that sailing race? The America's Cup?" Superstoe asked.

Furth shrugged to indicate he didn't know of such a thing.

"Well, they have one. And they have auto races, as at Indianapolis."

Furth nodded. He had heard of that. "The Four Hundred, they call it," he said.

"That refers to another race," said Superstoe. "Anyway, I thought we could conduct submarine races. Make them big sporting events."

The stenographer shook his head in wonder.

"I wonder if they could design one-man or two-man subs," Superstoe continued. "That way it would be more like auto racing. Like a rally, you know?"

Furth shook his head.

"Go north-northwest at sixty knots and at two hundred fathoms until you reach fifteen degrees, five minutes, twenty seconds latitude and eighty degrees, two minutes, ten seconds longitude. Then go, and so on. *Or,*" he exclaimed, the idea just coming to him, "conduct mock wars. *That* would appeal to the masses!"

Superstoe poured himself more coffee. "We'll turn the Army training camps into summer camps for kids," he said.

The Labor Secretary reminded, "There will be a sudden surplus of manpower when everyone is released from military service."

"Some will be absorbed in the PF and IS," Superstoe said. "But we'll institute a national vocational guidance system. We'll use computers. With all our projects, unemployment should be zero. The economy will be stronger than ever."

Furth raised the dagger he used as a letter opener. "Paxton," he inquired, "have you by chance thought of a solution for the uniform industry?"

Superstoe's cup was poised at his lips. "Yes." He sipped.

"They'll convert to Ivy League patterns and we'll sell the suits to China. They're introducing a new look in clothes, to go with their de-Stalinization program."

"Excellent," said Furth.

Superstoe consulted a memo. "One hundred million olive-green three-button narrow-lapel suits," he read, "to be accompanied by one hundred million red silk ties." He looked up. "Unfortunately they're making the ties themselves. But Charley has promised to send me one. Would you like one too, Lazarus? I could take a few orders for him, I suppose."

"Charley?"

"Mr. Chan."

9   The day after that meeting the Secretary of Labor—a Knutson appointee—resigned.

So, a week later, three men were sworn into office: Allen T. (Thundercloud) Smith became Commissioner of Indian Affairs; W. C. H. (Wild Crazy Horse) Samson became Secretary of the Interior; and Thomas Hanson, a Negro, became Secretary of Labor.

The following day several new ambassadors were appointed—Ishogu Nisakomi, ambassador to Japan; William Lee, ambassador to China; Abdul Barushi, ambassador to Pakistan; and others.

After congratulating and advising the new ambassadors, Superstoe returned to his office to find Zorr talking on the phone. Zorr quickly hung up.

"Who was that?" asked Superstoe.

"A girl."

"I gathered."

"She's the younger sister of the ambassador from Mali."

"I want you to draft the statement announcing the abolishment of the Department of Defense," Superstoe said, sitting at his desk. "It will in the future be known as the Department of Planning. It will coordinate the reform of society. Lazarus will stay on there. We'll split HEW into two departments, Health and Welfare, and Education. Ed will be in charge of Health and Welfare. He'll work out eugenic selection. That correlates with welfare. The Department of Education will supervise the new system of federally sponsored colleges, as well as general education for the populace. How would you like to be Secretary of Education?"

Zorr pulled a cheroot from his coat pocket and lit it. "I guess that would be all right."

"Good. I expect in a year or so Ben will want to head that department, and then you can hop over to Secretary of State."

"All right," he said nonchalantly.

"As for Arthur—where is Arthur, anyway?"

"Moscow."

"Ah, yes. I was talking with the Secretary-General of the UN the other day. I was telling him about Arthur's abilities. So it seems that the Secretary-General is thinking of appointing Arthur Director of the Biological and Chemical Supervision Section of the IS." Superstoe smiled with satisfaction. "Arrange an appointment with that fellow Lamont Cornwall, who writes spy stories," he went on. "I may appoint him Director of the CIA."

"We're keeping the CIA?"

"Just to keep an eye on things. That leaves one vacancy to fill. My Press Secretary. I don't want to lose you, Isen."

"I think I'd like a change."

"I see. Then whom shall we pick?"

"What about Jack Smith?"

"Fine," said Superstoe. "Who's Jack Smith?"

Zorr, holding the cheroot in his teeth and squinting his eyes in the smoke, pretended to drive a car.

"A racing driver?" asked Superstoe.

"Ours. One of our germ-truck drivers."

"That Jack Smith."

"Director of Public Relations for Manichean Laboratories, which now owns six subsidiary companies and is building plants in New Jersey, Michigan, California, New Mexico, and Louisiana and is negotiating to build labs in Germany, Italy, Nigeria, India, Poland, and Yugoslavia."

"They're doing rather well, aren't they?"

"Yes, we are."

Zorr, Pall, Furth, Johanneson, and Watt each owned six percent of the stocks in Manichean Laboratories. Superstoe and Adams had refused their shares.

"Love of money is the root of some evil," Superstoe remarked.

"I don't love money," Zorr said. "I love the Good Life."

Superstoe cast a suspicious eye upward. Then he looked back at his desk, saying, "And I'll appoint Josh Cohen Attorney-General."

Joshua Cohen had attained eminence by representing numerous life-insurance beneficiaries in suits lodged against the insurance companies. The companies refused to honor the policies of persons who died in the epidemics, maintaining the deaths were the results of acts of war.

Cohen argued that death from disease is always death by natural causes. Moreover, he said, it had never been conclusively proved that the epidemics were spread by enemy agents.

The case reached the Supreme Court, and the court found in favor of the plaintiffs, 5 to 4.

10   In addition to the economic conversion plans and the construction bills Superstoe sent to Congress, he submitted a prison-reform bill and an American Indian Restitution Act.

The prison-reform bill provided for the building of new prisons, which would not be known as prisons but as rehabilitation centers. Prisoners would live in comfortable, colorful, fully furnished cottages. Their families or girl friends could live with them. Prisoners would be given vocational training and psychological counseling. Most important, however, would be the facts that the environment would be pleasant and natural and that the members of the communities—as the prisoners would be called—would be allowed to satisfy their natural hungers: enjoy a pleasant shelter, wear ordinary clothes, eat home-cooked meals, and fulfill their sexual needs.

If anyone did not respond to this rehabilitation, he would undergo an operation on his brain.

"Consider," said Superstoe, "why people commit acts of violence. They either suffer from psychological problems or they suffer from a quick temper. In either case, they can be rehabilitated, by counseling or by drugs or by surgery. It is time we left the middle ages behind."

The old prisons would be converted to zoos or museums of natural history.

The American Indian Restitution Act would allocate millions of dollars with which fertile land would be purchased and turned over to Indians who wanted to farm. They would be provided with equipment. Failure to use the land profitably, however, would result in loss of the land.

Other funds would be assigned to educating Indians.

Large areas of land in the West would be purchased and stocked with fish and game. There the Indians, or anyone else who wished to live as the Indians had once lived, hunting and fishing and residing in teepees, could do so. Special attention would be paid to increasing the buffalo herds.

And those Indians who did not desire to hunt or farm or work in other fields would be given simple but comfortable and hygienic homes—built of stone or brick, with electricity, water, and appliances—free; plus free medical care.

"This," said Superstoe, "simply as a token compensation for the host of injustices we have inflicted upon them and their forefathers."

Furthermore, each tribe was encouraged to maintain its traditional customs and culture.

He also submitted a constitutional amendment abolishing the death penalty. "Simply that no innocent person will be murdered by the state," said Superstoe.

11 The Superstoe bills poured into Congress. Congressmen gasped, struggled, thrashed, nearly drowned.

Zorr and Furth moved from hearing to hearing. They argued, they reasoned, they enlightened. The congressional committees listened, nodded, and knuckled down. The members of Congress had been uncertain before, but now they knew which way the tide was running. They ran with it.

Gideon Shiloh Geaseman continued to swim bravely, resolutely, upstream.

Superstoe chatted to the people over color television. He wore a mauve sweatshirt emblazoned across the chest with the presidential seal.

It looked like good times ahead.

After a few minor incidents the UN Inspection Service functioned smoothly and efficiently. There were problems, of course, and a few scandals; but eventually the Russians and the Chinese and even the French decided the Americans were sincere. Gradually trust begat trust.

Each UNIS Disarmament Observer Team consisted of five men: an American, a Russian, a Chinese, and two neutrals. One team would arrive at an American missile complex, another team at a Russian missile site. Telephone communication would be established between the two teams.

At the American site the Russian observer would take the phone and say to his countryman in Russia, "I watch now the dismantling of three intercontinental ballistics missiles in North Dakota, under a beautiful blue sky flecked with white clouds, accompanied by the pleasant trill of small brown birds with yellow breasts."

And at the Russian site the American observer, watching the technicians, would take the telephone and say, "Checkout here, Charley. Stripping three birds. Pop the balloons."

12   By the spring preceding the presidential nominating conventions disarmament was nearly completed.

Congress had passed all the Superstoe bills.

Superstoe made an announcement.

"I have never," he said, "considered myself a member of either political party. I have rather thought of myself as belonging to what we might call the American Party.

"Therefore, in answer to queries concerning my political intentions, I am forced to admit that I have no intentions.

"I became president, as it were, accidentally. I became president in a time of grave peril. I sought to surmount the peril. Happily, we succeeded.

"Then, looking about me, I perceived in our country grave injustices which had long gone uncorrected. I sought to rectify those injustices. Happily, our Congress was as concerned as I about those injustices, and together we have begun the labor of correcting them.

"Still, there remains a lot to be done.

"For example, I would like to see our system of government made more democratic. I would like to see a national referendum instituted to allow every single citizen a vote in the most important matters confronting our country. In the past such democracy was not possible. We hadn't the facilities to cope with millions of votes in an efficient manner. We hadn't the means of communication. We hadn't the time to devote to government while we went about our own individual labors.

"But now that is not true. Now a true government of the people and by the people is possible.

"We no longer have to work sixty, fifty, or even forty hours a week. There are those who wonder what we should do with all our leisure time. To them I have a suggestion. Why not use a fraction of that leisure time to participate directly in our national government?

"For now it is technologically possible. With electronic voting facilities, connected by a nationwide computer system and by television, men and women could gather, say, once a month, or once a week, if necessary, and watch and listen to debates, could themselves engage in debate, and then, at a scheduled time, press a button before them, vote aye or nay, and within ten seconds the votes would be in, counted, and posted.

"Nor is that all we could do," Superstoe continued. "We could propose new rules which would ensure a responsible Congress—rules which I am sure every honest, loyal member of Congress would wholeheartedly approve.

"I would suggest higher salaries for congressmen. And then, to guarantee their dedication to their post, I would rule that any member who missed more than ten percent of the roll-call votes in any session for any reason other than illness would receive no pay for that session. And if he missed more than twenty percent of the votes, or if he missed more than ten percent in two succeeding sessions, he would not only receive no pay but he would be fined an amount equal to his pay and be automatically removed from office and ineligible to run for public office again.

"There are other reforms we might suggest as well, but this is not the time to talk about reform. My point is rather this. There is still much to be done—a great deal to be done. But since I have—thanks to you—accomplished our most pressing goals—world peace, secure disarmament, certain domestic legislation—I feel I should no longer impose myself upon you. I do not wish to take advantage of my position as chief executive. I wish the American people to be free to choose whomever they wish as their next president.

"I am not, therefore, declaring myself a candidate of either political party."

Later a reporter inquired, "If you were nominated, would you run?"

"Run?" asked Superstoe. "Where?"

"For office, Mr. President."

"Oh, for office. Well, it would be my duty, wouldn't it?"

13   Geaseman was no fool. He stopped swimming. He began to float.

"We know one thing for sure," he told the party's national committee. "Superstoe will win the election. The only question is, which party will ride his coattails?"

The chairman of the national committee tried to sound out Superstoe.

But Superstoe would not be sounded. "I shall not declare myself a member of your party," he told him, "nor shall I declare myself a member of the late President Knutson's party. I am available to all the people." He patted the chairman's arm and handed him the keys to a new Maseratti.

Geaseman's party held their convention first. On July 21 they nominated Superstoe for President. Geaseman seconded the nomination.

Superstoe happened to be cruising in the Caribbean on July 21. It was reported that he was suffering from a slight bronchial infection. He regretted he would be unable to come to Los Angeles to address the convention. However, since he had been asked to suggest a running mate, he would, with all diffidence, suggest Lazarus Furth.

Furth was on the yacht with Superstoe.

Furth accepted the invitation to address the convention, but the helicopter experienced engine difficulty, and the second helicopter failed to find the yacht. The third found the yacht, but a sudden storm came up and it was unable to take Furth off. So Zorr appeared at the convention to accept the nominations for Superstoe and Furth.

Knutson's party had no choice. They nominated Superstoe and Furth, protesting that the other party had "stolen our candidates."

Furth made it to that convention to accept his and Superstoe's nominations. Superstoe was said to be suffering from a severe sunburn.

But a few days later a tanned Superstoe met with the leaders of both parties. As a result of that meeting the two parties merged to become the American Party.

The new party, however, faced the dilemma of having two candidates running for each office. Again Superstoe came to the rescue.

He reviewed the records and the CIA reports on each of the candidates, and then he chose the one who was to run on the American Party ticket. The rejected candidates, he suggested, should run as independents.

He pondered a long while over Geaseman. His inclination was to reject him, but at the same time he felt obliged to him for leading the party, finally, into his hands. He left his name on the American Party list.

Zorr and Adams objected. But Superstoe reminded, "We don't want to stifle *all* opposition. After all, we're not a dictatorship."

The rejected candidates gathered and formed a new second party. They called it the Freedom Party. They asked Geaseman to join them. They promised to make him their candidate for President.

Geaseman wavered. But he decided to float awhile longer. Especially since he was still on the bobbing coattail.

14 Superstoe, Adams, Furth, and Johanneson flew to Crossbar the day before the election to vote.

From Air Force I they looked down on the strictly geometric North Dakota fields. Not even the tortuously winding river that separated the state from Minnesota broke the monotony, for the twists in the river were as unvaried as the squares of yellow and brown and black.

As the plane flew parallel to the highway, however, they noticed construction in progress, widening the highway from two to six lanes. And as they passed over the Great Spoons airport they read, in large green letters on the runway: WELCOME TO NORTH DAKOTA HOME OF PRESIDENT SUPERSTOE.

The jet banked left and headed west for the former SAC base. The base would eventually become a commercial terminal servicing an industrial complex which was being planned for the area.

Johanneson and Adams were playing chess.

Superstoe was in the co-pilot's seat learning to fly.

Furth was across the aisle from Adams and Johanneson reading a newspaper aloud, when he reached a statement he thought worth sharing.

"Listen," said Furth, "to Don Winterback's column." Adams and Johanneson did not look up, but he read anyway. "It seems impossible that less than four years have passed since the election of Bryan Knutson. It seems even less possible that it has been but three years and six months since Paxton S. Superstoe succeeded to the presidency.

"Surely the world has never witnessed so much so quickly. Surely there have never been such nightmares, followed by such dreams . . ." Furth tossed the paper to the floor and picked up another. He leafed through the pages. "Say, Jason," he called, "you know what?"

Johanneson looked up.

"It appears that a gang of pirates have killed Daddy Warbucks and are in the process of suffocating Li'l Annie in a fiendish computer. One of the pirates is a mad scientist with thick glasses. Another one is short, fat, and bald; he's the leader. Another one is tall and has a big ugly mustache. Then they have two midgets who do their dirty work."

Furth took a pen from his pocket and drew pupils in all the eye sockets.

"Li'l Abner," he continued, "is running for President of the United Counties of Candyland. His opponent is Daisy Mae. And Pogo is showing his cousin around the swamp."

"His cousin?" asked Johanneson.

"A portly, likable possum, named Super S. Possum."

"I'd say the comics were more acute than Don Winterback," Adams said, taking a bishop and checking the king.

Furth turned the page. "Here's L. T. Traugett's column: 'The most amazing thing about Superstoe is not all that he has accomplished—which is amazing enough, if not miraculous. The most amazing thing is that he has done and is promising to do all the things everyone agrees should have been done but which no previous President ever bothered to do.'

"And further on he says, 'Despite his pretended political naiveté, Superstoe is undoubtedly the shrewdest politician America has seen for generations. Yet—most miraculous of all—his shrewdness seems to be directed not only toward his own gain but toward the good of the country as well.'

"And," Furth continued, "still further on he says, 'Superstoe stands out as one of America's greatest—and most unusual—charismatic leaders. Undaunted by the howls of criticism that greeted his policies at the beginning of his presidency, he resolutely maintained those policies, even in the face of ignominy and threatened impeachment, until his policies were proved by time to be not only advantageous but incredibly wise and farsighted.

"'Thus, finally, the people rallied behind him. He did not have to beg or compromise to win his nomination. The people wanted Superstoe. They would have no one else. He needed no party. He could have run without the endorsement of any party, and he would still win the election tomorrow. He could have run on the Bull Moose ticket. He could have run on the Prohibition ticket—though that would be unlikely.

"'As for a platform, he is his own platform. The candidates running with him under the aegis of the American Party are committed simply to support Superstoe and whatever he thinks of in the next four years.'"

The plane banked sharply, rose, dipped, tossed, banked again, and straightened out. A familiar voice came over the intercom.

"Ladies and gentlemen, this is your captain speaking. I have the pleasure to announce that you have the privilege of being the first passengers to break the Superstoe barrier. Now fasten your seat belts. I'm taking the plane down." The intercom clicked off. The plane dived forward.

Furth leaped to his feet but was thrown down the carpeted corridor. From the floor he cried, "He's not really going to land it!"

The plane banked sharply.

"Looks like it," said Johanneson, tightening his seat belt and reading the crash instructions printed on the wall.

"But the pilot can't let him!" Furth screamed.

"He's the President," Adams said. "Nobody gives him orders." Adams's normally ruddy face was pale.

The plane swooped toward the ground, shuddered, teetered, and then zoomed back into the sky. Superstoe's voice came over the intercom again. "Didn't quite make her that time. We'll try her again, folks. Alley-oop!"

Furth, still on the floor, crossed one ankle over the other and buried his head in his arms.

The plane swerved. The plane descended. The concrete runway neared, rapidly.

With a rattle of drums and a blare of trumpets, "The Star-Spangled Banner" resounded through the cabin. Then it stopped, and a melancholy organ pealed out "Swing Low, Sweet Chariot."

Superstoe stood in the doorway to the cockpit. He looked down at Furth. He inquired, "Are you ill, Lazarus?"

One of Furth's eyes opened and appeared above an elbow. He mumbled something.

Superstoe bent over. "What, Lazarus? Do you want a bag?"

"I said I suppose now no one's at the controls."

The plane bounced. Then it whizzed smoothly down the runway and gradually slowed. Superstoe peered out the window at the snow flurries and said, "Home sweet home."

15   When, exactly four years before, Superstoe had bounced in his jeep up the same road on his way to the SAC base to catch the jet that took him and Knutson to Washington, the road had been of dirt, and it had been barely wide enough for two cars.

Now it was a four-lane highway.

When they had left Crossbar, it had possessed one old hotel which was seldom occupied and one motel at which a salesman occasionally stopped.

But now as they approached the town in the limousine they saw new motels, restaurants, and service stations begin ten miles from the town. A five-story motel, named *El Presidente,* was in construction.

Crossbar itself had changed, too. Now the town had taxis and parking lots and even rent-a-car signs. The railway crossing had a signal—although traffic was still delayed half an hour whenever a freight train passed through, backed, switched, and went on. Three intersections had traffic lights; but one of them wasn't working.

There were more bars: The Cabinet Bar, The Secretaries of State, Defense, and Agriculture Bar, The Presidential Lounge, The Presidential Tavern, The President's Bar and Grill, The Crossbar Home of Greatness Cocktail Lounge.

The Happy Corral Bar had been renovated and renamed The Happy Nation Bar. And the Saddle Up had been refurnished. For fifty cents one could visit the room where Vice President and Secretary of Defense Lazarus Furth once lived, still containing a hot plate, a pot, a tin cup, a can of chicken noodle soup, a few mathematical journals, and a pair of overalls; and on the walls one could see strange symbols and equations written in orange chalk.

Crossbar High School, however, remained unchanged. It was overcrowded now and needed repairs, but the school board was building a hockey rink before they built more classrooms. The name, on the other hand, had been altered. Now it was Superstoe High School.

The limousine swept out of town, trailed by reporters in buses and rented cars.

"I wish they hadn't paved this road," Superstoe said. "I always enjoyed arriving in a cloud of dust."

A high wire fence had been erected around Superstoe's house for security. But the house and barn were still unpainted. The barn stood empty. The equipment was at Manichean Laboratories, which stood four miles south.

They stepped from the limousine and walked to the house through the dead, knee-high grass. A Secret Service agent stood to attention at the door.

Adams, then Furth, then Johanneson passed into the house without a glance at the young agent. But Superstoe looked at him closely and realized he had not seen him before. He stopped before him, looked shrewdly up into his face, and fingered the lapel of the agent's topcoat.

"Have you," asked Superstoe, "inspected my house?"

The agent stiffened. "Yes, sir."

Casually Superstoe asked, "What's your name?"

"Mark Capwell, sir."

Snow was gathering on the shoulders of the two men, but Mark Capwell's forehead was perspiring. Furth, curious, had turned back and was watching from the doorway.

"You've inspected it thoroughly?" asked Superstoe.

"Yes, *sir!*"

"Excellent, Mark. Now tell me, what did you find in the house?"

"Nothing, sir."

"Nothing!" Panic-stricken, apparently, Superstoe clutched both of Capwell's lapels.

"No, sir." Capwell shifted his weight. His face wore the expression Superstoe had seen so often on men he had interrogated—an expression that implied a sudden, horrible loss of confidence in a predictable universe.

"You found no books?" cried Superstoe.

Capwell sighed in relief. "Yes. Yes, the books are there."

"How many?" Superstoe asked quickly.

"I didn't count them, sir. There were many books."

"Very many?"

"It looked like the Library of Congress."

Superstoe breathed more easily. "What else did you find, Mark?"

Mark Capwell thought. "A moldy skillet. A pair of dirty socks." He paused. "A chamber pot."

Superstoe gave him a congratulatory grin. "A chamber pot."

"Yes sir."

Superstoe stepped closer. He whispered, "What color was it?"

Capwell hesitated a second, and then he said, "Blue."

"Blue! *Blue!*"

Even Furth looked worried.

Capwell bent down and whispered into Superstoe's ear, "An oak tree was growing out of it, and there were nightingales singing in the branches."

"How lovely," said Superstoe and hopped up the step and into the kitchen.

He entered the Dialectic Room, observed the empty red chamber pot on the table, and said, "I must promote Mark Capwell."

He made a careful tour of the house to inspect his books—not that he thought they had been tampered with, but for the sheer joy of seeing them again. Two hours later Johanneson found him behind a stack of novels, asleep, his head cushioned by *The Tempest* and *A Midsummer Night's Dream.*

He had not slept a great deal during the past weeks, for he had campaigned vigorously. Everyone said he could win the election without a single speech, could win it even if he came out against God and Mother.

But he did not want to merely win. He wanted to landslide.

16   Sixty-four percent of the registered citizens voted. Ninety-four percent of them voted for Superstoe.

A spirit of elation, a mood of nervous excitement, flowed like an electric current across the land. Men and women, boys and girls, rich and poor and middle class agreed: a new day was at hand.

Superstoe rested in Crossbar for three days after the election. Then he flew to Bermuda, where he stayed four weeks. He swam, fished, skied, scuba dived, and wrote.

Next he flew to a resort on the Black Sea and there conferred with Soznolopak and Borozov. They went hunting. Superstoe wounded a rabbit; Borozov killed a bear.

From there he flew to China for four days of talks. Furth accompanied him to China, and Pall was there already, as a representative of the UNIS. When the four days had passed, the Premier, a man of twenty-nine who had been a journalist in Changsha, invited them to stay another week.

They stayed eight more days. Then Furth returned to Washington by way of Thailand, Cambodia, Laos, Vietnam, the Philippines, Formosa, Korea, Japan, Australia, and Hawaii. Pall's assignment took him to Indonesia, where the IS was experiencing some difficulty. Superstoe made a pilgrimage to Tibet.

Adams meanwhile toured Africa. He was accompanied by Ambrose Washington, Thomas Hanson, and Mohammed Ali T, who was then a New York City councilman.

Zorr was overseeing things at home. He caused a slight scandal when various young ladies were observed to stay overnight at the White House. The White House denied the accusation.

Superstoe arrived back in Washington on Christmas Eve.

The inauguration ball was the liveliest reporters could remember. At 10:25 P.M. the Marine Band stopped midway in a waltz and launched into "Hail to the Chief."

All eyes turned to the doorway.

The eyes watched. They waited.

No one appeared.

The band played "Hail to the Chief" a second time.

A dejected bloodhound loped through the entrance, looked about, sat, and howled.

On the bandstand a short, portly Marine stood and played a thrilling rendition of "The Bugler's Holiday."

The hound yelped in delight and raced to the bandstand, knocked over the snare drum and licked the bugler's face.

Superstoe handed the trumpet to the Marine beside him, took off his cap, bowed, stepped down, grabbed the nearest woman—she happened to be Mrs. Ambrose Washington—and waltzed her about to the tune of "Greensleeves."

Later, dressed in a tuxedo and accompanied by timpani and cymbals from the New York Philharmonic, he recited Lear's soliloquy in the storm, followed by a segment of Socrates' "Apology," in Greek.

As dawn broke, he won an impromptu dance contest by performing the frug with the young wife of the Indian ambassador.

Furth repeated his Zulu war dance; and Pall led a spontaneous, improvised, avant-garde ballet.

The ball ended, after a sumptuous breakfast, at 11 A.M. with a concert of Renaissance tunes. Zorr played the harpsichord, Pall and Superstoe played recorders, and Furth played the rebec.

17   Three days later Congress began debating the stack of bills and constitutional amendments submitted by Superstoe.

The White House announced that Vice President Furth would retain his post of Secretary of the Department of Planning, that Adams had been appointed Secretary of Education, and that Zorr had been appointed Secretary of State. Watt of course remained Secretary of Health and Welfare, Johanneson remained Secretary of Agriculture, and Cohen remained Attorney-General.

Congressmen doubled their salaries and voted the Superstoe Rules into effect.

More bills affecting the conversion to peacetime economy were passed.

The electoral college was abolished.

The first President's Cup submarine race was held.

The hollow shells of hydrogen bombs were sold by the government as souvenirs.

The government-owned herd of American bison increased by twenty percent.

Congress debated the constitutional amendment providing for a national referendum.

Opponents of the amendment argued that the populace would be unable to understand bills and knowledgeably vote on them. They said the average man did not have time to study legislation, much less the time to debate and vote.

Supporters of the amendment asked, "Do our opponents believe Congress is an intellectual elite, superior to the common man? Do they think congressmen are smarter than their constituents?"

"Of course not," the opponents replied.

The House passed the amendment; but in the Senate, Geaseman began a filibuster.

About the same time three new syndicated columnists appeared in the newspapers.

One of the columnists was noted for his erudite but homey wit. His name was Solomon Towe, and his column, which appeared thrice weekly, was written by Superstoe.

Another, characterized by his vigorous style and political savvy, was known as Canfield Collander; he appeared thrice weekly, and his copy was written by Zorr.

The third columnist, Jacob Allworthy, quickly famous— or notorious, some said—for his merciless satire, appeared only once a week, on Sundays, because Pall was extremely busy with the UNIS.

All three columnists supported the referendum amendment, and they were credited with rallying public opinion until the filibuster was stopped and the amendment passed. Perhaps the most influential columns were those by Solomon Towe which revealed how certain congressmen, especially senators, spent their time. Towe showed that the man who worked forty hours a week would have as much time to study legislation, debate, and vote as the average congressman, considering the time a congressman spent in committee hearings, writing letters, appearing on television, making speeches, conducting filibusters, talking to lobbyists, attending luncheons, cocktail parties, receptions, dinners, and conferences, touring Europe, Asia, and Africa, and reminding constituents of his indispensability.

Geaseman's voice failed. The Senate rode the waves.

Any bill or constitutional revision could be submitted to a national referendum by the President, or by Congress, or by petition of ten percent of the voters.

A referendum vote could not be overruled by Congress; it could not be vetoed by the President—unless less than sixty percent of the voters approved the measure. If less than sixty percent approved the bill in question, the President could veto it. But his veto could be overruled by two-thirds of Congress.

To prevent an energetic minority from taking advantage of a lethargic majority, a referendum would be valid only if at least forty percent of the registered voters voted.

By the time the states had ratified the amendment, most of the referendum voting facilities had been installed.

The installations for the National Referendum Communications and Voting System—usually referred to as Recomvote—were to be permanent and used in elections as well as referendums.

New, small, compact voting machines were set up. They were connected to regional computers; the regional computers relayed the votes to a central tabulator in Washington. The final vote could be electronically computed and published twelve seconds after the polls closed.

The electronics of Recomvote presented no problem. Finding a sufficient number of facilities did.

Recomvote equipment was installed in school auditoriums, meeting halls, theatres, state fair buildings, club buildings, garages, and taverns.

To prevent electronic ballot stuffing, every registered voter was issued a card bearing a unique number. He would insert his card into the slot in the voting machine. The machine would "read" the number; the voter would press the Yes button or the No button.

During each voting period the computers would record only one vote for each card. If the same card was inserted more than once, its subsequent votes would be disregarded.

If a voter lost his card, a new one bearing another number would be issued. The numbers of all lost or stolen cards would be fed into the computers and would be rejected in all future ballotings.

A voter need not be in his home town, or even his home state, to vote.

The computers would not correlate individual numbers with individual votes. It would not be possible to know who voted Yes or No.

An Anti-Computer Card League was organized in California. Branches followed in other states. The league filed suit against the federal government, contending the cards were unconstitutional, an invasion of privacy, and a denial of human rights.

The suit reached the Supreme Court, where Joshua Cohen argued the case for the government. "A man is not a number," Cohen said, "a man is not a plastic card. If anyone thinks the possession of a little card will diminish his dignity or his individuality, he has obviously never had any understanding of dignity or individuality. Man is above numbers and cards and even ZIP codes and direct digit dialing. Such things are merely the necessary epiphenomena of modern existence, like clothes and automobiles. I haven't heard any members of the Anti-Computer Card League complain of the credit cards they carry."

The Supreme Court found in favor of the government, seven to two.

18   It was almost two years after Superstoe's election when Recomvote was declared ready for operation.

To assay the popular response, Superstoe submitted the national budget.

The budget was substantially the same as that which had been passed by Congress; but Superstoe restored a few appropriations which Congress had deleted and expunged some that Congress had added.

During the two weeks previous to the vote newspapers, radio, and television published the budget in detail. Round-table discussions were broadcast. Town meetings were called.

The vote was scheduled for a Friday. Both Thursday and Friday were declared national holidays.

On Thursday congressional debate on the bill was televised. The House debate was televised from 8 A.M. to noon, and the Senate debate from 1 to 5. Then, from 8 P.M. to 11 a summing-up discussion was televised in which representatives, senators, distinguished citizens, professors, and Superstoe participated.

The Recomvote centers opened Friday at 6 A.M. Citizens gathered to discuss the budget among themselves. Some of the meetings, such as those held in municipal auditoriums, were chaired by mayors, city councilmen, or other prominent members of the community. Other meetings, of a less formal nature, were supervised by the bartender or a respected steady customer.

When each assembly decided they had debated the budget sufficiently, they voted. Votes could be cast between 6 A.M. and midnight Saturday, local time.

No tabulation was announced until all votes were in at midnight Hawaii time.

Fifty-nine percent of the card-carrying citizens voted. Eighty-one percent of them approved the Superstoe budget.

19 They even danced in the streets. Neighbors shook hands, enemies spoke, bartenders set out free beers, and news analysts declared it was the greatest event since the signing of the Magna Charta.

"At last a true democracy such as has not existed since the golden age of Athens—an even truer democracy than Athens's, for we have no slaves," wrote Don Winterback.

"At a single stroke the genius of Superstoe has restored faith in the common man, secured democracy so firmly it will never be uprooted by man or time, and solved the most perplexing problem of the modern age—what to do with leisure time," wrote L. T. Traugett.

"It will restore man to the community and dissolve the nagging neurosis of alienation," wrote a famous psychologist.

"No greater blow for freedom, democracy, and self-government has ever in the history of man been dealt. Not even the signing of the Declaration of Independence can be compared with it." So wrote Canfield Collander.

"For once the government has acted nobly. It has surrendered its power to the rightful possessors of power—the people. The critics of the Superstoe administration who cried that it was paternalistic, socialistic, and undemocratic have had their accusations shoved down their throats." Thus Solomon Towe.

It was as if the entire nation had suddenly entered into blissful, optimistic childhood. The blasé, the disenchanted, the cynical were rejuvenated; or, if not rejuvenated, then ostracized by the faithful. Those who had predicted a dry, lifeless, uninspired future, a future of mass nonentity smothered in bureaucracy and technocracy, were given the lie. Superstoe had turned the tables on the prophets of doom. He had proved that technology need not be an evil, a dehumanizer; he had proved that, in wise hands, it could be good, and make man more human, restore him to being a political animal, a shaper of his own destiny.

There was talk of making Superstoe President for life.

Only the members of Congress were uneasy.

But Superstoe remained unaffected by the elation and the adulation.

When Zorr would cry, "Isn't it fantastic?" Superstoe would simply smile and continue typing.

The typewriter clattered on and on, late into the night.

Adams, in his hotel suite, wrote slowly, carefully, in brown ink on lined yellow foolscap. He too wrote late into the night.

Furth rose before dawn and pounded his secondhand typewriter. It was the same typewriter from which had come the articles by Matthew Bumm and Fillmore Thumb. In the afternoons Zorr, feet on desk, dictated into a tape recorder, his words to be transcribed by a trusted secretary —a loyal, efficient woman of fifty-six who thought of Zorr as her son.

And in Pakistan, in Iran, in Rhodesia, in China, in Russia, in Argentina, in Cuba, in Estonia, in New York, Pall, whenever he found a few minutes' spare time, unzipped his portable typewriter, inserted two sheets of cheap yellow paper, and wrote.

New names began to appear in magazines and journals. Solomon Towe had an essay in *Reader's Digest;* P. P. Sorrel had an article in *Ladies' Home Journal;* S. S. Pluck and S. P. Pikklemier authored essays in other magazines and Sunday newspaper supplements.

Adams concentrated on the learned journals. K. P. Kobb, M. M. Athens, D. T. Tuck, and Robert A. Fischbein appeared in *Foreign Affairs, American Scholar, Partisan Review,* and *Commentary.*

The dazzling, unconventional prose of Fillmore Thumb appeared in *Esquire.* And, from the same hand, came the articles in *Fortune, Harper's, Atlantic,* and *Playboy,* by Lee Po Tong, M. B. Sindoulli, Lash Togurik, and L. Antisthenes.

The women's magazines were not neglected. Housewives came to talk about the articles by Plato Jackson, Roger Roll, F. Simpson Spamm, Robert F. Rinksfeller, and Humphrey Lump, which flowed, unbeknownst to them, from the transcribing typewriter of a sweet, efficient, white-haired secretary in the State Department Building.

Readers of *Ramparts, Saturday Review, Life, Esquire,* and *Look* began to discuss the humor, insight, and satire of C. R. A. Pittfell, P. D. Pimm, and A. T. Talmutt, all of whom might have reminded a very perceptive reader of the columnist Jacob Allworthy.

But the newspaper columns and the magazine articles only mirrored public sentiment—or so it seemed. For, amidst the success of Recomvote, amidst the great return to true democracy, more and more people began to wonder why the United States Congress should even exist.

As the articles, essays, and columns pointed out, Congress had become an antiquated, unnecessary institution, an obstacle in the way of complete democracy.

Jacob Allworthy's satire of Congress as a retired gentlemen's club with oligarchic ambitions became a literary classic overnight, and within a year it was included in anthologies, along with "A Modest Proposal" and "Self-Reliance," for use in college English courses.

Meanwhile the third year of Superstoe's first elected term as President passed.

And amidst the popular clamor for the abolition of Congress—most cities had an Abomcong Committee—President Superstoe advised caution.

"We must," he said, "consider long and carefully before making fundamental changes in our system of government."

Demonstrations were held.

Abomcong staged a sit-in in the capitol building which lasted for ninety-three hours.

So in the fourth year, after Superstoe and Furth had been nominated for second terms by the American Party, Superstoe submitted the abolishment of Congress to Recomvote.

It would be voted on the same day as the presidential election.

20   Ninety-three out of every hundred voters voted for Superstoe and Furth.

Eighty-six out of every hundred voted to abolish Congress.

The amendment to the Constitution that abolished Congress and placed legislation in the hands of the people provided for a Recomvote Advisory Council. It had twenty-five members, twelve appointed by the President and thirteen appointed by the governors of the states acting in concert. Its duties were to oversee the maintenance of the Recomvote centers, publish proposed bills and supporting material, arrange televised debates, and schedule bills for voting.

Legislation and constitutional revisions could be submitted to the council from two sources: from the President, and from the people.

The government facilitated petitioning by converting former Draft Board offices into Recomvote petition offices. If citizens managed to obtain signatures amounting in number to 0.1 percent of the voting population, the proposal would be displayed at the petition offices (as well as in newspapers), and there citizens could go to affix their signatures. If within six months ten percent of the voters had signed the petition, it would be forwarded to the Advisory Council.

In the Recomvote balloting the forty percent quorum remained in effect: if less than forty percent of the registered voters participated, the vote was declared invalid. The measure in question could then be signed into law or vetoed at the President's discretion. Such legislation was called legislation by default.

21 In January, a week before his inauguration, Superstoe gave a farewell party for the members of Congress.

Some representatives and senators—Gideon Shiloh Geaseman was among them—refused to attend. But for those who attended, the gloom was lightened as Superstoe presented to each legislator a new car and a signed certificate of faithful and meritorious service—on the back of which was a five-year extension of his franking privilege.

Some were made even gladder when Superstoe told them he was appointing them to various executive, judicial, or diplomatic posts. He awarded his faithful supporters with positions of importance. His most influential opponents, those who might continue to foment trouble, he offered lucrative jobs without influence. Some of his opponents accepted the jobs.

Then the bottles of champagne were opened, famous performers staged a variety show, and Superstoe invited all the congressmen to a private stag party the following night.

The stag party gave rise to rumors of congressional lasciviousness and aberration, which only confirmed the people's belief that they had acted wisely—and, some added, just in time.

22 The day after the inauguration (seven days after the stag party) Geaseman, who had not attended the stag party, called a press conference and announced the formation of a new political party, the Congress Party. It would incorporate the principles and members of the aborted Freedom Party and "what's more, dedicate itself to the restoration of representative government."

Geaseman had more support than met the eye.

A number of ex-congressmen were hanging on to the Superstoe bandwagon only until it hit a bump. They smiled in public, but privately they mourned their loss of fame, prestige, and testimonial dinners.

Despite the autographed photos showing Superstoe's arm around them, despite the cars and franking privileges, despite the plain brown wrappers enclosing crisp thousand-dollar bills, they discovered that their former constituents did not look at them with the same awe and respect. A member of the President's Permanent Peace Parliament (a post with a high salary but without a trace of authority) was not the same as a senator, was not even the same as a representative. And even an ambassador to Luxembourg or a consul in Beirut longed for the crowds, the rostrum, and the thrill of victory.

They told Geaseman he could count on them. They could not, of course, declare themselves openly. Not yet. The mortgage payments depended on the monthly check they received for attending the monthly meeting of the President's Permanent Peace Parliament. But some went so far as to contribute the crisp thousand-dollar bills to the Congress Party coffer.

Geaseman was clearly a man to be reckoned with.

Superstoe reckoned.

He offered him the ambassadorship to the United Kingdom (America and Great Britain were such fast friends not even Geaseman could wreck that union) and a hundred thousand dollars.

But Geaseman was a man of principle. He spread the money before the television cameras and cried he would not be a Judas to his country, not for thirty pieces, not for a hundred grand. He set the bills on fire, and an uneasy audience watched.

Superstoe responded to the Geaseman pyromania with the deed to a Puerto Rican estate, the deed to a Swiss chalet, and an account book to a Swiss bank showing a balance of one million American dollars.

Geaseman stepped suddenly and, to the public, inexplicably out of the spotlight.

But Jacob Allworthy could not resist a last arrow. His humorous and indecorous article interpreting the Congress Party's aims and name in a physical rather than political sense was printed in *Playboy* and picked up by the national news magazines.

The Congress Party announced it would henceforth be known as the Popular Party—the name would symbolize not only its dedication to the restoration of representative government but also its loyalty to "all the American people everywhere." And Geaseman, deeds and bank account secure come what might, returned to the battle.

"Sorry," said Pall.

"Still," Superstoe replied, "I thought he *was* a man of principle. But he didn't even return the gratuities."

Geaseman fought hard. The Popular Party leased billboards, bought full-page ads, and commissioned comic strips.

But the people repealed the constitutional amendment limiting a President to two elected terms, anyway. Geaseman charged the repeal originated in the White House. The White House swore it came from the people. The Recomvote Advisory Council wasn't talking.

The people ignored the controversy. They were in the saddle. Why should they give it back to Geaseman? Or to anyone?

23   The Department of Legislation was added to the cabinet and Zorr named Secretary.

Ambrose Washington became Secretary of State.

Ivan Borozov, much to Soznolopak's regret, departed from Moscow to become the United States ambassador to the United Nations. His first speech before the body caused some confusion in the translating booth. He was delivering his speech in Russian.

Superstoe appointed a friend of Borozov, Dmitri Vassyliovitch Tserensky, ambassador to Russia.

Enthusiasm for the new democracy surged on through May and into June. Between forty-three and fifty percent of the voters assembled at the Recomvote centers, talked, had beers, inserted their cards, and voted on bills.

Studies, schedules, copies of speeches, and copies of proposed measures were mailed daily to every household in the country. Votes were held every Friday and Saturday; one could go to the center either day, between 6 A.M. and midnight, and vote on the week's bills—usually one to ten bills, depending on the length and complexity of each measure.

Then the computers were turned off for July and August. And when they were turned on again, three weeks after the Labor Day weekend, and fourteen bills were up for consideration, only eighteen percent of the voters, as Superstoe had expected, came to insert their cards.

The following week twelve percent voted. Then four percent.

Legislation settled into an uneventful pattern. Government agencies and departments sent requests for bills and appropriations to the Department of Legislation. After study, discussion, and drafting, the bills reached Zorr's desk. Zorr conferred with Superstoe. Those bills approved by Superstoe were submitted by Zorr to the Recomvote Advisory Council, who scheduled them for voting, along with the bills submitted by the people. The balloting was held. On Monday the preceding week's bills were placed on Superstoe's desk marked RECOMVOTE INVALID. Superstoe signed some and vetoed others. He signed quite a few which had been submitted not by the government but by the people.

The Popular Party condemned the apathy. They renewed their billboard leases. But their newspaper ads appeared less frequently, and they were half-page ads, and then quarter-page ads.

Geaseman was interviewed (in Puerto Rico) for a television news special. The ratings indicated almost no audience at all. At the same hour another network was interviewing Jacob Allworthy, whose pseudonymity was preserved behind a bright red devil's mask. And the third network was running *The Greatest Story Ever Told.*

Pall said Geaseman was through, but Adams wasn't sure. Superstoe smiled and said nothing; but he retained the CIA surveillance teams, and they sent him weekly reports on Geaseman's activities.

24   They were busy years, the four years of Superstoe's second elected term. And at times it was not Superstoe who made the headlines but Johanneson and Adams and Watt.

Johanneson received the least attention. He was merely straightening out the farm mess.

Adams made the papers when the Adams Curricula was published.

The Adams Curricula would be employed in all the new federal colleges. The first ten would open that autumn; six were coeducational, three were all-male, and one was for women. The colleges were known collectively as the University of America, but each college had its own distinct name. Furth had named two of them: Gauss College and Cantor College. Superstoe named one: Lookalive College (named, it was said, after the obscure but prophetic educator Aston Angus Lookalive). Pall christened Diogenes College, Medici College, and Malfunkt College. Adams named the other four: Hume, Voltaire, Peirce, and Henry Adams Colleges.

Some of the colleges were in large cities; others were in the country. Each had its own character and distinction and was in large measure autonomous. Eighteen others were in construction, and thirty-six more were in the planning stage.

Many private and state colleges and universities talked of adopting the Adams Curricula, for federal funds always accompanied adoption.

For large institutions the Adams Curricula provided two sets of courses and two degrees, one for average students and one for above average students. The average students were taught principally by teaching machines and televised lectures. The aim was admittedly to produce degree holders with a minimum of professorial time. The faculties were to concentrate on the exceptional students, who could pursue interdisciplinary studies and learn in small discussion groups.

In June Superstoe and Adams, with much fanfare, announced the creation of the Academy of Philosophy.

The ultimate intention of the academy—training philosopher-kings for future generations—was not revealed. All the necessary reforms had not been accomplished; the American Constitution had not yet been rewritten.

But the general purpose of the Academy of Philosophy was no secret. The academy was to be the intellectual acme of the world.

After announcing the creation of the academy, adding that it would be built in the New Hampshire hills, Superstoe issued the prospectus. It read as follows:

1. Membership in the Academy of Philosophy will not be determined on the basis of age, sex, nationality, academic degrees, profession, color, religion, physical characteristics, publications, or personality tests.

2. Applicants will be admitted to membership if they demonstrate
   (a) a thorough knowledge of mathematics,
   (b) a comprehensive knowledge of all major branches of science and of most minor branches,
   (c) the ability to read French, German, Latin, ancient Greek, and English,
   and if they agree to seek wisdom by means of the science of dialectic.

3. Applicants who cannot demonstrate all of the above may be admitted to provisional membership at the discretion of the admissions committee. Provisional members will be given scholarships or fellowships to appropriate universities or institutions, where they will study those disciplines in which they are deficient. When the deficiency is repaired, they will be admitted to full membership.

4. Members will live together in plain but adequate facilities. They will hold most things in common. They will eat at a common board. However, each member may maintain a private study where he can retire for study and meditation and a private kitchen. Each member will be allowed to keep personal possessions such as clothes, books, and diaries.

5. A member must relinquish all commitments. While at the academy he must not engage in business activities, hold a job, or labor under the distractions of family life. The academy will provide all his needs. If necessary, the academy will contribute an adequate sum to the maintenance of a member's family.

6. Members will be free to come and go as they please.
7. The academy will be located in natural surroundings, away from cities and industries. No internal-combustion vehicles will be allowed in the area.
8. After several years at the academy a member will be encouraged to leave so that he may contribute his wisdom to society. It is expected that members will become community leaders, teachers, and government officials. The academy will be not merely a refuge from the distractions of ordinary society; it will be a school, the aim of which is the attainment of wisdom.

The Department of Education received 7,682 applications.

Tests were administered to determine the applicants' knowledge of mathematics, science, and languages.

As a result of the tests 724 persons were admitted to provisional membership and awarded grants for further study. The others were advised to pursue regular university courses of study.

Forty-six persons were admitted as the first members. They came from eighteen countries. Forty-one were men; five were women. They ranged in age from seventeen to seventy-eight.

The academy consisted of log and frame buildings of a rustic design. Cottages were designed for one, two, three, or four persons; each member chose which cottage he wished to live in. There was a common kitchen and dining hall to which was attached a series of dialectic rooms, each containing a table, comfortable chairs, books, glasses, and beverages.

The library stood on the north side of the campus. Members contributed their own books to it. Superstoe and Furth sent most of their books. The library also contained listening rooms where members might listen to records.

A small theatre-concert hall was built on the south side of the campus. There members delivered lectures, recited poetry, and gave music and dance recitals. Every six months a Platonic dialogue was acted out by some of the members. Superstoe attended the first performance—it was of the *Protagorus*—and suggested filming the performances for educational television and distribution to universities. (The next year Superstoe took part in a performance of the *Symposium*. He played the role of Aristophanes. Pall took the part of Socrates, Watt played Eryximachus, Furth played Alcibiades, and Zorr, Agathon.)

Behind the cottages stood the gymnasium.

In one small, soundproof room in the basement of the library stood a radio and a television set; but no one was ever seen in that room.

No newspapers, magazines, or journals were sold on the campus; and after a few weeks most of the members canceled all their subscriptions.

25   While Adams improved education, Watt began his eugenic program.

Watt's first step was to write articles dealing with the population explosion and unemployment in the technological age. Subsequent articles revealed the extent to which eugenic selection was already a reality, in the forms of voluntary sterilization, artificial insemination, planned parenthood, and family counseling. The articles also pointed out the deficiencies in those methods.

His articles appeared in *Reader's Digest* under the name Y. D. Malone. Canelli Cartwright wrote for *Fortune*. John Eudaemon wrote for *Playboy*; and A. S. Klepius sent articles to *Life*, *McCall's*, and *The Saturday Evening Post*. He also wrote for medical and learned journals as William X. Youngberg-son, S. Fred Angstrom, L. S. Muffet, and A. P. Markrest.

At the same time he created the Bureau of Population Analysis which, among other duties, issued certain directives to public health agencies and government clinics and mailed select literature to the nation's doctors.

But when the activities of the Bureau of Population Analysis became known to the public, Watt, and the BPA, were attacked.

Protest groups formed: the Anti-Eugenics Committee, the Keep Sex Pure League, WOMB (Women's Organization for Motherhood and Babies), and the American Parents for Constitutional Liberty.

To protest the protest groups, students at Harvard, and then at other universities, formed ORGASM: Organon for Rodomontadism, Gymnosophism, Aphrodisiacism, Sanguinity, and Mastoeroticism.

Embarrassed by the publicity, Watt gave a press conference. He assured the people the government had no intention of imposing eugenic control over them.

"Perhaps," Superstoe said to Watt, "we'd better slow down the eugenic program. Until our political position is more secure. Have a sandwich?"

Watt accepted the chicken salad on toast, and Superstoe poured him a glass of Riesling.

"Did you see," asked Watt, "that survey?"

"Which survey?"

"Eighty percent of the persons interviewed had not read a single book in the past year."

Superstoe ceased chewing. "Full speed ahead," he ordered through the mouthful of sandwich.

Swallowing, he added, "But take care. Remember, Newton's parents were average folks. So were mine, for that matter."

Quietly the Bureau of Population Analysis drew up its programs, set up clinics providing free medical care, and hired doctors who were sympathetic with its aims at generous salaries and convenient hours.

At the clinics depressed or antagonistic patients were given free tranquilizers. Clearly defective persons were without their knowledge sterilized; their enjoyment of sex was unaffected. Above-average women were encouraged to enjoy artificial insemination; their husbands would not know.

BPA staff members conducted a careful survey of intellectuals and other individuals who read voluminously. The readers were awarded special tax exemptions and sometimes given additional financial aid for every child they produced.

Meanwhile the Department of Health and Welfare declared its concern for orphans and illegitimate children.

The Department's Bureau of Children began to build homes for orphans and underprivileged children.

The character of the homes, all observers agreed, was homelike. They did not resemble institutions at all.

Mothers, fathers, and teachers—as the staff were called—were carefully selected. Most of them had children of their own who also lived in the home.

Each home was comprised of ten to twenty families. Each family was supervised by a mother and a father, and they were aided by a maid who performed the menial work. Each family was composed of six to ten children, ranging in age from infancy to eighteen years. Adjoining each home was a kindergarten, a primary school, and sometimes even a high school. The better students from the nearby communities often attended the schools at the homes.

The homes were so successful the government announced that as new homes were built any parent might apply to send his children to the homes. If the child was gifted, he was admitted free. Inferior children were returned to their parents or to private orphanages.

Years later, when the government was relatively free from criticism, tax deductions and bonuses were given to the parents of exceptional children who sent their progeny as infants to the homes and thereby renounced future control over the children.

Wet nurses were employed to suckle the newborn, for Superstoe was a believer in breast feeding, although Watt asserted, "It doesn't matter a damn whether they get it from a breast or a bottle or a goat or a machine, so long as they get warm milk and are held in a warm, soft lap and hear cooing sounds. We're developing a nursing machine that handles forty infants at a time. The tads lie in soft warm cradles, they're gently rocked, the milk comes from a central tank through a simulated breast and soft music counterpoint with coos and sweet babykums is piped into the room.

Superstoe canceled the project.

The selection of Class A citizens was not a quick affair; but Superstoe's aim was quality, not quantity.

Class A persons were those the government wanted to become prolific parents. If a Class A individual was wealthy, he or she was fined for not producing at least one child every three years—provided there existed no medical reason why the person should not produce children. If a Class A individual was not wealthy, he was exempted from taxes for three years for every child produced; and a woman was awarded three thousand dollars for every child born to her.

There were problems, of course. Some Class A men were married to women of a lower class, and vice versa. But if artificial insemination did not appeal to them, a Class A couple could go to one of the private, exotic rooms on the top floor of a BPA clinic. When the woman became pregnant, the date of conception was checked with the BPA register.

It was not an infallible method. But, as Superstoe said, "We cannot hope for perfection; man is born to err. But we can come close if we keep our wits."

Other citizens were designated Class B or Class C.

Class B was the largest. Class B citizens might or might not procreate exceptional children. They were allowed to have as many or as few children as they wished. But those whose first child was above average were encouraged, with financial rewards, to have more. And those whose first two children were mediocre were given free contraceptives; if they had a third and it was mediocre, they suffered additional taxes.

Class C were sterilized.

26   The BPA report on Geaseman found its way to Superstoe's cluttered desk. It designated him Class A.

It gave Superstoe pause. But he was busy, and for once he failed to pursue a problem to its conclusion. Besides, Geaseman was a childless widower, sixty-three years old.

Geaseman led the Popular Party attack on the BPA. Invigorated by the largess of several millionaires (all Class B except one, who was Class C), the party spawned a monthly magazine. A famous Hollywood actor was appointed editor-in-chief. The third number, escorted by considerable advance publicity, laid bare "the BPA top-floor scandal." The exposé was written by a former clinic physician whose issue had been rejected by the artificial insemination bank, and the article was illustrated by photos taken through a two-way mirror installed in one of the top-floor bedrooms by three shifty-eyed technicians.

One of the Superstoe bills, now in effect three years, forbade the Post Office to confiscate material deemed obscene. The magazine sold out the first day and was reprinted twelve times.

The public rose from its apathy like a hungry lion after a long sleep. It demanded a cessation of BPA activities. Superstoe promised an investigation.

"Is this a crisis?" asked Watt, removing the pipe from his mouth.

Superstoe removed the dark glasses and false beard and looked around the lushly furnished bedroom on the top floor of the Georgetown clinic. "I'm afraid it is," he mused. He glanced right and left to see them both reflected in the expansive wall mirrors, and then he tipped his head backward and gazed into the eyes of his somber twin on the ceiling. He inquired, "Who authorized these mirrors?"

Watt chewed the pipe. "We wanted to make the surroundings as conducive to pleasure as possible. Some couples find it a creative environment." He sucked on the gurgling pipe. "You said you didn't want it to be mechanical or animalistic. You didn't want cold, calculated breeding." He searched for a match.

"I do want them to have fun," Superstoe agreed.

"Well," Watt countered.

Superstoe patted the neatly tucked, royal purple bedspread. "You've checked these mirrors?'

"Oh, yes."

"Those shifty-eyed technicians?"

"Pall."

Superstoe opened the closet door. "No whips, I hope?"

"Paxton," Watt protested. "We don't encourage aberration. We want babies, not neurotics." Watt sucked on the rasping pipe. Superstoe fingered the satin dressing gown in the closet.

"They don't all have mirrors," Watt added. "Each room has its own décor."

"Yes, I remember your telling me." Superstoe opened the drawer of the bedside table and eyed the specially printed *Kamasutra*.

"Illustrated," Watt commented.

"I see," said Superstoe.

Watt tamped the cold ashes with an index finger and watched Superstoe in the mirror. "We excluded windows to foil anyone with a telephoto lens," he explained.

"Very wise," Superstoe said to the Watt reflection.

"What should we do?"

"Lie low," Superstoe advised, head down, eyes lowered.

"Should I resign? To save you face?"

"Heavens no!"

Side by side each spoke to the other's left-handed image. "Should I deny it?" Watt queried.

"I don't know."

"Well?"

"Let me think." Superstoe donned the dark glasses, appraised the effect, and sat on the bed. Watt sat beside him. Superstoe bounced gently, steadily. Watt stood and watched the mirror. Superstoe bounced higher. Watt forsook the illusion and faced the high-bouncing reality.

Superstoe reclined in midair, landed, and jiggled to rest, arms behind his head, eyes on the chief of state in the ceiling.

"The lewd photos," he announced, "were taken at a private orgy. The orgy had nothing to do with the BPA clinics." He bounced to his feet and, attaching the beard, crossed to the wall. Nose to nose with the black-bearded phantom he continued. "The top-floor rooms are used exclusively for scientific research into the physiological responses to erogenous stimulation." He bared his teeth at the steam-effaced phantom.

"We have a lot of top-floor rooms."

"I'm speaking of the rooms at the clinic in question."

"The reporters will be curious about the other clinics."

Superstoe turned and looked at Watt over the tops of the glasses. "Those rooms," he observed solemnly, "are strictly reserved for married government employees for free rest and relaxation away from the kids." He strode boldly to the door. "Invite the reporters in. Show them around."

"*Invite*—?"

"To every clinic in the country. *Carte blanche*. Except to the files." He stood in the hall and waited while Watt smoothed the bedspread.

He bounded down the three flights and out into the sunlight. He flourished his right arm and declaimed through the beard to the panting Watt behind him, "We have nothing to hide!" Then, the *Kamasutra* in his left hand, he ducked into the back of the dirty, dented 1960 Chevrolet and, followed by the Secret Service agents in the Edsel, was conveyed quietly back to the White House.

The three shifty-eyed technicians were thoroughly discredited. Shortly after the scandal one suffered a fatal case of ptomaine poisoning; another succumbed to a coronary thrombosis during an interview with a free-lance journalist; and the third was diagnosed a hopeless paranoid schizophrenic and committed.

The author of the exposé clearly suffered from delusions of grandeur. His family removed him to Europe, hoping to clear his mind, but he drowned, quite accidentally, in a sudden storm in the Aegean.

The majority of the journalists thought the rest and relaxation centers very nice indeed. The minority, most of whom represented small-town weeklies, found their protests upstaged by the government announcement that promised to build more rest and relaxation centers which would be open to the public at a minimal fee.

The National Motel Association objected. After some negotiation the government agreed to make its rates conform to the motels' rates. Then the Internal Revenue Service ruled that rest and relaxation expenses were tax deductible.

By the time the motel controversy died, the public had wearied of the BPA scandal. The report of the investigating committee, headed by Watt, received only perfunctory attention from the press.

The lion was sated, and slept.

27 Summer faded; leaves turned scarlet and gold; apples were pressed into cider. It was election time again.

Twenty percent of the voters went to the polls. Sixty-six percent pressed the button for Superstoe, thirty-four percent jabbed at the button for Geaseman.

Even Superstoe felt sorry for him.

But more and more younger politicians were swelling the membership of the Popular Party. Superstoe kept an eye on them. He feared they would cause trouble, and he was right.

Meanwhile he created two committees.

The first committee, that of Statutory Analysis and Codification, was headed by Joshua Cohen. Its task was to study the entire corpus of American law. Antiquated, ambiguous, and conflicting laws would be annulled. New laws would be written which would redress blatant differences among state laws and recast federal laws in a simpler and more comprehensive manner.

Cohen called it the Loophole-Plugging Committee.

The study was expected to take twelve years: eight years to transcribe the laws into computer notation and write instructions for the computer analysis and four years to rewrite the laws.

Adams was appointed chairman of the second committee —the Committee for Constitutional Analysis. It was to investigate the advisability of drawing up a new American constitution.

The members of the Adams Committee, in addition to Adams, were Furth, Johanneson, Cohen, eight professors, and the nine members of the Supreme Court, which then included Ambrose Washington and James Water, a Seminole Indian.

Certain famous but never-seen-in-public writers greeted the Adams Committee with enthusiasm.

Solomon Towe wrote: "A new constitution, setting forth more explicitly and completely our fundamental human rights, is long overdue."

Jacob Allworthy satirized the "archaic" constitution as a mass of amendments repealing other amendments, followed by more amendments repealing the repeals. He called it "an exercise in second thoughts."

K. P. Kobb pointed out the "fuzzy thinking" and "undefined terms" in the "makeshift document."

Adams told a news analyst interviewing him on a television program, "We will have two goals before us: the definition and preservation of basic human rights and the establishment of the best possible government."

28   As the Adams Committee completed its study, in Puerto Rico Gideon Shiloh Geaseman died a natural death in the arms of a black-haired virgin.

The Popular Party did not mourn long. The empty shoes were not only filled but stretched, and the Geaseman circle was shoved aside by the throng of bright-eyed, restless men. They were young politicians who had won office in the governments of cities and states but could go no further. The federal government did not want them.

They pledged their talents and their personalities to the unseating of Superstoe. At their head was the charming, blond, blue-eyed Tim Taylor.

At twenty-one he had been elected to the city council of Lincoln, Nebraska. At twenty-six he had been elected Mayor. At thirty he was Governor, and at thirty-four he was Governor again.

The millionaires watched him, listened to him, and signed their checks. They knew a winner when they saw one.

Superstoe kept a sharp eye on Taylor, too. He knew he would have to deal with him, sometime, somehow.

He summoned his advisers to a dialectic.

29

"Ben," he asked, filling Adams's glass with claret, "why don't you run for President?"

"You mean run against you?" asked Zorr.

"Oh, my goodness no," said Superstoe. "Instead."

"No," said Adams.

"Are you really so humble?" asked Superstoe, sipping with his eyes on Adams.

"On the contrary."

"I see," said Superstoe quietly. Then he brightened and turned to Furth, who was gazing intently at a large stain on the tablecloth. "Would you like to run for President, Lazarus?"

Furth made no reply.

Superstoe looked discouraged.

"Off," Zorr observed, pointing vaguely to the ether.

Superstoe shouted at the top of his lungs, *"Lazarus!"*

Furth eyed the stain and scribbled on the tablecloth with a stubby pencil.

"I think he's thinking about his book that's coming out," Watt said. *"Furthian Mathematical-Physical Principles, Problems, Theories, and Guesses."*

"I think he's figuring out the formula to describe that stain," said Pall, brushing his recent red mustache.

"Maybe the formula for the stain contradicts one of his Guesses," Zorr suggested.

"That wouldn't bother him," said Watt.

"Do you think he'd like to run for President?" Superstoe asked the rest of the assembly.

"What's wrong?" asked Watt. "Don't you want to run?"

"Certainly. I just want to be fair to everyone. I don't want you to think I'm greedy."

"I'll run," said Zorr.

"I didn't ask you. You're young yet."

"I was just volunteering my services."

"Thanks," said Pall.

"Don't mention it."

"No thanks, Paxton," Furth said.

"Don't you want to be President?" asked Superstoe.

"If I have to be, I will. But what's the point?"

"All right then. That's settled. We'll begin educating the people."

"I beg your pardon?" Adams inquired, his glass midway to his lips.

"We're going to televise our dialectics," said Superstoe.

"Didn't he tell you?" asked Watt.

The premier color telecast began at 10 on a Friday evening. It ended at 6:22 Saturday morning. The dialecticians were Superstoe, Furth, Watt, Pall, Zorr, Cohen, and Washington.

Adams had gone to a ballet.

TV Guide said they would discuss Truth.

The cameras and microphones were set up in the White House Dialectic Room.

Superstoe wore a green sweatshirt, blue slacks, and sneakers.

Furth considered overalls, but at the last moment he put on a sports shirt and slacks.

Printed in archaic letters, the word DIALECTIC appeared on television screens. From the audio was heard a merry medieval danserie.

Then the seven men gathered about the table appeared. Ashtrays, glasses, and bottles were on the table.

"Good evening," said Superstoe. "This is *Dialectic*. Dialectic is the science of asking questions and answering them. It is the way we arrive at truth. This is unrehearsed."

"Anything may happen," Furth said and filled his glass.

"And will," said Pall.

"I can see the switchboards lighting," Cohen said. "Millions asking, '*What* are they drinking?'"

"Whiskey," said Superstoe with a toast to the number-one camera.

Pall said, "Maybe we should talk about"—drinking—"temperance."

"I thought we were discussing justice," said Zorr.

"A good reason for discussing temperance. Have a snort."

"Josh, how would you define temperance?" asked Superstoe.

The program received mixed reviews.

Solomon Towe thought Superstoe had monopolized the discussion.

Some observers thought there was too much spontaneity. Participants left the room without apology and returned to ask what had been said in their absence. Furth, on one return, had forgotten to zip his fly. Zorr left at 2 A.M., announcing he had a date with Janet Jumper. Furth and Washington, blinded by the light, took to wearing dark glasses. A bottle was accidentally broken; Superstoe left, returned with a broom, and swept up the broken glass. Furth passed a bottle among the technicians, and a cameraman entered the argument.

They ate sandwiches between midnight and one. They ate chocolate cake and vanilla ice cream and drank coffee at two. At three they returned to whiskey and munched potato salad and fried chicken.

Cohen, to sharpen the argument, had taken the position that temperance was the same as abstinence. Watt had enumerated the medicinal benefits of alcohol taken internally. Thanks to Zorr, the dialectic moved to the consideration of sex. Superstoe asked if celibacy was temperance or insanity. Watt suggested it might be either impotence or psychosis.

Eventually they debated whether temperance was the same as justice—that was at 5:15 in the morning. At the conclusion—necessitated by a technician's falling asleep—they had agreed that temperance had some things in common with justice but that the two were not identical.

The following Friday they were scheduled to discuss Justice.

They talked of beauty.

At 11 Superstoe made a phone call, and at midnight Mrs. Ambrose Washington, two Miss America contestants, and a model appeared to provide illustrations to the argument, or, as Zorr expressed it, inspiration.

Before long the women joined the argument. Mrs. Washington silenced Furth, who was maintaining that a man could embody as much beauty as a woman, by raising her skirt.

Superstoe, sensing that things might become too spontaneous even for him, in view of a thirty-million audience, inquired if one could say a woman's soul was more beautiful than a man's. One of the Miss America contestants, emboldened by her drink, gave her opinion. Furth summarily refuted her, and she departed in tears. "Incontrovertible proof," he concluded with a wave of his hand.

They concluded, at 8:57 A.M., that temperance and justice were beautiful, but probably no more beautiful than Mrs. Washington and the model.

Adams joined them for the third program. He could no longer resist the fray.

The next week Johanneson came, unexpectedly, and shocked everyone into speechlessness so that Johanneson was left to talk for several hours on cartography and its relation to the real world.

30 Big Business and languishing ex-military men threw in with the Popular Party.

The FBI and CIA reports on the party grew longer and less coherent. Even Pall was at a loss. "We can't kill them all," he said. "Not without suspicion, anyway."

The President's Permanent Peace Parliament dissolved itself and joined the Popular Party.

Seven national committeemen of the American Party defected. The rank and file began to follow.

Adams bit his cigar. "Rats leaving a sound ship in smooth waters," he growled.

"A metastasized carcinoma," Watt diagnosed.

Tim Taylor stumped the country. The reporters followed. He was news.

31   Superstoe countered (feebly, some said) by unveiling the new constitution.

The public, however, was not immediately cognizant of the unveiling. It occurred, as it were, accidentally, during a dialectic on Reason. Superstoe was not present.

"The tyrant, for example," said Adams at 1:17 in the morning, "employs his reason to evoke the emotional acclaim of the masses. That's how tyrants secure power: with the applause of the crowd. The crowd deceives itself. It thinks democracy ensures individual rights."

Pall, moderator, asked, "How does that apply to America?"

"It's obvious," snapped Adams.

"But the American President, although elected by the people, is constrained by the law," Cohen observed.

"He can change the law."

"There's the Supreme Court," Cohen argued.

"He could wipe them out."

The discussion moved to the presidential nominating conventions. Everyone agreed they were shameful spectacles—not as shameful as they had been before Superstoe, but shameful enough.

"To entrust the selection of presidential candidates to a small mob of self-seekers and bandwagon jumpers inspires me with little confidence," Adams said. "A George Washington and a Paxton Superstoe are lucky accidents, proving the people can be right some of the time but are never right all of the time."

"Then," said Pall, "the point is not that the people are not wise in their choice. The point is that the method of nominating the candidates is not a sound one."

"That's one of the points," said Adams.

"Then," Pall continued, "in order to ensure the best government we must provide the best method for choosing presidential candidates." Despite the air conditioning, the lights heated the room. Pall removed his sports coat and tie and rolled up his sleeves. "But, before we can determine the best method of choosing the candidates, we must consider who would make the best President. Mustn't we?"

"We must," said Furth.

Pall rubbed his perspiring palms together, winked into the camera (he knew Superstoe was watching), and said, "What sort of individual would make the best President? Would we say, the wisest?"

"I think we would," said Cohen.

"Can there be any doubt about that?" asked Pall.

"How can there be any doubt?" asked Furth.

"Then the wisest man in the country should be President," Pall concluded.

"Obviously," said Furth.

"And the Vice President and the President's advisers should be as wise as he, or at least the wisest after him."

"Nothing could be more self-evident," said Furth.

"Now how shall we determine what we mean by *wise?*"

"That is a more difficult question," Furth said.

"But not impossible."

"Of course not."

"It occurs to me," Pall began, looking into the air and wiping his forehead with his wrist, "that the question might be approached two ways. We could begin by defining wisdom. We might say wisdom is the ability to act always in the best interests of the state. We might add that the wise man is courageous, temperate, just, intelligent, knowledgeable, able to reason quickly, clearly, and accurately; a man whose reason always controls his emotions, but a man who nevertheless is warm-hearted, sensitive, and alert to human strivings and fallibilities."

"You might say all that," said Adams.

"But then," Pall continued, "I'm not sure we would have progressed very far in our search for the wise man. For how are we to find the man—or woman—who possesses these attributes?"

"A damn good question," said Furth.

"On the other hand," Pall went on, "we could approach the question a second way. We could ask, 'What qualities would a child have to be born with in order to become wise?' We would agree, would we not, that not everyone who is born can become wise—wise, that is, in statecraft? Every child *can* become President. But not every child when grown, would make the best President. Isn't that true?"

"Is it?" asked Cohen.

"Would you want an idiot to be President?"

"Hell no," said Furth.

"Well, let's leave the question of what inherent qualities a child would need to become wise. Let us ask instead, 'What education will he have to have?'"

"A fine idea," Furth said.

"We agree he would need some sort of education?"

"Certainly."

"We couldn't have someone with no education at all?"

"Christ no."

"And by education we do not mean mere academic degrees. We mean education."

"Right," said Furth.

"Then what education will make a boy wise? As we answer that, we will discover if he needs to have been born with any inherent qualities or talents."

"Most likely."

"And we must remember," said Pall, "we are not speaking of the education of a merely competent President, a makeshift President, a mediocre President ..."

"Lord no."

"But the best possible President."

"Right."

"And if there is a way of finding such a person, and educating him, and nominating him, and electing him, then that is what should be done."

"No doubt."

"We want to arrive at the ideal President."

"Naturally."

"And if we find it impossible to find the ideal, we shall choose the man who comes closest to the ideal."

"That's logical."

"The best possible."

"Yes yes yes," said Adams. "Get on with it."

"I am," said Pall. "Tell us, Ben: what education will the child need? What will he need to know?"

"Everything." Adams filled his glass with a vengeance.

"Why?"

"Don't ask stupid questions."

"Perhaps we should elucidate, Ben. We don't want anyone ..."

"Elucidate, then, elucidate."

"The President must make decisions affecting every aspect of life. He must be well read, to know what decisions have been made before and what their results were."

"Yes," said Adams.

Pall: He must know history and literature.

Adams: Yes.

Pall: He will affect in one way or another the life of the home, the life of the arts, the life of mankind.

Adams: Clearly.

Pall: So in addition to literature he will know drama, painting, sculpture, architecture, music, dance. A nation without culture (as people are wont to call these things) is a nation of barbarians.

Adams: It is indeed. *(He glared at the number-two camera. Then he noticed the red light on the number-one camera. He glared into it. Its light went off and the number-two camera's light came on and moved in for a closeup of Pall. Adams glared at the control booth.)*

Pall: In addition to history and the arts, what must the President know?

Furth: Mathematics and science.

Cohen: Law. Sociology and psychology.

Adams: Plato.

Pall (smiling): Mathematics and science because ...

Furth: Christ, they're life itself, like elimination.

Pall (refilling Furth's glass): Not to know math and science would be like being unable to read and write?

Furth: Worse.

Pall: Especially for the President, who must make decisions in those areas. Space travel, research, new ways of producing food, new ways of obtaining natural resources. *(Furth, swallowing, nodded.)* But he needn't be a practicing scientist. *(Furth shook his head and wiped his chin.)* But couldn't he simply rely on his experts? His advisers? As the Presidents previous to President Superstoe did? *(Furth dropped his glass.)*

Furth: Good God, Arthur! Who's to know whether his *experts* know what they're talking about? Who's to know if they're *lying?* I could write a book about the mistakes and stupidities perpetrated by Presidents who took the advice of *experts* because they themselves didn't know a reactor from a reagent. Experts! *(He grabbed Pall's glass.)*

Pall: Then the best President will know math and science. And I think the advantages of law, sociology, and psychology are obvious.

Cohen: Since Ed isn't here, I'll add medicine, too.

Furth: Sure.

Pall: All science: physics, chemistry, biophysics, bio-chemistry, astrophysics, geophysics ...

Furth: A little of everything. Genetics, cybernetics—the most crucial fields.

Pall (turning to Adams): And Plato. And we might say, philosophy in general? Since philosophy is the love of wisdom? He should know all philosophers, to obtain a clear vision of metaphysics, to distinguish reality from non-reality, to reason cogently, to comprehend ethical principles—in short, he should know all the branches of traditional philosophy.

Adams: It wouldn't do him any harm.

Pall: Perhaps he should even know logical positivism.

Adams: If he hasn't anything better to do.

Furth: I'm hungry.

(Pall ordered sandwiches.)

Pall: Now. Need he possess any other knowledge? The knowledge to build a house, for example?

Furth: The White House might collapse.

Cohen: Oh, really ...

Furth: Ben can build a house. Can't you, Ben?

Washington: Urban renewal. Suburban renewal.

Pall: Exactly. So he should have a fundamental knowledge of the practical arts, as we might term them. We might even include plumbing.

Cohen: Why not?

Furth: Agriculture, engineering, electronics ...

Washington: What about cooking, sewing, and embroidering?

Pall (uneasily): What about them?

Washington: Well?

Furth: Paxton's a damn fine cook.

Cohen: Ambrose, come off it.

Washington: Half the population is female. They cook, sew. Doesn't the President affect them?

Cohen: This is a serious discussion ...

Washington: I'm serious.

Cohen: I don't anticipate legislation dealing with sewing or cooking.

Pall: I suppose he should know a good diet from a bad one.

Washington: Of course he should.

Pall: But sewing is pretty much a family thing. It's not likely to affect the state.

Furth: You never know.

Pall: Well, if it does, he can learn it quick enough!

Washington (soothingly): Of course he can.

Pall: So. Now. What else?

Adams: Languages.

Pall: Ah yes! Languages! *(Sitting up straighter, smiling.)* The President deals with other nations. How is he to communicate accurately with them, reach agreements, if he doesn't know their languages?

Adams: How, indeed?

Pall: To depend on translators is an inferior method.

Adams: Much.

Pall: But he can't know every foreign language.

Adams: Some are more important than others.

Pall: Then what languages should he be able to speak?

Adams: English.

(A long silence.)

Pall: Yes?

Adams: French, German, Russian, Chinese. That's a minimum. It would be nice if he spoke *(tipping his head back and closing his eyes)* Arabic, Hebrew, Spanish, Italian, Swedish, Norwegian, Polish, Hungarian, Roumanian, Japanese, Portuguese, Czech, Bulgarian, Persian ...

Pall: Well ...

Adams: At least two or three others, if possible.

Pall: And what would you say of ancient languages?

Adams: Obviously.

Pall: I beg your pardon?

Adams: Why?

Cohen: Classical languages, Ben, Greek, Latin, Sanskrit.

Adams: I said, yes.

Pall (inhaling deeply): The ideal President would read the classical languages: Greek, Latin, and perhaps even Sanskrit?

Adams: How many times do I have to tell you?

Washington: He should be in good physical condition.

Pall: Oh, yes. In good health, and also strong, able to run, swim, walk long distances ...

Cohen: He needn't be the decathlon champion.

Pall: No, no.

Furth: Nor waste his time playing baseball or some other half-ass game.

Pall: (with a quick glance at the control booth): No.

Furth: He could dance.

Pall: Yes.

Furth: Dancing is extremely tiring.

Pall: Indeed it is.

Furth: It looks easy, but it's the most exhausting activity you can engage in.

Pall: I know.

Furth: It develops physical harmony.

Cohen: All right. We know what the ideal President needs to know. We know he has to be healthy. Will that mean he's wise?

Pall: I was coming to that.

Cohen: Good.

Pall: Will it?

Cohen: No.

Pall: What will make him wise?

Cohen: You tell me.

Pall (taking a swallow): The wise man is master of his emotions, passions, and desires.

Cohen: He is?

Pall: Yes. So, if a man possesses the knowledge we have spoken of, our next step will be to see if he is master of himself.

Cohen: How?

Pall: Test him.

Cohen: How?

Pall: Put him in situations wherein lesser men would lose their heads.

Cohen: Good.

Pall: Invite him to a party and try to get him drunk.

Cohen (sipping): Right.

Pall: Present him with other temptations.

Furth (eagerly): Yes.

Pall: Set his house on fire and see if he panics. Threaten him with death.

Cohen: It would be like fraternity hazing.

Pall: Simulate a situation in which he could, if he were of that nature, be a tyrant. Give him absolute control over a group of people.

Washington: Make him a drill instructor in the Marines.

Furth (yelling): More sandwiches! *(To Pall)* In other words the wise man is in harmony with himself.

Cohen: Let's not get off on harmony.

Furth: Why not?

Cohen: That's another subject.

Adams: The entire discussion is about harmony. *(Silence.)*

Pall (warily): You mean, if the best possible President is governing the best possible state, the entire state will be in harmony.

Adams: Isn't anyone listening to me tonight?

Pall: So if ...

Adams: Is that bottle empty?

Washington: I'm afraid so.

(Three more bottles were brought. Adams opened two and passed one across the table. Silence.)

Furth: I can't express what satisfaction it gives me to appear on the only television program in which ten seconds of silence can intentionally occur. An hour of silence, if we like.

Washington: It's a fantastic step forward.

Furth: Damn right it is.

Pall: We should probably make a habit of stopping now and then so that the audience can go to the bathroom, get a beer and a sandwich—since we have no commercials.

Adams: The entire program is a commercial.

Furth: Do you really think we have an audience, Arthur?

Washington: I think we should make one thing clear.

Furth: What isn't clear?

Washington: By a well-balanced individual, by a man in harmony with himself, we don't mean a nonentity. We don't mean a conformist.

Furth: Hell, the wise man always looks odd to the rest of the people. The rest of the people aren't wise.

Pall: He's likely to be an individualist.

Adams: Likely isn't the word.

Pall (peering into the camera, fingering his mustache and screwing up his right eye): He might even be eccentric. *(Furth hiccupped.)*

Cohen: Would we agree that we have now theoretically found, educated, tested, and proven our ideal President?

Washington: There's another thing. He must be a leader. He must possess that quality which some men have and some do not which enables him to lead. Which inspires in others trust, confidence, and the willingness to carry out directions with efficiency and enthusiasm.

Pall: Yes, he should be a leader. And that could be tested, couldn't it?

Furth: But, if he were President, his authority would be in the office. He wouldn't have to be a leader.

Pall: But his subordinates would obey him more promptly, they would do better jobs, they would be devoted to him if he were.

Furth: Well ...

Pall: He'd inspire the people.

Furth: The people?

Pall: Yes.

(Silence.)

Cohen: You know, this ideal President is going to be a paragon. I don't think it's possible to find one.

Furth: Well, say we need one President every generation. At any moment there exist three generations. Or: we need one President for every third of the population. Anticipating the future ...

Cohen: Careful.

Furth: Oh, hell, nobody's watching.

Pall: For simplicity's sake, say two hundred ten million, divided by three: seventy million.

Furth: Whatever you like, Arthur. One man out of ...

Washington: Or woman.

Furth: Whatever you say, Ambrose. Out of seventy million. That's ... *(scribbling on a note pad)* Point oh oh oh oh oh ...

Pall: Write it on the blackboard.

Furth: Why?

Pall (patiently): For the television audience.

Furth: You write it out.

(Cohen walked to the blackboard. He smiled at the camera, found the chalk, and, as Furth dictated, wrote 0.000001428-57142.) The interesting thing is, it's a repeating decimal. *(Cohen continued writing until the number read 0.0000014285714 2857142857142857142857 ...)* And so on percent of the population will be needed for the job of President.

Cohen (sitting): That's not many percent.

Furth: But isn't it interesting that it's a repeating decimal?

Cohen (staring at the number, and then at Furth): I suppose.

Pall: Well, the point is, there are a lot of people to choose from.

Furth: No, the point is, it's a re—

Cohen: I suggest we forget numbers and decide *how* we're going to find this prodigy.

Furth: Finding him won't be any problem.

Pall (quickly): Then it only remains to ask: *Who* shall choose the President?

Cohen: Maybe the voters should elect him. In a democracy.

Pall: Ah. Yes. Then who shall nominate him? A political nominating convention? *(Furth, swallowing, laughed, choked, and gasped. Pall waited patiently until the paroxysm subsided.)* It's an important question.

Washington: Extremely important.

Furth (repressing another outburst): No doubt about it. *(Silence.)*

Pall: Let's assume we have a President who is the best possible.

Cohen: Okay, let's assume that, for the sake of the argument.

Pall: Let's also say that President has appointed the wisest men after him to be his counselors. We'll call the President, Vice President, and the counselors the High Council. Or the Presidential Council. Or whatever you want to call it.

Cohen: Okay.

Pall: Now. Would not that council be the ones to choose the next President? Wouldn't the wisest men in the country be the only ones qualified to nominate the next generation of wise men?

Cohen: I'd say that made sense.

Furth: Why, it's obvious.

Pall: But let's not be hasty.

Furth: Who's being hasty?

Pall: Well, Lazarus, I can imagine some people saying the *people* should choose.

Furth (throwing out his arms, grazing a bottle, speaking louder than necessary): How the hell could the *people* . . .

Pall: It would be a cumbersome process. Over a hundred million persons going through ...

Furth: How the shi—

Pall: Not everyone could verify that he had the necessary knowledge ...

Furth: That's not half ...

Pall: Look at the present method, for example. *(Furth, mouth gaping, was speechless.)* The people don't nominate the presidential candidates. Political conventions do. The people put their faith in a few hundred men and women whose only qualification is faithfulness to the party ...

Cohen: Even that qualification is a dubious one.

Pall: Then we might conclude the present method is a highly questionable one?

Furth: Might?

Pall: I doubt if anyone—except those who attend nominating conventions—would say the present method is the best.

Furth: Impossible.

Pall: Or even a reliable method.

Washington: Remember in the old days, before Superstoe, everyone said at election time, "It's not a question of who's the best man; it's a question of who's the lesser of two evils."

Cohen: Exactly.

Pall: So no one could honestly argue that a political convention is a better means of nominating candidates than a council of wise men.

Furth: He'd be a fool.

Washington: An idiot.

Furth: A ninny.

Pall: Therefore, if the Presidential Council nominated the candidates, that system would be much better than the present system.

Washington: Infinitely better.

256 SUPERSTOE

Furth: A nearly incalculable improvement.

Pall: Even with the primaries a convention can nominate whomever they please. The people have no voice.

Cohen: No.

Pall: Then we can conclude—can we not?—that our method would be the best possible method.

Furth, Cohen, Washington: Agreed.

Pall: And the rest of the electoral process would remain unchanged. The council would nominate, say, two candidates, and the people would vote.

Adams: Now look here. What kind of idiocy is that? Two wise men fighting for the election! And what if one is manifestly wiser than the other?

Pall: What would you suggest?

Adams: The council nominates one man for President. The populace votes: Yes or No. If a majority vote No, the council nominates another. The people vote again.

Pall: And if they vote No again?

Adams (with a gesture of contempt): Then let the council nominate two or three or a dozen and let the people choose.

Pall (to the others): How does that strike you?

Washington: Cool.

Cohen: Very intelligent.

Furth: Not a bad idea.

Pall (with great happiness): And now it only remains to ask: Who is the best possible President, now?

32 "Solomon Towe."

"What's he say?"

"Says *Dialectic* last night presented some intriguing ideas."

"Did you see it?"

"No. I've gotta sleep sometime. You?"

"No. What's he mean, intriguing ideas?"

Preceded by considerable publicity, the salient portions of the discussion were rerun on Wednesday evening beginning at eight o'clock.

That morning the Adams Committee had released its report.

The report was published in four volumes: three thick ones and one thin one.

Two of the thick ones summarized the research and reproduced some of the discussions which had been conducted by the committee. The first was entitled *Individual Rights*. The second was entitled *The Best Government and How to Achieve It*.

The thin volume was *The New Constitution*. It contained the text of the proposed constitution accompanied by explanatory and hortatory notes.

The fourth volume was *Minority Reports*.

The new constitution was in part similar to the old, although amendments which had later been repealed were expunged, along with their repeals.

Individual rights were more explicitly defined. The right to privacy, for example, had been elaborated, and electronic spying devices had been taken into account. Wiretapping was illegal. Any device which permitted a person to listen or see into another's home or private office was unconstitutional.

Even devices which were only speculative were dealt with. Any device or power which allowed one to perceive another's thoughts without his consent was declared unconstitutional; its invention, production, or use was prohibited.

The sexual rights of man were defined. A human being could not be involuntarily deprived of the enjoyment of sexual relations. Persons judged by a panel of doctors to be genetically deficient could, however, be rendered sterile.

"Man has the right," one note read, "to the pursuit of happiness, which includes the pursuit of sexual relations. But man does not have the right to burden the state with useless and inferior progeny."

Another note read: "Men do not have the right to deform the moral, physical, and intellectual growth of the young. If parents are incompetent, it is the duty of the state to ensure their children a sound rearing."

All of the committee members endorsed the articles which expanded individual rights. But a few members voiced, in *Minority Reports,* varying degrees of dissension with the Right of Parenthood and Right of Child Rearing articles.

Some committee members also dissented from the new method of nominating and electing the President and Vice President.

By the terms of the new constitution the Presidential Council would consist of seven members, including the President and Vice President. The first Council would be appointed by the President in office on the day of the new constitution's adoption. Thereafter new members would be elected by the Council itself.

Every four years the Council would nominate one candidate for President and another for Vice President. The voters would vote Yes or No. If the voters rejected the nominees, the Council would submit another pair of candidates. If the voters rejected them, state primaries would be held to determine the candidates.

There would be no definite term for members of the Council. A member could remain on the Council as long as he chose. But five members could dismiss another member, providing he was not then serving as President or Vice President.

A member of the Council, or ten percent of the voters, could initiate a Recomvote impeachment proceeding against the President. To effect impeachment fifty percent of the registered voters would have to vote, and two-thirds of them would have to vote for impeachment.

Thus democracy would be preserved.

PART FIVE

The Challenge

1 Superstoe's plan was to put off the Recomvote balloting on the new constitution for two years.

During those two years an easy-going, soft-sell, patient, educative program would be carried out. The program, known in the White House by Furth's code name, Operation Woolpull, would accustom the populace to the new constitution. It would be discussed casually, confidently; the beautiful picture of the future it would bring would be painted; it would become a familiar, friendly object. Then, when it was submitted to Recomvote, no one would pay it much attention. For, by the terms of the Recomvote amendment to the old constitution, if the forty percent quorum was not met, the new constitution, upon Superstoe's signature, would automatically supersede the old.

Meanwhile, a few months before the new constitution would be submitted to the voters, Superstoe would be elected to his fourth term.

But the plan was foiled.

Tim Taylor led the attack.

In July, at a rousing convention in Atlantic City, the Popular Party nominated Tim Taylor on the first ballot.

In August the American Party, at a brief, businesslike convention in San Francisco, nominated Superstoe and Furth.

Newspapers expressed satisfaction at Taylor's nomination. They said it was time the country saw a serious contender to Superstoe.

2   Tim Taylor was married to a pretty, sensible girl, had three children (three boys), and faithfully attended the Episcopalian church.

His position was clear. He represented the common man, the common interest, family, fatherhood, husbandhood, free enterprise, youth, love, romance, marriage, church attendance, Sunday school, and the old constitution.

He promised an investigation of the "highly suspect Cohen Committee."

He called for the repeal of the Recomvote quorum.

He called for a reappraisal of "the Congress question."

He swore to abolish the Bureau of Population Analysis, which he called "an invidious, evil, totalitarian design to wipe out the common man."

He castigated the "Adams revolution in education." "We are not anti-intellectual," he orated. "This would be a sorry nation if it despised intellectuals, just for being intellectuals, and sorrier still if it had no intellectuals. But Adams—and Superstoe—want *everyone* to be intellectuals! And those that can't make the grade, those whose interests lie elsewhere, they throw away. They give them a second-rate education. Adams wants a nation of intellectuals! He wants everyone to be the same!"

(Queried by a reporter, Adams said, "Taylor thinks of the state as a beehive with intellectuals for the drones. That's the popular view. What I want is a community of idiosyncratic individuals with a common body of knowledge.")

"Superstoe and Adams talk about the rights of the individual," Taylor declared in Los Angeles. "They say their new constitution increases your rights. But I say to you, no right is more sacred than the right to have children! No right is more hallowed than the right to raise your children as you see fit! No right is more fundamental than the right to choose your own President!

"Adams talks of wisdom. But I say to you, no one—not one man, not one group of men, *no* intellectual *elite,* brainbound by more knowledge than *anyone* could hope to have or would ever need or would even *want* to have—I say, *no one* is wiser than the total voice of the American people, voting together and exercising their collective judgment and wisdom. One man knows more about farming than another; another man knows more about business. But all together, all our citizens know more about nominating a President than any so-called council!"

And in Chicago he asked, "Is not fifteen years long enough for one man to be President? If he is elected again, he will have ruled for nineteen years. Nineteen years, ladies and gentlemen, is a long, long time. President Superstoe is not a young man. If he was employed by a corporation, he would have been retired five years ago!"

There were innuendoes, too, about the fact that Superstoe was not a family man and about the fact that he had never been known to attend church. Some commentators even pointed out that it seemed odd that neither Superstoe nor his "closest advisers," with the exception of Watt, were married.

3 Many persons were made uneasy by the constitution's statements on parenthood and child rearing; and some, but not as many, were opposed to the new method of nominating the presidential candidate.

But Superstoe maintained that the constitution should have a long and thorough study by the people. "We must not act rashly," he said. "Let us elect the President. Then there will be time to vote on the new constitution."

That was why Taylor, in a series of secret meetings, persuaded the Recomvote Advisory Council to schedule the vote on the new constitution the same day as the presidential election.

Taylor gathered massive crowds. For the faithful, a Taylor speech was a religious experience.

"Are we for motherhood?" he cried, flinging his arms and bending his knees.

"*Yes!*" shouted the crowd deliriously.

"Are we for fatherhood?"

"*Yes!*"

"Are we for childhood?"

"*Yes!*"

"Are we for *God?*"

"*Yes!*"

"Are we for *democracy?*"

"*Yes! Yes!*"

"*Then we are against the new constitution!*"

Frantic cheering.

"*We are against Superstoe, Adams, and Furth!*"

4   Superstoe called a strategy meeting. He served hot dogs.

"Ed could slip him some tranquilizers," Furth suggested.

"Can't we pin something on him?" asked Zorr.

"He's clean," said Pall. "He cheated once in college, but so did everyone else. His first child was born six months after the wedding, but ..."

"We could make something up," said Zorr.

"It wouldn't do any good."

"Let's examine Taylor's appeal point by point," Zorr said, "and see how we can counteract it. One, he stands for the family."

"Not even Paxton could produce three kids in a month," said Furth.

"He'd need a little help, at any rate," Watt observed.

"Just a wife would help," Zorr said. "A mother figure." He turned to Superstoe, who was cross-legged on the desk, a canny Buddha in khaki and gray Thomas Jefferson sweatshirt. "I have a sweet, white-haired secretary, Paxton, a widow ..."

"Isen," said Superstoe, "I am too old to have a mother."

"What about an Italian movie actress?"

Superstoe looked interested.

Zorr tried another tack. "Taylor represents churchgoing. You might ..."

"Never. But I might become an evangelist." He started singing "Rock of Ages."

"You've been an evangelist all your life," said Adams.

"Could you issue a statement expressing your religious beliefs?" asked Pall.

"Would that be in the national interest?" asked Watt.

"I believe in Superstoe," said Superstoe.

"That won't set church bells ringing," Said Zorr.

"I doubt if it would even bring in the Unitarians," said Watt.

"Superstoe is Love?" suggested Furth.

"What about stressing your confidence in the common man?" asked Pall.

"But, Arthur," said Furth, "the basis of the new constitution is that we *have* no confidence in the common man."

"Now look here," said Adams. "Do you really think Taylor can beat you?"

Everyone looked at him.

"It seems to be possible," said Pall.

"Disassociate yourself from the new constitution," said Zorr. "If they defeat it, you can submit it again in a couple of years."

"The constitution is our capstone," said Superstoe. "I stand on it."

"Our only hope is that the forty percent quorum won't be met," said Watt.

"Don't bet on that," said Pall. "Taylor reminds every audience that if they don't vote, they'll be sterilized and their children taken away in the middle of the night."

"Surely they don't believe that," said Superstoe.

Watt spoke to Furth: "Can you fix the Recomvote computer?"

"I wish I could. Paxton insisted it be unfixable. An honest computer."

Superstoe looked apologetic. "It seemed the least I could do."

Zorr turned to Adams. "Did you have to be so damned explicit in that constitution?" he demanded.

"Did you have to bully the Advisory Council until they threw in with Taylor?" Adams snapped.

"Why the hell screw around with this constitution anyway?" Zorr cried.

"We began all this," Superstoe explained quietly, "in order to reform society."

"And now this sonofabitch Taylor will fuck the whole thing up!" Zorr shouted.

"Sit down, Isen," said Superstoe. Zorr sat. Superstoe scratched the tip of his nose. "Obviously," he said, "there's only one thing to do. I must urge the people to vote. I must persuade them to vote for me and for the new constitution."

"And if you lose?" asked Adams.

Superstoe frowned. "If I lose, then—but Ben, how can I lose?"

5   As the election neared, Superstoe's confidence increased. He had faith in the people.

He knew the people were consuming an average of 1.7 tranquilizers per adult per day.

The Manichean Laboratories' aspirin, Carelessin, containing H-57, a tranquilizer, was the best-selling aspirin in the country.

And the country was prosperous.

Nevertheless, Operation Woolpull had been accelerated. Articles were published and movies were shown stressing the benefits of the new constitution and showing that the common man would never be adversely affected by it. Who is unfit to have children? the articles and movies asked. Morons, they replied. Who is unfit to rear his own children? Idiots and moral degenerates.

It was pointed out that the Department of Health and Welfare had no intention of compelling anyone to be, or not to be, a parent. The department merely dispensed drugs, released information, provided medical care, and saw to the welfare of orphans and underprivileged children.

Although thirty-four years older than Taylor, Superstoe made more appearances and more speeches and shook more hands.

Some people said Superstoe's methods had been highhanded. But, said others, look at the results. And, said others, were his methods so highhanded, at that? Was it

Superstoe's fault the Recomvote quorums were never met? Wasn't there *more* democracy under Superstoe? Was *he to* blame for public lethargy?

But what about this new constitution? Are we to vote against it, and vote against the right to privacy? What do you have to hide, asked Taylor's supporters, that you're so worried about privacy? Besides, don't you want the right to have children?

Well, who are they going to stop from having children? Not you and me. Our children are smart; they're going to college. If we don't have the money, the government pays their tuition. What more can we ask? The earth will be over-populated unless something is done. Isn't it reasonable to encourage the procreation of the most intelligent?

And, after all, it was an age of innovation. The new was good; the old was bad.

Some said it was a decadent age. But decadence, as well as power and glory, has its termination in time. Wasn't this the beginning of a glorious, golden age?

6   Superstoe invited Tim Taylor to appear with him on *Dialectic.*

Tim Taylor declined the invitation. He told reporters, "I have expressed myself clearly, again and again, on the new constitution. I will shortly appear on nationwide television myself, with a distinguished panel of journalists, to answer questions. But to appear on *Dialectic*—gentlemen, I would be a babe in the lion's den! It's like the fox inviting the goose to come to his lair for a chat about which tastes better, fox or goose! President Superstoe and his friends are very clever men. They have a way with words. They've studied how to twist words and arguments and make an ordinary man say the opposite of what he means. I don't pretend to be as smart as Mr. Superstoe. I'm just an ordinary man. I represent ordinary people. The kind of people who have families, and worries, and debts, and dogs, and cats, and go to church on Sunday. They say Mr. Superstoe still reads schoolbooks. Well, that's all right. But I've graduated from school. I read newspapers now.

Jacob Allworthy wrote a satire on Tim Taylor. Many said it was the most brilliant, and the most acid, of Jacob Allworthy's career.

That morning Tim Taylor, for the first time in public, lost his temper. His face was flushed his breathing was heavy, his speech was nearly incoherent. He called Jacob Allworthy "a sniveling, viperous, vicious, unprincipled hatemonger who hides behind a false name to libel God-fearing, innocent citizens!"

7   That evening more people than ever before gathered before their television sets to watch *Dialectic.*

On the table were coffee cups, a coffee pot, and a brandy bottle.

Superstoe, Pall, Washington, and Cohen sat around the table. Two chairs were vacant.

"Our two guests are coming a little later," Superstoe announced.

They discussed whether a President should ever allow his anger to control his judgment.

They asked, if a man cannot control his emotions before he becomes President, is he likely to learn to control them after he becomes President, when he is subjected to even more criticism?

Obviously not, they concluded.

Cohen recollected the vituperation that had assaulted Superstoe the first months after his succession to the presidency. He recalled that Superstoe had never lost his temper.

They spoke of the knowledge a President needs if he is not to be the ignorant victim of experts. "Popularity may be all a man needs to win an election," said Cohen, "but he needs more than popularity to govern a nation wisely and efficiently in this day and age."

Superstoe read a list of the subjects he had dealt with that day. To many viewers the list was incomprehensible.

Superstoe recalled the day he had journeyed to Moscow to meet with Soznolopak and the Central Committee. "A translator would have meant chaos," he said.

Slyly Cohen asked, "Do you speak Chinese?"

"Not very well," Superstoe answered. "I've been studying it only three years. Arthur, Lazarus, Ben, and I study it together with a professor from Columbia."

Pall observed that the President must often debate, discuss, and argue with a variety of people, some clever, some even dishonest. "If a man were afraid to discuss issues before the American people, I wouldn't have much confidence in him," he said.

"I'd say he was trying to hide something," Washington said.

"A quick temper, for example," said Cohen.

"Or his ignorance," Pall added.

At that moment the two guests arrived: Theodore F. Lawrence, an Episcopal bishop, and Father A. J. Dolman, S.J.

They continued their discussion of wisdom and Presidents for a while, and then they talked of children, parents, and the common man.

"I know a man who loves children when I see him," the bishop said, patting Superstoe on the knee.

Eventually they talked of religion.

Superstoe seemed to remember church history more accurately than the bishop. A learned viewer might have observed that both Superstoe and Father Dolman expressed the subtleties of Anglican doctrine more acutely than the bishop.

By 3:40 A.M., having consumed numerous cups of brandy-laced coffee, the bishop allowed that none of the members of his congregations could in any sense be termed religious.

At 4:10, having eaten a snack and drunk two more cups, he asserted that an atheist could be a better President than an Episcopalian. "But I can tell, Mr. President," he said, "you are not an atheist. You are an Episcopalian."

Superstoe poured more brandy into everyone's cup.

"I beg to differ," the Jesuit said. "Paxton is above denominations. Technically he is a heretic—as are you, though for different reasons, my dear Theodore—but in his bones, in the depths of his being, in his soul, Paxton is . . . a Jesuit."

Superstoe winked at the camera.

"Church attendance today is the greatest heresy on earth," the bishop said, taking the bottle and filling his cup. "There's more piety in Superstoe's little finger than there is in my entire church," he added.

Superstoe made the sign of the cross over the bishop, and the bishop passed out.

Cohen and Washington excused themselves at 6:15, pleading business engagements in a couple of hours. Pall left at 9:20 to attend a meeting.

The program ended at noon with Superstoe and Father Dolman discussing eschatology.

8   Three days before election day Tim Taylor spoke in Madison Square Garden. His address was televised.

Near the end of his speech he asked, in ringing tones, "Does Superstoe think he's smarter than George Washington, Thomas Jefferson, James Madison, and Alexander Hamilton, the original writers of the original, *true* constitution?

"Who does Superstoe think he is, anyway? *God?*"

9   "God knows who will win the election," the journalist said, "but who do *you* think will win, Mr. President?"

"Search me," said Superstoe.

It was the following evening, and Superstoe was holding a quiet, informal, televised press conference. The five journalists, elected by their colleagues to represent them, sat in easy chairs in a guest room of the White House. Superstoe was in shirtsleeves, but he was wearing a tie. A red silk tie.

They were drinking cream sherry.

"Would you say that passage of the new constitution depends on your election?"

"Just the reverse," said Superstoe. "My election depends on approval of the constitution. Because common sense says the new constitution is better than the old. It will provide the best possible state. If the people don't want the best possible state, then I would not care to be their President."

"What would you do if the people elected you but rejected the constitution?"

"Do you think they would do that?"

The journalist hesitated for only a second; he was an old hand at interviewing Superstoe. "But if they did?"

"I would resign."

"Surely you're joking," said a young hand.

"No."

"But, Mr. President ..."

"If Lazarus wanted to fumble along with an antiquated system, that would be up to him. But now that we have, after all these years, re-examined the old constitution, after we have labored to reshape it into a better, more workable, clearer document, it would be silly to reject it. Why, we might as well go back to the cold war days."

Another reporter spoke up. "About Mr. Taylor's accusation that you think you're smarter than Jefferson, Madison ..."

"Tom Jefferson was one of the most intelligent, well-read men who ever lived. I'm flattered by the comparison. But there's no question of who is smarter, he or I. It's simply that Tom didn't have to worry about electronic spying devices, tapped phones, computers, satellites, and a population of two hundred million."

"Mr. President, if the new constitution is approved, you will appoint the first Presidential Council. If it is approved, who will you appoint?"

"Whom will I appoint? The wisest men I know, of course."

10   Forty point two percent of the eligible voters went to the polls.

Of them fifty-seven percent voted for Superstoe.

Forty-one percent voted for the new constitution. Forty percent voted against it. Nineteen percent did not vote on that question.

On the day after the election the five men strolled slowly down the dirt road. Three of them, Superstoe, Johanneson, and Adams, were old men; Adams was eighty-two. Watt and Furth had gray hair. There was no one in sight except three Secret Service agents a hundred yards in the rear. Three helicopters were in the air observing the area.

It was a sunless, windy, cold morning. On either side of the road were Johanneson's fields; the fields were covered with the brown stubble of cut wheat. Elsewhere the fields were black; the stubble had been ploughed under so the fields would dry more quickly in the spring, that the wheat might be planted earlier, and harvested earlier, and sold sooner. Johanneson left the stubble until spring because the ploughed fields lost a quarter inch of topsoil in the spring winds. The other farmers didn't care; the topsoil would last out their lives; that was enough for them.

They needn't have returned to Crossbar to vote. As card-carrying Recomvoters they could have voted anywhere. But Adams had wanted to return. The others came with him.

They had their topcoats buttoned against the wind, and their hands were in their pockets. They walked for an hour without a word. Most people would have expected them to be elated. Although it had never been said, anyone who bothered to think of such things would have sensed the truth: the last of Superstoe's reforms had been effected. Now their program could proceed unhindered: principally eugenic selection.

That would still take generations, for Superstoe insisted on caution; but eventually, they hoped, the so-called common man would no longer exist. His progeny would either die out or be educated out of that class. When that happened, Recomvote would no longer be a farce, a mechanism by which the President legislated at will by virtue of a careless populace. It would become the means by which a true democracy would be realized. All citizens, or most, would by inheritance be intelligent; and by education they would be knowledgeable, alert, and concerned. They would have even more leisure time, and they would not expend it making more money than they needed or waste it in idle pleasures. ("I hope," said Superstoe.) They would spend their leisure time in politics: meeting together, discussing, and voting. The Recomvote quorum would always be fulfilled.

They were counting on that. For they also expected the quality of the Presidential Council to decline, at least periodically. They knew it would be easy for such a body to become conservative, inbred, cynical, and even tyrannical. By the time that happened they wanted the populace to be ready to exert its own power and its own wisdom.

So on that cold, gray November morning the five men were not elated. They were reflective. An observer might even have said they were depressed.

Their silence enwrapped them like their topcoats, buttoned them up and united them in a warmth of mutual understanding.

Earlier, as the others breakfasted, Superstoe had phoned Pall in Washington. He had asked him what he was doing.

"Reading reports," Pall had replied.

"What reports?"

"Judicial reform."

"Did you go to the party last night?" Superstoe had asked.

"Isen's party?"

"Yes."

"No."

"What are you doing this afternoon?"

"A couple of meetings. This evening a chess game with Ivan. We speak Russian to take my mind off the game so he wins. Why do you ask?"

"Goodbye, Arthur."

"Goodbye, Paxton."

Then he called Zorr. A woman's voice had answered and said Isen was sleeping. Superstoe hung up.

The dirt road led past a small graveyard. It looked incongruous, alone on the plains. There wasn't even a church nearby. Since his youth Adams had made a hobby of scrutinizing graveyards; it always cheered him. Adams pulled open the gate and the five men entered the graveyard and sat on gravestones.

"I think," said Superstoe, "in a year or two I'll resign."

"What the hell for?" asked Adams. "Are you going to run for Secretary-General?"

"I thought I'd go live at the Academy of Philosophy. Read and talk and live a quiet life. The presidency's not so much fun any more. There are no more crises." He bent over and read the tombstone upside down. "Maybe I'll write my memoirs."

Furth, leaning against a one-winged angel, slipped and nearly fell.

"It's time I let Lazarus be President," Superstoe went on. "I'm afraid I've been selfish. Wouldn't you like to be President, Lazarus?"

Furth blew his nose. "I couldn't care less," he said.

"Actually," Watt mused, "I think I might resign in a few months. I'd like to become head of a nice medical school for a couple of years. There are a few things to be done in that line."

"Oh, I don't think we could do without you," said Superstoe.

"Shit, now's a fine time for everybody to be talking of retiring," Furth said to the angel, who, he noticed, was without a nose.

"We all retire eventually," Superstoe observed.

"Come on," said Furth. "Let's walk. I'm cold."

Watt started for the gate. Furth absently gave the angel's wing a tug as he left, and the wing broke off. He jumped aside as it crashed to the ground.

They walked on down the road.

"We five," said Superstoe, who walked on Adams's left, "are the first Presidential Council. We have two others to choose."

Johanneson walked on Superstoe's left. Adams was in the middle, and on his right were Furth and then Watt.

"The trouble is," Superstoe continued, "I am in doubt as to whom to choose. I think it would be wise, for example, to appoint Josh or Ambrose, or both of them. But, on the other hand, Ivan deserves to be one. He was with us almost from the beginning, and he was one of us originally, back at our dialectics at the university. On still another hand, Arthur and Isen were with us then, too; and they have worked with us since the beginning. We couldn't have succeeded without them. Especially Arthur."

"Ivan doesn't care about being on the Council," Watt said.

"I know. But he belongs."

"So do Isen and Arthur," said Furth.

No one spoke for several hundred yards.

Then Adams said, "You have to put Arthur on the Council."

"That leaves one vacancy," said Superstoe.

"Why didn't you make it so there'd be ten members?" asked Johanneson.

"Seven's a nice size for an advanced seminar," Superstoe replied.

"One thing is obvious," Watt said. "Isen is counting on being appointed."

"In the beginning I expected more of Isen than of Arthur," Adams remarked.

"It will be very unpleasant if you appoint Arthur but not Isen," Watt said.

"Yes," said Superstoe. "And Isen has served us faithfully, don't forget."

Epilogue

1 The Presidential Council met officially on Thursday mornings and unofficially on Friday evenings. Meetings were attended not only by the seven members but also by Borozov, Cohen, Washington, and three other members of the Academy of Philosophy whom they expected eventually to become members of the Council.

"The Inner Ten," as reporters called them, formulated a "Rules of the Council."

The "Rules" advised that the candidates for President and Vice President should be members of the Council; that at least one new member should be elected to the Council every two to four years; that members should first be residents of the Academy of Philosophy.

Final decisions would always be the President's.

But the majority vote of the Council would determine who would be the presidential and vice presidential candidates every four years.

The Council members decided among themselves the line of succession to the presidency.

If the entire Council but one were permanently incapacitated, the remaining member would become President and appoint the new members.

If the entire Council were permanently incapacitated, the presidency would fall to the Chief Justice of the Supreme Court.

2   Furth began a series of journeys to foreign capitals to explain the new American constitution and encourage its adoption by other countries.

Watt called a World Conference on Eugenic Study. It was held in New Delhi.

Superstoe appeared on the cover of *Time* magazine for the fifty-sixth time.

The next week Furth appeared for the eighteenth time.

Zorr married a famous Hollywood actress. She appeared on the cover of *Time* for the third time.

Finally, on a mild, sunny afternoon, less than a year after the adoption of the new constitution, as he strode sturdily along the boulevard on his way to Watt's house for dinner, Adams faltered, wavered, and crashed to the pavement. A minute later he was dead of a cerebral hemorrhage.

3   In Washington there were the eulogies and the procession with the muffled drums and the flags and the dignitaries and the horses and the coffin.

Then there was the jet and the quick drive to, and through, Crossbar. The townspeople stood silently on the pavements.

The vehicles hardly slowed. They fled through the town like black, blind ghosts, heeding no one.

They pulled into Johanneson's drive. Superstoe, Furth, and Pall emerged from the first limousine, Johanneson, Borozov, and Zorr from the second, Watt and his wife and a nun from the third.

Secret Service agents slid the pine coffin from the hearse and, followed by the others, carried it half a mile behind Johanneson's house to a small grove of pine trees. Without a pause, without a word, ropes were looped around the coffin and it was lowered into the dark fresh hole. It thudded against the bottom. The ropes were hauled up. They could smell the fresh earth. It began to rain.

Johanneson took a shovel and began filling the hole.

Superstoe picked up a second shovel, heaved a spadeful into the hole, and handed the shovel to Furth.

They passed it from hand to hand while Johanneson, with the other, shoveled steadily, efficiently, until the dirt mound rose above the wet, trampled grass.

They returned to the cars along a path of mud. Johanneson carried both shovels on his right shoulder and the ropes coiled in his left hand.

He stored the shovels and ropes in the barn, and they climbed into the limousines.

It was dusk as they sped back through Crossbar. It was still raining, and the pavements were empty.

The limousines drove on to the airfield, and all but one of the passengers boarded the plane. The nun, the former Sophia Adams, was driven to the railway station in Great Spoons.

Rachel, accompanied by her husband and five children, had attended the ceremonies in Washington.

A few hours later they seated themselves around the table in the White House Dialectic Room. Superstoe filled eight pewter cups with John Jameson. The eighth stood at the head of the table before an empty chair.

They raised their cups into the air, and then they drank. They stared at the untouched cup.

"Who'll come for it first, Elijah or Ben?" asked Furth.

Suddenly Superstoe's arm flew out and spun the cup to the floor. The whiskey spread in the air and collapsed to the carpet. The cup rolled against the wall. He fled from the room.

Another bottle was passed around. Furth said, "Paxton slipped a bottle of Jameson into the coffin. And a box of cigars. But no matches."

"We all grow old," Borozov said. "It is best quick. Look at my friend Alexei Mikhailovich. In a wheelchair now five, six years. He cannot even speak."

No one spoke.

"Wakes should be joyous," Pall said morosely.

Furth ordered the food.

The food was brought.

Superstoe entered. He had showered, shaved, and changed clothes. He wore a red sweatshirt, blue trousers, and sneakers.

Resolutely he moved the empty chair to the wall and placed his chair at the head of the table. He drank, refilled his cup, and sat. He took a plate and piled it with food. "There's talk of monuments and statues," he said, "but I'll have none of that. Stone breaks."

He took a mouthful, chewed, and swallowed. "The academy will be the Benjamin Franklin Adams Academy of Philosophy," he said. "We'll publish the marginalia in his Plato. And of course we'll publish the ten volumes. Finally."

"He burned them," Johanneson said.

Superstoe looked at him.

"Two weeks ago," Johanneson said. "Two weeks ago tomorrow. I was eating supper with him. He'd just come back from the academy. He'd spent a week there."

"Yes," said Superstoe.

"I asked him how it seemed to him. He said it was a dream made flesh and blood. Men and women from seventeen to ninety talking; every damn one of them able to quote Plato or Cicero or Heisenberg; every damn one of them able to talk about aleph numbers or the Cyrenaics. But he said he still didn't approve of the signs Lazarus had tacked on the walls."

(Furth had inscribed the mottoes on the spur of the moment on a visit to the academy two years before. They read:

> *Is everyone agreed? You're all damn idiots.*
> *The fool thinks he knows everything.*
> *Who is this that darkeneth counsel without knowledge?*
> *Are you wise now? Get the hell out.*
> *It's a long way to Tipperary, and longer still to Nirvana.*)

"He mentioned a boy he met there," Johanneson continued. "About twenty. A sharp lad—I remember him—with an ornery streak. Ben and the boy argued for thirty hours straight. Ben said the lad's mind was the first he'd met that he thought might be superior to his. Said the boy nearly had him on the ropes toward the end."

Johanneson ate a few mouthfuls and then resumed: "The boy's parents died in one of the epidemics." He took another mouthful.

"But the ten volumes," said Pall.

"You know they were in the academy library," Johanneson said. "One day he heard four or five people discussing them. He said at first he didn't know they were talking about *his* work. They had it all ass backwards. Then one of them said, 'It's not the ideas that bother me. It's that they're hard to read. I can't read his writing. Why the hell didn't he *type* the manuscripts?' Ben said that was what did it. He said he might have tolerated their getting the ideas ass-backwards—he *might* have—but the handwriting set him off. He charged into the library and pulled out nine of the volumes and grabbed the tenth out of the hands of a girl sitting nearby and walked into the woods and burned them. Burned two fingers, too, he said."

They finished the meal.

Afterward they talked aimlessly for an hour, and then Zorr, Watt, and Borozov departed.

Pall went for a swim in the White House pool.

Furth, who was living in the White House, went to bed.

A few minutes later Superstoe went to his room, undressed, and climbed into bed. Finally, as dawn was breaking, he fell asleep.

Johanneson stayed in the Dialectic Room and drank until the room was lit by the sun; then he walked to his office.

4   Borozov was elected to the Council, but he resigned after three months to become president of the Russian-American Institute, where he devoted himself to philology.

Ambrose Washington took his place on the Council.

Superstoe began to have his bad days again. He would speak to no one, not even Furth or Pall. He ate less and drank less. Sometimes he failed to appear at Council meetings.

Nine months after Adams's death, having been President of the United States for seventeen years, he resigned and moved to the Adams Academy of Philosophy.

Furth became President and Watt Vice President. Cohen was elected to the Council.

Not long after that Johanneson retired to his farm. He supervised the ploughing and sowing and reaping, often driving a tractor himself, and he studied astronomy charts. He lived ten more years.

Superstoe revived at the academy. He had a cottage of his own, but he took his meals at the common table. He was a favorite of the younger members and frequently held dialectics in his cottage.

A year after his retirement he began a series of lectures at Harvard, initiating the Superstoe Chair of Political Philosophy. But after the second lecture he fell ill with a cold, and the cold developed into pneumonia.

When he had recovered, he left the Boston hospital and returned to the academy. A few days after his return a party was given in his honor in the dining hall. He performed a soft-shoe dance, with skimmer and cane, and at the end he sat down, exhausted and smiling, reached for a glass of champagne, and fell to the floor.

5   Furth declared a year of mourning and commissioned a monument to be built along the Potomac. "Not for him or for me," he said; "for the country."

Borozov returned to Russia, to the town of his birth, to spend the remainder of his days.

Eight months after Superstoe's death Watt injected a narcotic into his bloodstream. He had cancer.

Furth served a second term as President and then retired to write a book, *The Future of Mathematics*.

Ambrose Washington became President.

By that time there was dissension within the Council.

Zorr opposed Washington's nomination. He said Washington lacked authority; he tolerated too much opposition; he wasn't qualified. He was a member of the academy, but only a *de facto* member; he didn't understand mathematics, he knew little science, he couldn't read Greek or Latin.

But Pall insisted on Washington's nomination. He told Zorr he, Zorr, had forgotten all the Greek and Latin he had ever known, and he reminded him that Washington had learned Russian, which was more than Zorr had done.

So when Pall, at the end of Washington's term, was nominated for President, the Council split into factions. Three of the members sided with Pall; two supported Zorr.

Council meetings exploded in anger. Zorr shouted that Pall was inefficient and stupid. He said the eugenic program was not working; stricter controls were needed. He said it was insane to continue favoritism toward the American Indians. He said the United Nations was under the influence of the Chinese, and the UN would soon become a worldwide tyranny.

Pall offered Zorr a seat on the Supreme Court, but Zorr refused it.

There were only the official Council meetings now—on Tuesday mornings.

Occasionally, on Sunday evenings, Pall invited a few friends in for dinner, drinks, and discussions; but Zorr was never invited.

When it came time to nominate the President again, Zorr and his two followers threatened to wreck the government if Pall was renominated. They would boycott Council meetings, they would pursue their own aims within the departments they controlled, they would embarrass Pall and his supporters.

A Council member, one of Zorr's supporters, was killed by a drunken hit-and-run driver.

A new member was elected, and the Council voted 5 to 2 to remove Zorr's other supporter from the Council.

He was replaced by a woman from the academy who happened to be Pall's wife.

Pall was nominated, 6 to 1, to serve a second term as President. That was in June.

Zorr resigned and took his cause to the people. He thought he would repeat Superstoe's strategy.

He would woo the masses, champion the cause of the people, and persuade the populace to reject the Council candidates. Then he would be nominated by the state primaries, would be elected, and would put his own supporters on the Council.

If Superstoe could fool the people, he thought, so could he.

Pall thought the people couldn't care less.

And they didn't.

At the election twenty-eight percent voted. Sixty percent of them voted Yes for Pall.

But Zorr was not easily beaten. He continued to campaign. He urged the people to attend the Recomvotes.

Gradually he gathered followers. At the vote on the renewal of the Indian Land Restoration Act he managed to get forty-four percent to the Recomvote centers. The measure was defeated.

Pall began to employ some strategy of his own. He too followed Superstoe's example.

The trouble with the people, psychologists were saying, was that they were bored.

True, now the average IQ, by the old testing technique, was 141. But, although nearly everyone could be called an intellectual, there was a dearth of intellectual interests.

Even an intellectual tired of reading Plato, even in English. (There really wasn't any point in learning Greek—or Russian, for that matter; the Russians spoke English.) Not even an intellectual wanted to go to a ballet or a concert every night. Mathematics was still the province of mathematicians; understanding it took a knack, just as painting and poker playing required talent, and anyway there were so many systems no one could expect to know them all; why, some professors spent their lives just studying

Furthian numbers; besides, math had no bearing on everyday life.

And as for dialectic—was there really anything to talk about?

Politics? The government tended to politics. Maybe there should be more than one candidate; maybe there were some loose ends to tie up; but there was nothing vital to be done.

There were no fundamental problems to talk about.

There were no fundamental problems.

They might jabber about the meaning of life or the purpose of human existence or the relationship between mathematical constructs and the physical universe at the Academies of Philosophy (there were three academies now: the Adams, the Superstoe in Oregon, and the Borozov-Soznolopak in Leningrad), but the common intellectual wasn't interested.

So Pall created diversions to occupy people's time.

On the one hand he ordered computers programmed to invent and specify diversions; on the other hand he thought of some himself. They weren't original ideas. Even Pall was finding life a little dull. Neither the problems nor the answers were new.

The two war clubs, the Greens and the Blues, received government subsidies. They inducted and trained volunteers. Parts of California, Arizona, Utah, and Nevada were declared off limits to civilians, and there the Greens and the Blues conducted battles against one another. They used live ammunition; the participants, after all, wanted thrills.

Often above the whirr of slot machines, the rattle of a chuck-a-luck, and the banter of croupiers in Las Vegas could be heard the rattle of machine guns and the thunder of howitzers.

A religious leader, Euphraim Brozzle, appeared, claimed to be the Messiah, with a new message of happiness and earthly euphoria, attracted followers, and occupied the minds and time of the latent religionists in the country.

And the other organizations which were already flourishing without Pall's encouragement, the Pleasure Society, the Physical Relaxation League, Bedwarmers, Pillow-jumpers, Ecstasy, Thrills, New Thrills, Society of Eros, and Anything Goes, to mention the more popular ones, were given official government sanction.

But Zorr was clever too. He campaigned against the government subsidies and sanctions. He said they destroyed private initiative.

People supported Zorr.

Half the people who supported him belonged to a pleasure club, or maybe to more than one.

They would fight any attempt to abolish their organizations. But they supported Zorr because they opposed the government's sanctioning the clubs. It wasn't respectable. Besides, they liked their activities to be clandestine. They savored the flavor of illegality and innocent perversion. How could they enjoy perversions if the government refused to recognize perversion? If perversion, as well as morality, no longer existed? (Remember the furor when Furth legalized prostitution?) They didn't want government approval; they wanted excitement. God (supposing he existed) knew they needed a little excitement.

A year and a half after Pall's re-election a poll found that forty-two percent of the people wanted Zorr as their next President.

It looked as if Zorr had outsmarted Pall.

But Pall was shrewd.

He seduced Zorr's mistress.

It was not concupiscence; it was strategy. It was cunning, too; another man might have seduced Zorr's wife.

Zorr of course found it out. He always had both his wife and his mistress watched by detectives. While Pall was holidaying in Maine, Zorr, as Pall expected, arrived at his house for a showdown.

Pall received him graciously, led him into his study, took out two glasses, and, his back to Zorr, poured two drinks, dropping poison into one.

Smiling, he handed Zorr the harmless glass of Scotch.

Cannily Zorr took the other glass, saying, "I don't think you'd poison me, Art—you know my supporters wouldn't stand for it. But I'm not going to take any chances."

Pall, showing no surprise, said, "That's very wise of you, Isen."

"I know you," Zorr said.

"I should hope so."

"You made a point of pouring the drinks so I couldn't see you. You're trying to unnerve me."

Pall sat in an easy chair. "I think you're getting paranoiac, Isen."

Zorr looked reflective. "Maybe you're right," he said. "But I'm going to fight you, Art. I'm not going to let you get away with ..."

"Isen, we've been together too long, we know too much about things, to fight like this. Let's call a truce."

"If you resign, and I'm nominated President, and the Council's filled with my men, I'll call a truce."

"You'd screw everything up if you were President."

"Hell, you've already screwed everything up!"

"Think of Paxton," said Pall. "He wouldn't want you to do this. He wouldn't want a tyranny."

"What do *you* have if it's not a tyranny?" Zorr shouted.

"Is it my fault no one votes?"

"I don't see you hustling them to the centers."

"That's their responsibility."

"What do *you* think Paxton would say if he saw war clubs and sex clubs?" Zorr cried.

"Maybe he'd join them."

"Shit."

"Well . . ."

"Our revolution's a failure. You know that. A country of intellectuals? They're no better than a bunch of aborigines. The only difference is, they need more sophisticated diversions." Zorr gestured, spilling some of his drink.

"Well, well," said Pall, "it's the age. It's a decadent age. You can't manufacture a renaissance. Here's to philosophy."

Zorr put the glass to his lips. But then he hesitated. "Of course you might have poisoned your drink, expecting me to suspect you and take yours."

Pall smiled a little wearily and offered his glass to Zorr. Zorr nearly took it. Then he stepped back and clutched his own. "Or is the one you have now poisoned?" he asked. "You know I'd be clever enough to see through your ruse and want the one you have now."

Pall waited patiently for the wheels to turn once more.

"Or did you think . . .?" Zorr smelled his whiskey.

"They're both poisoned," Pall said.

Zorr sniffed Pall's drink.

"Hell, don't drink at all," Pall said.

"I need it," Zorr said and drank.

So it was Pall's victory.

About the Author

William Borden was born in 1938 in Indianapolis. His short stories have won the PEN Syndicated Fiction Award and have appeared in numerous magazines and anthologies. His plays have been produced in New York and Los Angeles, among other cities, and have won many national playwriting competitions. The film adaptation of his play *The Last Prostitute* was produced by Universal Studios in 1990. A collection of his poetry, *Slow Step and Dance*, was published in 1991.

Borden is Chester Fritz Distinguished Professor of English at the University of North Dakota, where he teaches creative writing. In addition, he is a Core Playwright at the Playwrights' Center in Minneapolis and is fiction editor of *The North Dakota Quarterly*.

He lives on a lake in northern Minnesota with his wife, Nancy Lee-Borden.

A Note from the Publisher

Orloff Press appreciates your purchase of this book. We would like you to know that a great deal of care has gone into every phase of its production, from manuscript acquisition through editing, text design, cover design and illustration, typesetting, proofreading, printing, and binding. If you have comments or questions, we encourage you to write to us at Orloff Press, P.O. Box 8536, Berkeley, CA 94707-8536.

The typeface selected for this book is Palatino, a roman font with strong inclined serifs, designed by Hermann Zapf in 1950. It resembles a Venetian style and is named after a sixteenth-century Italian writing master. With broad letters and short descenders, it is notable for its strength and clarity in both roman and italic.